I0602502

CAUGHT ON CAMERA

CAUGHT ON CAMERA

A CAMERA CLUB MYSTERY

KARA LACEY

First published by Level Best Books 2024

Copyright © 2024 by Kara Lacey

All rights reserved. No part of this publication may be reproduced, stored or transmitted in any form or by any means, electronic, mechanical, photocopying, recording, scanning, or otherwise without written permission from the publisher. It is illegal to copy this book, post it to a website, or distribute it by any other means without permission.

This novel is entirely a work of fiction. The names, characters and incidents portrayed in it are the work of the author's imagination. Any resemblance to actual persons, living or dead, events or localities is entirely coincidental.

Kara Lacey asserts the moral right to be identified as the author of this work.

First edition

ISBN: 978-1-68512-747-3

Cover art by Level Best Designs

This book was professionally typeset on Reedsy.
Find out more at reedsy.com

To my mom, the original Bobbie, for sharing her love of cozy mysteries with me.

Praise for Caught on Camera

"With its well-drawn Vermont setting and page-turning mystery, *Caught on Camera* is a must-read debut mystery by Kara Lacey."—Trish Esden, author of the Scandal Mountain Antiques Mysteries

"Surrounded by early summer in a charming Vermont village, *Caught on Camera* is a page-turning mystery where the sleuth enlists her sharply focused photography club to help clear her name. Cozy mystery fans will love the quirky characters, well-placed doses of humor, and a heroine we can root for."—Janna Rollins, author of the Zen Goat Mystery series

"I was invested from page one…[A] well-developed mystery, fleshed-out characters, and an idyllic, small-town Vermont setting combine to deliver a picture-perfect storyline."—Leah Dobrinska, author of the Larkspur Library Mystery series

"Kara Lacey's debut novel is charming, intense, and beguiling. I was mesmerized by *Caught on Camera*."—Laurie Buchanan, author of the Sean McPherson novels

"Kara Lacey's debut novel, *Caught on Camera*, perfectly captures everything readers want in a cozy mystery—three-dimensional characters who feel like friends, a picturesque Vermont setting, and most of all, a well-plotted puzzle of a mystery to solve. I'm thrilled that this is the first in a series. I can't wait to see how the Camera Club Mysteries develop!"—Lori Roberts Herbst, author of the Callie Cassidy Mysteries

"*Caught on Camera* was enthralling, atmospheric and captivating. It captures picture-perfect small-town life with a deadly twist. I 'shutter' to think that a killer could be so close to home."—J.R. Lancaster, author of *Someone's Always Watching*

Chapter One

I set my backpack on the park bench and raised my camera to pan the scene across Main Street. Country store, Victorian-house-turned coffee shop, white farmhouse cottage… I stopped, focusing my lens without finishing the panorama that I knew included a second cottage followed by a non-denominational church whose tall white steeple pierced the blue sky. I let out a slow breath and clicked.

"It looks like home, right?" I bent to rub the belly of my four-legged partner in crime and photographer's assistant. Darcy wriggled in the grass with a disinterested groan while warming his yellow fur in the late May sunshine. As an assistant, my Labrador retriever's skills were dubious at best, but these days, the value of his companionship was immeasurable.

I stood upright and tucked an errant strand of hair behind my ear before aiming my lens at the farmhouse cottage. Leaves of a giant maple tree formed a natural frame for my new home, their vivid green a welcome sight after the long winter. I adjusted my lens and zoomed in on the freshly painted door—bright yellow, like daffodils—optimistic and audacious. The color of hope.

"Hey, girl," a familiar voice called. Only one person called me *girl* rather than Bobbie. With forty-six years under my belt, it was a misnomer, but one I wouldn't squabble over. I fired off several shots of my next-door neighbor, Rose Lavoie, whose purposeful stride contradicted the playful tilt of her head. Fiery red curls escaped a messy bun, framing her broad grin. In each hand, she carried a takeout cup from her coffee shop, the Rosebud Café.

"Liquid courage. I think you might need it for our camera club's photo shoot tonight." Rose handed me a cup while leaning to pat Darcy's head. He sat upright, tail thumping. "Hey there, Darce." She dug a dog biscuit from her pocket and held out her hand. "You're the most chill doggo ever."

I wrapped my hands around the cup's warmth and laughed. "You must not remember his puppy days."

After another pat on Darcy's head, Rose plopped onto a park bench, her bright pink Croc-shod feet barely touching the ground.

I held my cup aloft. "Why would I need courage?"

"You didn't see today's post on the Stonebridge Scandal page?" Rose asked.

I dropped onto the seat next to her. "I'm not on social media, remember?"

"Mm-hmm," she said. "That needs to change. I'm setting up a group for our camera club. After everything you went through to get this club going— with a huge assist from yours truly—it would be totally wrong if you didn't take part in our prompts. The first one is the rule of threes, correct?"

I groaned. Thinking about rejoining social media made me queasy. It wasn't that I was particularly introverted. I wasn't. I used to post photos and status updates with the best of them. That all changed with my husband's sudden death a little more than a year ago. Well-meaning friends wrote messages and comments filled with kind words of sympathy and support. At our age, this sort of thing wasn't supposed to happen.

Inevitably, their lives returned to normal. I'd tried to stay positive, truly I had. I'd clicked the happy emoji on all their painfully cheerful posts. But the more I missed Dan, the harder it was to bear. I'd given up and deactivated my accounts.

"You're right," I said. "And yes, the rule of thirds. We'll start our photography challenges with composition." I forced a tight smile. "Okay, I give. What does The Scandal say?"

"You want me to read it to you?" Rose asked.

I slumped in my seat. "Sure, why not?"

Rose's thumbs flew over the screen of her cell phone. "After a contentious meeting last night, the Stonebridge Keep it Snappy Shutter Club, led by newcomer Bobbie Brooks—" Rose stopped to peek over her phone. "Alicia came up with the cutest club name, don't you think?"

"Mmm," I murmured. It was a little cute for my liking, but knowing Alicia Crowley, aka my big sister and owner of the Stonebridge Village Market, her suggestion had been facetious. That hadn't stopped Rose's enthusiasm from spreading. Before we knew it, we'd chosen the club's name.

"What else does the post say?"

Rose seemed hesitant to continue. "It just goes on to mention tonight's photo shoot."

I sensed there was more, but let the subject drop. We'd held our first club meeting at my house the night before. Except for a few minor hiccups, I thought it had gone well enough.

Contentious, indeed. It was probably better if I didn't know who'd offered that gem. I was looking forward to leading the group on our first shoot and couldn't let idle village gossip ruin the fun.

I touched my ponytail, reaching for the comforting silk of the scarf I'd tied in my hair. Unable to find it, my fingers fumbled, combing through wavy strands.

"Hey, I thought you were wearing a scarf when you came in for coffee this morning." Rose watched my frenzied search with a concerned expression. "It was so pretty. The pink and purple flowers brought out the gold flecks in those big brown eyes of yours, making them look uber glittery."

"I was." My voice trailed off, confused. In my mind's eye, I visualized myself unpacking a box of clothes earlier in the morning, excited to wear a springy scarf for a change. So where was it? I let my hand fall to my lap, shaking off uneasiness.

"Maybe you should retrace your steps?" Rose suggested.

The afternoon was too nice to spend worrying about a misplaced scarf. "It's probably stuffed in the bottom of my backpack. I'll look for it later."

Rose tipped her face to the sun. "What a bea-u-ti-ful day." She drew out the word, pronouncing every syllable. "Can you believe this weather? It's been months since I've seen so many people wandering the green."

"I was beginning to think winter would never end." I followed Rose's cue and angled my face skyward, closing my eyes to let the sun's rays warm my face. Spring had finally sprung in southern Vermont, and just in time for summer.

Back in February, when I'd left Boston, Vermont had been in the throes of winter. During the long, cold months since, the cacophony of hammers, drills, and heavy-footed contractors had provided the accompaniment to my second thoughts and misgivings. Throughout the upheaval of modernizing my cottage, I'd become the master of rationalization, trying to convince my twenty-three-year-old daughter, Emma, as well as myself, that moving was the correct decision. The jury was still out on that one.

Vermont winters weren't completely new to me, though. Dan, Emma, and I had been coming to the village for years to visit Alicia, who lived on a nearby farm with her husband, Nate, a Stonebridge native.

"Uh-oh. Don't look now." Rose's voice broke my reverie.

Reluctantly, I opened my eyes and watched Tiffanee Jacobsen sashay toward us. In her early thirties, if I were to guess, she wore tiny cutoff shorts and an even tinier tank top that flaunted every curve. The weather was warm, but not *that* warm.

As she approached, Darcy raised his head and sniffed. My dog, it seemed, categorized humans into two distinct groups—those who carried dog treats and those who didn't. I was certain Tiffanee fell into the latter category, and it appeared Darcy agreed. He tossed me a side-eyed glance, as though it was my fault, and let out a disgruntled sigh before dropping his head back to the ground to resume his nap.

I plastered on a smile. "Hi, Tiffanee. Excited for our club's photo shoot?"

Tiffanee's bug-eyed sunglasses did little to hide her exaggerated eye roll. "Oh, sure, Bobbie. Like a bunch of amateur photographers at the covered bridge won't look ridiculously cliché." She flipped her long blonde hair behind her shoulders, and I couldn't help envying the way it fell down her back like a satin sheet. My fingers reached for my chestnut waves, knowing the hair flip was something I'd never pull off.

"The club voted." Even as I said it, I knew I sounded lame. Not that I'd admit it to her. The covered bridge was the club's choice, and I wouldn't override them.

"Yeah, like, I know that." Shifting her weight from one slim leg to the other, Tiffanee lifted her glasses and peered at Rose. "Pretty blouse."

Rose smoothed the soft folds over her maroon leggings. The surprised flush on her cheeks was impossible to miss.

With a manicured finger, Tiffanee pointed at Rose's shoulder. "Yeah, the bright colors and large flowers are, like, suitable for your—fuller figure. It reminds me of my grandma's muumuus."

My chin dropped. It wasn't the first time I'd witnessed Tiffanee's insults. And yet, I hadn't seen this one coming. I was speechless.

"Thanks a million," Rose deadpanned.

"No probs." Tiffanee gave her hair another flip. "Gotta run. Travis is waiting. I'm sure you, of all people, know how impatient he can be."

As Tiffanee sauntered away, Rose puffed her cheeks, brushing her flowered shoulder as if sweeping off the callous words. "First, she compares me to an old lady, then she rubs it in my face that she's dating my ex-husband."

"Obviously, her grandma is a hot pistol." I loved the way Rose dressed. Bright colors and bold patterns paired perfectly with her exuberant personality.

Rose huffed. "Oh please, that girl doesn't have a grandma. Aren't dragons hatched?"

I laughed, admiring my friend's spunk.

"She can have Travis, for all I care. Sadly, she's right about my fuller figure." Rose gestured air quotes. "I need to give up scones before I become a giant butterball. My fortieth birthday is looming large."

"Pfft. Fortieth birthdays are a piece of cake," I said. "Take my word for it. I've had a few of them. You definitely look nothing like a butterball."

"I can always count on you," Rose said with a weak laugh.

"I hope Tiffanee changes her attitude before tonight. After everything we've put into getting the club started, the last thing I need is for her to ruin our outing."

"I wouldn't count on it," Rose said. "It's too bad we can't just, I don't know, get rid of her somehow."

"Let's pretend you didn't say that," I whispered as a triumvirate of middle-aged church ladies marched past, peering at us.

With a giggle, Rose's hand flew to her mouth. "Now I'm in for it. The Righteous Sisters are going to pin me with their most pious stares in my café tomorrow morning." She pinched her face, attempting an imitation that looked anything but pious. But then, I doubted acting saintly was part of her repertoire.

"If it doesn't wind up in the Stonebridge Scandal first." Honestly, whoever owned the page didn't miss a trick.

"Forget about it," Rose said. "No one actually takes The Scandal seriously."

"It's just that the post makes me feel unwelcome. You know, like I don't belong here. Aren't small towns supposed to be friendly?"

Rose waved a dismissive hand. "Girl, get over it. Feeling like you belong? That's going to be up to you."

Small-town life was completely new to me, and I wasn't used to being an outsider. I was eager to fit in—to feel like a part of the community. The process seemed excruciatingly slow.

Rose stood, brushing dust from her leggings. "I wish I could stay and chat, but I'd better get moving. Today was crazy busy. Thursdays seem to be the new Fridays these days. The weekenders were all so prickly." She paused, tipping her head toward a woman seated on a bench nearby. Slim with a tight blonde ponytail, crossed legs in skinny jeans, and heels with telltale red soles, the woman sipped an iced beverage while reading a book. "Especially that one," Rose said. "Sheesh. I'm not Starbucks."

"They'd be disappointed if you were." As a former member of the prickly weekender club, escaping the city on Friday afternoons with Dan and Emma for the relative quiet of the mountains, I knew all too well what Rose was complaining about. Despite our flatlander notion of Vermont being lost in time, we still expected our soymilk no-foam-extra-shot-vanilla-caramel macchiato—it just needed to be quaint. And Rose didn't disappoint, serving a steaming cup of charm with a splash of friendly banter.

Rose shrugged. "Good grief, it's almost five already. I'd better get Ethan to his baseball game." She referred to her teenaged son. "He's cleaning up the café—payback for me being such a cool mom and allowing him to go out for pizza on a school night. I'm totally bummed I won't be at the photo shoot, but if I make it back in time, I'll stop by the bridge to join you. Toodles." Rose waggled her fingers, then turned and hurried across the village green.

I rested back against the wooden bench, taking the last sip of coffee as Rose crossed Main Street to her apartment above her café. My sight settled on my home next door. In all the years I'd been coming to Stonebridge, walking past the little house and waving to the elderly woman with the kind smile, I'd never thought I might live there. With its inviting porch and flowered window boxes, the house had always drawn me in. I imagined summer afternoons swaying languidly on the wooden swing, watching life go by—not that I expected much to happen in this sleepy village.

My mind went back to the Stonebridge Scandal. I couldn't help it. The post bothered me more than I wanted to admit. The club was meant to be fun, a way to bring photography enthusiasts together. Through regular meetings, photography outings, and challenges, I hoped to explore the various facets of photography, from composition to editing. With Rose's and Alicia's help, we'd managed to drum up six members, including ourselves. It wasn't exactly a rousing beginning, but I was new in Stonebridge, and I'd take it. Small seemed like a good way to start.

I stood to click one last photo before leaning to ruffle Darcy's warm, yellow fur. He had been my husband's dog, all ninety pounds of overgrown teddy bear. His mournful brown eyes told me he missed Dan as much as I did. Widowhood hadn't come with a manual, though, and we were muddling through.

"You and me, buddy." I gave his broad head another pat. "Let's head home. I've got more boxes to unpack."

Together, we walked across the village green. *Liquid courage.* I crumpled my cup and tossed it into the bin. Why would I need that?

Chapter Two

Sunlight streamed through my bedroom windows as I rummaged through the mound of shoes strewn across my closet floor. Late afternoon had turned to evening, and I'd lost track of time sorting through boxes of belongings that seemed incongruous with my new life. Unpacking and settling in had been a surprisingly slow slog for me. The tailored suits and leather pumps of my former life would be of little use here. I couldn't help feeling somewhat shell-shocked.

To be fair, only six months before, moving to Vermont hadn't even been on my radar. My life had been settled. Too settled, maybe, but comfortable in its familiarity. Then, last December, when Alicia heard about the little house in the center of the village coming on the market, she'd been quick to call me.

"This is exactly what you need, Bobbie," Alicia said in that way only big sisters could get away with. "It's time for you to stop wallowing and move forward with your life."

Easy for her to say.

Once I'd seen the house with its cute barn at the end of a short driveway—perfect for a photography studio—my dream of turning my hobby into a profession had taken on a life of its own. Rose's squeal of delight over being neighbors had sealed the deal. Before I could stop myself, I'd sold my home of twenty-five years, quit my soul-crushing administrative job, traded my city-smart hybrid for a mountain-smart all-wheel drive, and left the only city I'd ever known for the tiny village of Stonebridge, Vermont.

Alicia had been right about one thing. I no longer had time to wallow.

I pushed the memory aside. If I didn't hurry, I'd be late for my camera club's first outing. Inwardly groaning at the heap of footwear in my tiny closet, I gave my duck boots an uncertain glance. They'd gotten me through mud season, but I cringed at the thought of wearing them with my linen slacks. Still, this was Vermont. No one would care—or even notice.

Pulling my favorite gray slip-on sneakers from the bottom of the pile, I smiled. Minor victories. I grabbed another flowered scarf from my dresser and tied it around my ponytail, stepped into my sneakers, and sped downstairs. A quick check of my backpack—my lenses were packed and ready to go. I glanced at my reflection in the hall mirror, adding a swipe of berry lip balm and a spritz of eau de bug spray. My earlier trepidation had vanished. Rose had been joking about needing courage—hadn't she? *Good grief, this is only a photo outing.*

A bright red notification glowed on my phone as I grabbed it from the hall table. A missed call from my daughter, Emma. Filled with indecision, I checked the time. I only had a few minutes to spare. Remembering she was working the night shift at the hospital, I made a mental note to call her in the morning and tucked the phone in my pocket.

I was right on time. I rushed outside and caught a glimpse of my neighbor, who sat on his porch in an oversized chair that appeared suspiciously like a worn-out recliner. How it didn't get soggy in the rain was a mystery to me.

"Hello, Mr. Miller," I called with a cheerful wave, always hopeful he'd offer more than his usual harumph in return. He didn't.

Lester Miller's family dated back to the town founders, which made him village royalty. A woodchuck, as Vermonters would say. With his unruly mop of white hair, a bushy beard, and faded overalls over an even more faded plaid shirt, he looked the part. Perched on his tweed Barcalounger-turned-throne overlooking the center of the village, he appeared to be surveying his kingdom.

I paused to roll my shoulders before heading across the street. Joining villagers on the green, I strolled the sidewalks that crisscrossed patches of grass like a spiderweb. When I arrived at the gazebo, two of the club members were waiting.

"Bonsoir, Madame." Jackson Gilbert brushed his hand along the side of his balding head, his eyes grazing me from head to toe. Dressed in dark jeans, a buffalo plaid shirt—blue, rather than the ubiquitous red most often worn in Vermont—and weathered hiking boots, he looked the part of an outdoorsy Vermonter with a flair of his own.

"Hey there," I said with all the politeness I could conjure, hiding my annoyance at his blatant once-over before turning to greet our other member. Hunched on the gazebo steps, Penny Wright pinned the bangs of her asymmetrical hairstyle behind her ear and tentatively lifted her fingers. In her late twenties, she was the club's youngest member. She'd been the first to join, and despite looking bored, I sensed an eagerness that brought out the tutor in me.

When I looked up, I saw Alicia approach from the direction of the village market, her long, muscular legs making purposeful strides. To look at her, you'd never know she'd once been a city girl like me. Her look suited her. Fresh-faced and wearing jeans with a simple top, her style was as practical as her personality. Strands of silver-streaked blonde hair escaped the oversized barrette she wore at her nape, and a slantwise grin slid across her face. My sister and I had inherited our tall, slim physique from our father, while our mother gifted us with her amber-brown eyes. As far as I could tell, that was where our similarities ended.

Penny gave Alicia the same finger wave she'd given me while Jackson swiped the side of his head.

With a quick smile to my sister, I asked, "Has anyone seen Tiffanee?"

"Not yet," Jackson replied.

Between Tiffanee's derisive comments the night before and her contempt for our shoot's chosen location, I wouldn't have been devastated if she'd decided not to show. Guilt sat heavily upon my shoulders at the thought, although I suspected Penny agreed.

"Poor little Penny," Tiffanee had said at our meeting. "How will you ever keep up with us? I mean, like, all you have is a cell phone." Then she'd turned to me with a phony pout and twirled her ponytail around her finger. Had she thought I wouldn't recognize bullying? I wasted no time in setting her straight. Faced with Tiffanee's ridicule, Penny barely reacted, seemingly unperturbed. Only the clicking of her tongue ring told me she felt otherwise.

"Gee, I'd hate to leave without her." To anyone else, Alicia probably sounded genuine. I knew better. *That makes two of us.*

Jackson tapped the toe of his boot on the sidewalk. "I hope we don't plan to wait too long."

Studying the sun's angle, I figured we had a little more than an hour before sunset. With the mountains and forest surrounding us, the light would grow dim much earlier. We probably should have planned for an earlier outing, but it was too late to worry about that.

"I'd rather not leave anyone behind on our first outing," I said. *Well, mostly true.*

Jackson let out an impatient huff, clearly ready to go, with or without Tiffanee. As much as I hated the idea of leaving without her, it wouldn't have surprised me to find out she was already at the bridge, unbothered that she'd kept us waiting. I made a quick decision. "Let's go ahead," I said. "I can call her."

While walking across the green, I left a cheerful message on Tiffanee's voicemail, claiming we looked forward to seeing her at the bridge. Hopefully, she'd get the message, but it wasn't a given. Around here, cell service was hit or miss—mostly miss.

From the edge of the village green, the red frame of the covered bridge came into view, glowing in the evening light. Steep embankments flanked each side, leading to the flowing river below. We crossed Main Street, rounding the corner onto Bridge Street, and I nearly bumped into Harmony Santos, our village yogi. Her long gauzy dress drifted behind her, giving her the appearance of floating as she skirted around me. The waning sunlight glinted off her tawny cheeks and black hair, and I found myself mesmerized by her ethereal beauty. She greeted us with a distracted smile, but passed by without stopping.

As we approached the bridge, our group scattered, ready to click. It had been a mistake to think this location a cliché. The quaint beauty of the red structure nestled in the mountains was more than picture-worthy, and I was glad I hadn't let my opinion sway the club. With any luck, I'd find time to wander on my own. But first, I'd spend a few moments with each member, answering questions and offering guidance.

Before entering the bridge, I scanned the area, on the lookout for Tiffanee. No luck. It had been less than three hours since I'd seen her on the village green. She'd been unenthusiastic about our location, but I didn't think I'd misunderstood her intention to join us. I checked my phone for new messages. No cell signal. Of course. Ignoring the feeling of disquiet that washed over me, I hurried inside the bridge.

Traffic was light in this part of the village, with only the occasional car driving through. Inside, Penny, the member I was most concerned about, ambled from one diamond-shaped opening to another. Also inside the bridge, Jackson stopped every few steps, holding his lens close to the bridge's frame before snapping an image.

When he glanced up, I gave him an approving nod. "Interesting idea to focus on the light and shadows hitting the interior structure."

He gave a nonchalant shrug and continued his slow saunter across the bridge.

Light shining through an opening illuminated Penny's face as she lifted her phone to catch the shimmering rays of sunshine on the river below. Her baggy tee worn over slouched shoulders made her tiny frame look tinier. Boyish almost. She appeared absorbed in her project, unaware of my approach.

Waiting until she snapped her photo, I stepped forward. "May I see?"

She smiled shyly, a look that contrasted with the tough-girl image her sleeve of vivid tattoos portrayed. She hesitated before showing me her phone, as though afraid of what I might say. It made me wonder whether criticism was something she expected.

I gave her photo an appraising look. "That's lovely," I said, meaning it. Framed by the rustic wooden window, her image captured the sun's rays glittering white and gold on the river below. "You have a good eye. Be sure to try different angles. Experimenting is helpful, even if you don't like the results."

Penny placed a finger to her chin as she stared at her phone's screen. I may not have cared for Tiffanee's snarky comments the night before, but they had sparked a useful discussion about the more essential elements of photography: light, composition, and perspective. We photographers loved our fancy cameras and lenses, but a good camera could only do so much.

I headed outside, where the sky had already turned a steely shade of blue, and the breeze had cooled. The sun's angle on the other side of the bridge was perfect for creating a sun flare from the riverbank. Shielding my eyes from the sun with my hand, I scanned the horizon. Alicia was no longer in sight, possibly under the bridge? Still no Tiffanee. It was becoming increasingly difficult to ignore the sense of dread weighing heavily in my chest. What was holding her? Clasping my jacket at my neck, I shivered. Something felt wrong—very wrong.

The slope leading to the river was steep, the soil, dry and rocky. I took a few careful steps before snapping a photo of the bridge, the lowering sun casting long shadows. As I peered through my camera's viewfinder toward the rushing water below, a large bundle caught my eye. No, not a bundle, a person. It was probably Alicia, lying on the ground near the bottom. I chuckled to myself. The things photographers did for an interesting angle.

Dusk was gathering, and the sun was falling fast. I continued to step closer, nearly losing my balance when my foot slipped on a loose rock. The rustling leaves played tricks with my eyes as their shadows danced across the ground. Something didn't feel right. I lifted my camera again, the zoom lens bringing the image closer. The bundle was still—too still. I took another cautious step.

Oh, no. No, no, no.

A lump lodged in my throat. Throwing caution to the wind, I rushed toward the dark, motionless shape. When I reached the bottom, I stopped and closed my eyes, shutting out the image before me.

Lying at my feet, Tiffanee had finally made her appearance—face down on the rocky riverbank.

Chapter Three

*N*o. *Oh no—tell me this isn't happening. Not at our first photo shoot!* Frantically, I shook off my earlier premonition and looked for my club members.

"Help!" My shout sounded hoarse—more like a whisper. I spun around and spotted Alicia at the top of the ridge. Waving my arm, I tried again. "Call for an ambulance." It was too late for an ambulance, I was pretty sure. Even so, I had to try.

Alicia peered down the hill with raised palms. I cupped my hands to my mouth and tried again. She waved back, and I let out a relieved sigh, grateful for my sister's no-nonsense style.

I crouched in the patchy grass. Tiffanee's hair fanned around her head, shimmering with the last rays of sun like a golden halo. The collar of her denim jacket was flipped up, hiding her neck and most of her face. If not for a pool of blood beneath her forehead, I might have thought she was napping.

Had Tiffanee come early rather than meet with the group as planned? Then what? I looked at the rock-strewn hill. She must have slipped and fallen, as I had almost done. The jagged rocks appeared deadly. With a shaky hand, I grabbed Tiffanee's wrist, willing the throb of a heartbeat through my fingers. *Come on, come on.* I knew better. Tiffanee's wrist was limp.

Clouds reflected in the camera's lens near Tiffanee's body, the strap still around her neck. I stretched to retrieve it and turned it over. The protective flap for the memory card was wide open, the slot inside empty. I froze, scanning the ground, somehow knowing I wouldn't find the missing card. Memory cards didn't fall out on their own. Losing one required human intervention. As I exhaled, the camera slipped from my shaking hand.

My legs stiffened while squatting next to Tiffanee's lifeless body, the discomfort a welcome distraction from my growing confusion. Tiffanee shouldn't be here. If she'd met our group at the gazebo as planned, this wouldn't have happened. I surveyed the trees along the river, not sure what I was looking for. I couldn't fathom the reason for Tiffanee's missing memory card. Had she been switching it with another when she slipped and fell? Maybe there was a spare in her pocket?

I turned back to Tiffanee, pulled my jacket tighter, and whispered to the young woman at my feet. "What happened? Why are you here?" A cool breeze blew but carried no answers.

A stone rolled down the embankment, announcing Penny's arrival. She stopped near my side and leaned to peer at Tiffanee. Her words barely audible, she whispered, "Is she dead?"

Before I could say anything, several more rocks tumbled downward. Jackson barreled toward me with his plaid-clad arms flapping like an out-of-control skier fighting to stay upright. He landed with a thud, almost knocking me over.

"*Mon Dieu!*" He stopped to stare at Tiffanee's inert body. "Well, that looks like quite the spill." If he was joking, I wasn't finding it funny.

"Except this was more than just a spill." I sidled away from him.

He ran his hand along the side of his head and, for a moment, sat motionless. "I hope you didn't touch anything." The return of his customary arrogance fueled anger I hadn't realized was simmering below the surface.

"I checked for her pulse," I said, my jaw clenching at his answering tsk. I bit my tongue to keep silent and slowly counted to myself before looking back toward the street a second time. Where was Alicia, and why were the police taking so long?

"No cell signal," Jackson said, as if reading my mind. "Alicia had to run toward Main Street to make the call."

Right. One more idiosyncrasy of rural life I needed to get used to. I sat on the ground and hugged my knees.

It wasn't long before Alicia reappeared and called to us. "Rescue squad is on its way."

The sky had darkened; only a dim glow spilled over the treetops. The river rippled with streaks of red, an eerie reflection of the bridge's walls, reminding me of the blood-splattered rocks beneath Tiffanee's head.

Alicia stepped sideways down the hill and placed a protective arm around me as she joined our somber gathering. I rested my chin on my knees. What seemed like hours, but was likely a few minutes, brought the flashing lights of a rescue vehicle. Rose's words came back to me. *Liquid courage.* There was no way she'd predicted this, but I couldn't shake the feeling I'd ignored a warning.

A middle-aged man and an older woman, both wearing the reflective coats of our volunteer fire department, strode down the embankment, sure-footed. The man's gray-streaked, brown hair framed a pleasant and authoritative face. He took charge. "Everyone needs to move back to the street while we secure the scene. Who discovered the accident?"

"Me." I lifted my hand like a timid schoolgirl while struggling to stand on wobbly legs. Jackson offered his hand and pulled me to my feet. Pasting on a weak smile, my earlier annoyance vanished at his gesture.

"State police are on their way," the man said. "Go on up to the road and wait. They'll want to ask you questions as soon as they arrive."

Alicia, Jackson, and Penny went ahead of me as instructed while I squared my shoulders, preparing to trudge up the hill. I took one last look at Tiffanee's lifeless form. "I'll find out what happened. I promise." It was a promise I didn't know how to keep, but I'd find a way.

"Bobbie!" Rose's breathless voice broke through the gathering crowd on the street. "What's going on?" She started down the hill, her ankles buckling in her wedge sandals.

"Ma'am, I need you to stay where you are." A police officer in a broad-brimmed hat materialized in the crowd.

"Excuse me, Officer, but I'm part of this group." With a stomp of her foot, she fisted her hands on ample hips. "I just got here, and I need to make sure my friend is all right."

I couldn't hear the police officer's reply, but Alicia appeared and took Rose by the arm.

A second police officer strode past me and kneeled next to Tiffanee's body. "No pulse," he said. "And a gash on her head." His tall, lanky frame unfolded like an accordion when he stood and stepped toward me. At five feet, nine inches, I rarely needed to crank my neck to meet a man's eye, but this man was well over six feet, and his beady eyes stared down at me over his beak-like nose.

"If you could move along," he said.

"Right." I started up the hill to where the first police officer was talking to the other club members, notebook and pen in hand.

"I'm told you found the body," he said as soon as I reached the top of the hill.

With a reluctant nod, I swallowed hard before answering him.

"How about starting at the beginning," he said. He was young and looked almost as nervous as I felt. His soft gaze appeared kind.

"I'm not sure what I can tell you. This was The Stonebridge Keep It Snappy Shutter Club's first photo outing. Or, at least, it was supposed to be." I motioned with a flick of my hand toward the rest of the group. "I guess it didn't go well."

He nodded, encouraging me to continue. "And?"

"And, like I said, I'm not sure what to tell you. We all met at the gazebo at seven o'clock. All of us, except for Tiffanee. We figured she was a no-show. Or maybe running late?" I hadn't meant it to be a question.

"If I have this right, you're saying the accident didn't happen during your outing. When did you find the deceased, then?"

"Oh, gosh, no!" I hadn't thought of that. "I found her after we got here. I'm not sure of the exact time. The sun was supposed to set a little before eight-thirty, and it was almost hidden behind the trees when I walked down the hill. So, about eight or a quarter past?" I paused. "What time did Alicia call it in? She called as soon as I found Tiffanee. As soon as she could get a cell signal, anyway."

"The body is the way you found it?" He pointed down the hill. "She likely fell."

"That's what I thought at first, but I don't know." My head was spinning, and I massaged the back of my neck. "Something doesn't feel right."

The officer stiffened. "What makes you say that?"

I pointed to Tiffanee's camera as if we could see the open slot from where we stood. "Her camera's memory card is missing. They don't fall out on their own. Here, I'll show you." I lifted my camera on its strap to open the slot, but he waved me off.

"Maybe she took it out herself," he said.

"It's possible." I paused, gathering my thoughts. "If she did, you should find a card somewhere. I didn't see it on the ground, but I suppose I could've missed it. Or maybe it's in her pocket? All I know is she wouldn't bother to come here without one. Her camera won't take photos without it."

The officer paused as though considering my words. "Are you sure no one from your group took it out?"

"I was the one who found her." At least, I assumed I had been. Alicia was the only member I'd lost track of. "The card was already missing. I noticed it right after I checked Tiffanee's wrist for a pulse."

He continued to ask questions about the outing and where each of the other members had been when I discovered Tiffanee. I did my best to answer him with minimal stammering. By the time I finished speaking with the young officer, everyone had left except for Rose, Alicia, and the members of the rescue squad.

"Bobbie! Holy moly! When I saw the lights and the ambulance, I freaked. What did I miss?" Rose grasped my arm, standing on tiptoe to peer down the dark slope. "Is that Tiffanee?"

"Yes." My voice shook as I fought back tears that always came much too easily.

Alicia wrapped me in a tight bear hug.

"I'm okay," I said, trying not to cry.

"No, you're not," Alicia said in that matter-of-fact way of hers. It wasn't like I could argue with her, so she released me, and the three of us walked toward Main Street, where she'd left her car.

"What happened?" Rose asked. "Did Tiffanee fall?"

I nodded, swiping the corner of my eye.

"That doesn't seem like her," Rose said. "Tiffanee grew up playing near this bridge. I'd think she's pretty sure-footed."

"Agreed," Alicia said.

My tears won the battle. "I know. Everything seems wrong."

Rose gave my arm a gentle squeeze. "She probably wasn't paying attention. You know how Tiffanee could be. The way she snuck around with that camera of hers gave everyone the heebie-jeebies."

"What do you mean?" I asked. "My camera is always with me, too. It doesn't seem all that weird to me."

"It's not the same thing. You don't creep up on people."

The sky grew darker as we walked away from the flashing lights. Across the village green, bluegrass music wafted through the open doors of The Mad Crow Tavern, known simply as The Crow to locals. The strum of the guitar contradicted the melee we'd left behind.

When we reached the corner, Alicia stopped. "My car's across the street. You're sure you're okay? You could spend the night at my house."

"I'll be fine." Then, noting her skeptical expression, I held out my hand. "Pinky swear. I'm fine." It was tempting to let her take care of me, but I held firm.

She gave me another quick hug before crossing the street.

"Let's go to your house." Rose grasped my arm. "If there was ever a time we both needed a glass of wine, tonight would be it."

Assured by my friend's presence, I let my tears flow. Rose was right; she had to be. Tiffanee had simply lost her footing while taking photos. Accidents like that were surprisingly common for photographers. As much as I wanted to believe this scenario, my neck prickled with apprehension. A fall didn't explain Tiffanee's missing memory card.

Chapter Four

The next morning, I woke to the clear whistle of a chickadee outside my window. "Fee bee, fee bee," it called. Before I'd even opened my eyes, Darcy nudged me with his nose.

"Too early," I grumbled while pulling the blanket to my chin.

Not one to give up easily, he nudged me again, his brown eyes shining and tail wagging. If Dan were here, he'd jump out of bed and take him for a run. Running was not my thing.

I rolled over, images of Tiffanee's lifeless body reeling through my mind. The previous night was a blur. After returning to the safety of my home, I'd been helpless to stop my torrent of tears. Rose and I had polished off a bottle of wine—my aching head reminded me of that much. I also remembered how she'd refused to believe there was anything strange about Tiffanee's death. With a shake of her head, she'd dismissed the missing memory card while vehemently insisting there was an innocent explanation. Finally, feeling silly, I'd agreed. I was a city girl, which by definition meant I was jaded. My suspicions had no place in Vermont.

Changing tactics, Darcy whined as though his life depended upon me getting out of bed. No longer able to ignore him, I pushed my covers aside, along with any lingering thoughts of the previous night. My clock read seven, not much later than my normal get-out-of-bed time.

"You really need to learn the art of sleeping in." I ruffled his fur, knowing he had no intention of sleeping in. Ever. As it was, I'd bought every extra minute of sleep time I could by using an automatic feeder for his breakfast. If only it took him for a walk, too.

I stood and reached for Dan's ratty bathrobe from a hook on the door and held it to my face, inhaling. His scent was long gone, but the act comforted me somehow. Darcy watched with knowing eyes, and I softened. A long walk with my camera suddenly felt like a good idea. It was the best way I knew to clear my head. Ignoring my early morning hunger, I hung Dan's robe back on the hook, threw on a pair of jeans with a fitted T-shirt, raked my hair back into a messy ponytail, and stepped into my hiking boots.

"Don't you dare think you talked me into this," I said in a stern voice while tying the laces.

Darcy's whole body wagged. He'd seen my boots and knew what was coming.

"Okay, you win. Let's go to the river."

Hidden near the dilapidated mill building and the crumbling stone bridge—the one from the Miller family's town-founding days—weeds and thistle nearly disguised the trailhead. Darcy and I had rushed down Main Street, avoiding the usual early morning chit-chat with other villagers. Before heading into the forest, I paused and removed my camera from my backpack. There wasn't another soul in sight, so I let Darcy off his leash. The fog was already lifting from my mind.

Darcy wasted no time pressing his snout to the ground, sniffing the newest woodland odors. This was our favorite trail, one we had walked many times with Dan and Emma. I stepped forward and adjusted the settings of my camera while gauging the light filtering through the towering trees above. My pace was slow as I, too, raised my nose to the fresh morning air and took in the forest aromas. Balsam, cedar, and pine. Christmas in May.

We ambled along in companionable silence. Darcy stopped to sniff now and then, and I crouched to the ground to snap pictures of woodland flowers while looking for the ever-elusive lady's slippers hidden among the ferns. It was early in the year to find them, but I was on the lookout.

Losing myself in the familiar motions of composing and focusing, my body relaxed. I twisted the dials and knobs as dappled sunlight danced along the path. Thoughts of Tiffanee slid to the back of my mind.

Under some brush, I spied a clump of delicate flowers whose yellow centers looked bright, surrounded by petals in a pale lavender hue. While kneeling to set my camera on the ground, I switched to live view and detected a movement in the background. Darcy seemed to sense it also, his body on full alert. I clicked my photo and stood. Beyond the flowers and across the river, a black bear stood on its hind legs, watching us.

"Darcy, stay," I commanded, holding my open palm near his nose. The rushing water separated us from the bear. She wasn't likely to cross the river, but her stiff posture was a warning. As we watched, two rambunctious cubs appeared, tumbling in the grass. The mama bear stood immobile and attentive, so much like a mother watching her children on the playground.

"Mama Bear," I whispered, raising my camera. I snapped, refocused, and snapped again. The morning sun shone on the bear family, illuminating patches of their black fur. I peered through the viewfinder, my lens bringing them closer. This was a photographer's dream—impossible to plan.

The cubs' comical antics lifted my spirits, but it was the mother bear's piercing stare that captivated me. I worked quickly, capturing as many images as my fingers allowed. Then, without warning, the bear gathered her cubs and led them back into the forest. I loosened my grasp, lowering my camera to my waist, and Darcy looked up, seeking permission to continue sniffing.

"Good boy," I said, digging a treat from my pocket, and the spell broke.

We continued our walk along the river. Reluctantly, my thoughts returned to the previous night. No matter how hard I tried, I couldn't shake the feeling something was off. I pulled a leaf from a nearby tree, shredding it before throwing it to the ground. An image of Tiffanee, her halo of golden hair in the evening sun, appeared in my mind. Tiffanee had been no angel. No one would dispute that. But surely no one wished her harm. I couldn't keep the question of the missing memory card from niggling at the back of my mind, finally convincing myself it must have been on the ground nearby and the police had found it.

I scratched the top of Darcy's head. "Let's go. It's time to check in with Alicia. If there's news, she'll know all about it."

After hooking Darcy's leash over the old hitching post outside The Stonebridge Country Market, he pinned me with a doleful gaze at being left outside. Even the promise of a treat did little to appease him.

"Sorry," I said. "I promise I'll be right out." I almost reminded him he's a dog, but I was the one talking to him, so maybe it was me who needed the reminder.

A bell jingled as I entered Alicia's store and stepped onto the scarred wooden floor. The earthy aroma of aged wood mingled with the spicy-sweet scent of fresh cinnamon rolls and pies cooling on the bakery counter. My stomach grumbled, reminding me I had skipped breakfast. I waved to my sister, who was boxing goods at the front counter while chatting with a customer, and strode past through cramped aisles brimming with an array of boxed and canned goods. At the far end of the store, I grabbed a bottle of milk and a container of yogurt from the dairy case, ignoring the temptation to snag a sweet, gooey roll on my way back to the front of the store.

"Hi, Sis," Alicia called from behind the cash register as the previous customer left, brushing past me with a cordial nod. Leaning on the counter, she shook her head. "I can't get over last night."

"It sure didn't go how we'd planned." I touched the smooth folds of my scarf.

Above her cherry-red reading glasses, Alicia's brows creased with concern. "It's all anyone is talking about." She lowered her voice. "It's so hard to believe Tiffanee would fall down that hill." Her fingers pecked the keys of the cash register.

"Has there been any news?" I asked.

"Nothing we don't already know. You found Tiffanee's body by the river. Looks like she took a terrible fall." Alicia stopped and pointed at my camera hanging from the strap around my neck. I sensed she'd grown tired of the subject. "You've been out taking pictures this morning?"

"Let me show you." I set my camera on the counter and opened the screen, eager to share my bear photos. I couldn't get over how lucky I'd been.

Alicia adjusted her glasses and peered at the images. "Oh, heavens."

I scrolled, giving her time to admire each snap, excited all over again. Even on the small screen, the playfulness of the cubs and their mother's stern countenance showed clearly.

"That mama bear!" Alicia said. "I've lived here most of my adult life, and I've never taken photos like these. Good thing you were across the river. Black bears rarely attack. But I wouldn't want to come between a mama bear and her cubs."

I was thinking about the bear when I bent to unhook Darcy's leash. A pair of hiking boots materialized beneath my bent head, and I blew a wavy wisp of hair from my forehead, managing a smile as I straightened.

"Hello, Jackson." I hoped my greeting sounded friendlier to his ears than it did to mine.

"*Bonjour.*" He patted my arm, his voice filled with a concern that sounded as false as my cheerful greeting. "Have the police come to speak with you this morning?"

"Not yet. I was planning to head to the station. I'm kind of in a rush, and I need to take Darcy home."

"You should probably wait for them to come to you." He continued to rub my arm.

Something about his hand on my arm set me on edge, and I couldn't ignore the odd tone in his voice. "Yes, well, I guess I'd better go home then." I gave Darcy's leash a gentle tug, shaking Jackson's offending hand away.

"*Bien sûr.*" Of course.

Over the past few months, I'd grown used to his solicitousness, despite the slimy way it made me feel. This seemed different, as if he was trying to tell me something. I shook my head to clear it. He was still speaking.

"...understand you can count on me, no matter what happens. I don't blame you for last night."

"Thanks, I appreciate that." I forced another smile and turned away. *Wait, what? Blame me for what?* I spun around, but Jackson had disappeared into the market.

Chapter Five

Chatter spilled from inside Rose's coffee shop as I walked past. A tempting aroma wafted from the café, impossible to ignore. My stomach grumbled again, a reminder I hadn't had breakfast, not to mention my morning cup of coffee.

It only took me a moment to decide to drop Darcy at home, brush the rat's nest from my hair, and return to the café, once again saving myself the need to figure out my ridiculously complicated coffee maker—the one my kitchen designer claimed ground the beans and brewed the perfect cup of coffee every time. Happy with my plan, I turned toward home, struggling to hold Darcy back as he tugged on his leash. A stiff ridge of fur rose along his neck.

"What's got you so tense?" I looked ahead and froze. Seated on my porch swing was a tall figure whose broad-brimmed hat could only belong to the lanky police officer from the night before. His attention appeared to be glued to his cell phone despite his body being taut and alert, giving him the look of someone who never relaxed. He lifted his hat and placed it in his lap, revealing a plume of gelled spikes. I couldn't help thinking he was the image of a hawk, ready to swoop down on unsuspecting prey.

The officer stood, towering over the porch railing as I approached. "You were told we'd have more questions for you."

I climbed my porch steps and mustered a weak smile, startled by his aggressive manner. "Oh…I…um…" I let out a long breath before speaking again. "I hope you weren't waiting long. I'm Bobbie Brooks."

"Detective Wyatt Cram," he said. "State police."

I swallowed. Staties had a way of appearing absurdly imposing. "I figured you'd want more details about Tiffanee's accident. Please come in." I opened the door and stood aside, allowing the detective to pass. It was unlike Darcy to growl, but he did then, a low, soft rumble.

"Watch your dog," Detective Cram said as he strode into my living room and settled on one of the two couches flanking my fireplace.

I gave Darcy an appreciative pat and followed behind. Sitting on the couch opposite the detective, I took a moment to skim the room. Gone were the dark floral wallpaper and velvet drapes that had suffocated me when I first moved in. The fresh coat of light, creamy-white paint, wooden blinds, and carelessly stacked books settled my nerves with their homey vibe. I ended my sweep, lingering on the framed photos clustered on my fireplace mantle. Seeking my favorite image from a happier time, I beheld the faces of my husband and daughter and found comfort in Dan's familiar smile.

"Let's get started." Detective Cram made clicking his pen seem menacing.

"Of course. Anything I can do to help with—"

"Tell me your version of what happened last night. Start at the beginning and leave nothing out."

"Okay." I blinked at his brusque tone, then looked back at Dan's photo, relaxing as I launched into an explanation about the camera club outing and how Tiffanee hadn't shown up at the gazebo as planned. "I was hoping she was just running late and would meet us there."

"What time was that?"

"We, the club members, met at the gazebo at seven. I'm not sure how long we waited. Maybe ten or fifteen minutes? I tried calling Tiffanee to tell her we were going ahead to the bridge. She didn't answer. Obviously." I let out a nervous laugh. "I left her a voicemail. If you want, I can look up the time on my phone."

Ignoring my offer to check my phone, he asked, "What happened after that?"

"We walked to the covered bridge." I frowned, rubbing the tail of my scarf. "When we got there, we split up to take photos. Photographers all have their own interests, you know, even when taking photos of the same subject."

"Describe your relationship with the deceased."

"Relationship?" I asked, wondering what he was getting at. "I wouldn't say we had one. I barely knew her."

"Tell me about the fight that took place at your club's meeting the night before last."

"Fight?" I startled. What was he talking about? "I don't know what you mean."

Darcy sat up, his fur standing at attention. "It's okay, boy," I whispered, scratching his head.

The detective glowered while flicking through the pages of his notebook. "Let's see. Ah yes, the two of you had a heated argument at your meeting on Wednesday night."

"Heated is not the way I would describe our discussion." My mind drifted back to our meeting. Tiffanee wouldn't have won any Miss Congeniality awards. Between mocking Penny and deriding our club's choice for the first photo shoot, she'd taxed my leadership skills. A heated argument, though? Someone was exaggerating.

"You deny arguing with the deceased? I have a witness who says otherwise." He cocked his head.

"We had a brief discussion about mutual respect."

"Mm-hmm." He scribbled in his notebook. "It sounds to me like you're saying your club is lying."

I squirmed in my seat. What was he insinuating?

Before I had time to think it through, he changed direction and asked when I'd last seen Tiffanee and where I'd been during the hours leading up to our photo shoot. I explained I'd seen her on the village green that afternoon before going home to unpack boxes.

"Can anyone verify that?" he asked.

"I was with Rose Lavoie on the village green."

"And at home?"

"Just Darcy," I said, patting Darcy's back. "Are you suggesting I'm a suspect?"

Detective Cram set his notebook and pen on the table with slow, precise motions and straightened. "Let me get straight to the point. Mrs. Brooks, can you identify this?" He drew a photo from his folder. "We found it at the scene." He slid it across the table and lifted his hand to reveal the image.

I gasped. My missing scarf.

I stared at the photo of my scarf's pink and purple flowers, knotted and twisted. Found at the scene? How could that be? As if acting on their own, my fingers reached for my ponytail and the scarf I'd tied around it earlier in the morning. I couldn't stop staring at the detective's photo. My mind reeled. "Where?"

"We found abrasions on the victim. And this"—He pushed the photo closer to me—"was wrapped around her neck. Most likely the murder weapon."

His words cut through me. I struggled to understand what he was saying. "Murder? B-but that's not possible."

"I assure you it is."

"Do I need a lawyer?" I asked.

"That's up to you," he said.

I took my phone from my pocket and texted Alicia. Her husband, Nate, was an attorney—the only attorney I knew and a brilliant one at that. She met my request for Nate's help with her usual efficiency. Most people I knew would have texted back a string of emoji-laced questions. Not my sister. Her quick response informed me she already had him on the phone.

Detective Cram and I waited without speaking. My hands shook at the sound of the detective flipping pages in his notebook as I peered at my screen, waiting for a reply. When Alicia's message flashed on my screen, I let out a relieved sigh.

Nate's on his way-Tell police you'll be at the barracks at 3

The wavering dots under her message showed she was typing her next message.

Heading over

I answered back with a thumb's-up and smile emoji, grateful her shop was only two doors away.

"My lawyer is on his way," I said. "We can come to the police station this afternoon at three o'clock. I hope that's agreeable."

Detective Cram sputtered while checking his watch. "Three o'clock will be fine. Don't be late." On his way out the door, he came to a stop.

Alicia's calm voice sounded from my front porch. "Hello, Detective."

Darcy's tail thumped at the sound of his favorite aunt. I touched his head and signaled for him to wait. The detective tipped his hat and held the door for Alicia to enter before tramping down the porch steps.

"Hey, boy." My sister stepped forward and patted Darcy's head. She drew a treat from her pocket and handed it to him before giving his head another scratch and shifting her attention to me.

I met Alicia's questioning gaze. "Did you know Tiffanee was murdered? That my scarf was wound around her neck?"

Alicia sat next to me. "I heard some scuttlebutt after you left. Apparently, Jackson had an early morning interview with the police. But what I don't get is how your scarf was involved."

"Rose and I noticed it missing earlier yesterday afternoon, but I forgot all about it, and I sure didn't see it last night." I thought back to the scene at the river, seeing it as though standing right there. Tiffanee's hair fanned around her head. I pictured her jacket collar and refocused on my sister. "Tiffanee's collar. It was turned up. It must have hidden the scarf."

"Okay. Nate is on his way over. He'll coach you before taking you to the police station."

It felt good to have Alicia's reassurance—to not be alone. Drawing a long, calming breath, I thought of Nate. I trusted him completely. I'd never forget how my sister, fresh out of graduate school, had shocked our family by announcing her engagement to Nate, along with her plans to move to his family's farm in Vermont. If we'd had a crystal ball to show us how she would take over the village market while raising goats and learning to make artisan cheese, we would have been flabbergasted. But really, it shouldn't have been a surprise. Alicia had always been someone who owned whatever situation she was in. Despite the disapproval of our urbane parents, I couldn't have been happier with the way things turned out. I loved Nate like my own big brother, and watching my sister defy our parents had been oddly liberating.

Never, though, had I expected to need my brother-in-law's help with a police inquiry. And I still couldn't get my mind wrapped around the detective's revelation. Someone had murdered Tiffanee. *With my scarf.*

Chapter Six

A short time later, Darcy jumped to his feet and ran to the door, announcing Nate's arrival.

"Hey there, buddy," Nate said with a laugh.

I sat up from where I'd been lying, cushioned in the warmth of my couch. "I sure am glad to see you."

Darcy appeared even more excited than I was. He wriggled around Nate's legs with a full-body wag.

"Sorry, bud. No treats today." He ruffled Darcy's fur before addressing me. "What's this about you getting into trouble with your camera club?" His furrowed brow contradicted his teasing tone. He stood in the doorway, and his neatly combed, light brown hair nearly touched the doorframe above his head. Even in his dress shirt and dark trousers with a knife-edge crease, Nate had the robust look of a man who was as comfortable on the seat of a tractor as pacing before a judge in the courtroom.

I stiffened. Trouble? Was I really in trouble?

"Thanks for coming." Alicia crossed the room and planted a kiss on his lips.

Nate took Detective Cram's place on the couch with a stiffness signaling his shift from good-humored brother-in-law to lawyer. "Okay, I need to hear a detailed account of everything that happened last night."

As Darcy settled on the floor next to him, I launched into my description of the events leading up to finding Tiffanee. He grilled me on even the most minute details.

"Think carefully. Did you touch anything or disturb the scene in any way?"

Staring across the room, I relived the scene once again. "I attempted to check Tiffanee's pulse. Then. Oh, no." I groaned.

Nate remained silent, waiting for me to continue.

"I thought it was an accident, you know? I mean, I figured Tiffanee had skipped meeting us at the gazebo and gone to the bridge on her own. I didn't know her well, but I got the impression she'd do something like that."

With a slight tip of his chin, Nate urged me forward.

"Her camera was lying on the ground, and I picked it up. That's when I saw the open flap. The memory card was missing, and I got the feeling something was wrong."

Nate nodded slowly. "You need to tell the police about touching the camera. They'll find your fingerprints on it, and it would be better if the information came from you first."

Detective Cram would think I was trying to hide something. How could I have been so dumb?

"We should head over." Nate held out his hand and helped me to my feet.

I untied the scarf around my ponytail, stroking the silk before dropping it to the table. Better not to draw attention to my scarf-wearing habit.

"Let's walk. That will give us a few minutes to talk." Nate and I patted Darcy's head before heading to the door.

When we stepped onto the front porch, I raised my hand to wave to Mr. Miller, who was lounging in his porch recliner.

"Hello, Mr. Miller," Nate called out.

"Well, hello yourself," Mr. Miller called back.

My mouth dropped open. *Is Mr. Miller smiling?* "What the…?"

Nate shrugged, giving me an impish grin. "I've known him all my life."

I pinched my mouth closed and reminded myself I had more important things to worry about than feeling like I didn't belong.

It was a normal Friday afternoon in Stonebridge, and stressed-out drivers in cars sporting out-of-state license plates formed a procession on Main Street. As we wove our way across the street, Nate turned to me. "Keep your answers as short as you can. Yes or no, if possible."

I listened to Nate's instructions, chewing my lower lip. My mind was a tumult of confusion and anger. Earlier, I'd been convinced Tiffanee's death was a tragic accident despite the suspicions I'd pushed aside. If only that were true.

"Don't answer questions that aren't asked, and if I put my hand on your arm, stop talking." The calmness of Nate's voice, his quiet confidence, did little to ease my growing dread.

We stopped at the walkway leading to the single-story building, more modern than most in the village. Nate placed a reassuring hand on my arm, and his hazel eyes locked with mine. "Everything will be all right. Detective Cram will try to rattle you. Stay calm."

I crossed my arms at my waist, the bitter taste of fear filling my mouth as we walked to the double doors.

The young woman at the front desk of the police station straightened when we entered. She'd just popped a fry into her mouth, leaving a spot of ketchup at the corner of her lips. My already fluttering stomach somersaulted at the greasy smell of fried food, making me glad I hadn't eaten all day. She licked the blob of ketchup while wiping her oily fingers on the napkin and flashed Nate a coy smile.

"Hi, Olivia. I've brought Mrs. Brooks to see Detective Cram," Nate said.

Olivia threw the remnants of her lunch in the trash and cast a wary glance my way. "Follow me." Her brown ponytail bobbed as she led us down a long, narrow corridor. I tried to ignore my stomach's flip-flops, their intervals shortening as the pea-green walls closed in around me. Grasping Nate's arm, I scanned the corridor for a restroom. I was preparing to make a run for it when Olivia opened a door and reached inside to flip a switch.

Harsh light glared from the ceiling, illuminating the stark gray walls and a table with four metal chairs. I tensed, swiping at my damp forehead, not expecting the room to look so much like a set from a television show. Thankfully, the dizzying feeling of the endless hallway lessened, and my stomach eased.

Olivia pointed toward the empty chairs. "Have a seat. Detective Cram will be right with you." She appeared hesitant to leave.

"Is there something else?" Nate asked.

With a flutter of eyelashes, she asked, "Can I bring you some water?"

Water sounded good, and I nodded.

"That would be nice," Nate said before sitting in the chair next to mine.

Out in the hallway, a door slammed, and the sound of heavy boots echoed.

"Mrs. Brooks, Mr. Crowley." The pompous detective strode into the already too-small room. He puffed his chest as he made a ceremony of plunking a tape recorder on the table, followed by his notebook and pen. "I am leading this investigation."

Nate greeted the police detective and reached across the table to shake hands.

"Sorry for interrupting." Olivia ducked into the room and placed two glasses of water on the table. "Let me know if you need anything else." She twirled her ponytail as she closed the door behind her.

Detective Cram grasped Nate's hand for a cursory shake before jabbing a button on the tape recorder. "Let's get started." In a loud monotone, he stated our names, the date, and the time of day before turning to me. "For the record, could you repeat your version of the events leading to your, ahem, finding the deceased?"

Version. This was the second time he'd used that word. The implication that I was lying wasn't lost on me. I recounted everything I remembered about the previous night, stopping at the point where I found Tiffanee, lifeless on the ground.

"How did your scarf wind up around the victim's neck?" He shoved a clear bag containing my scarf across the table. "This is yours, is it not?"

I remembered Nate's instructions. "I don't know, and yes."

Detective Cram's forehead wrinkled.

"I believe Mrs. Brooks is saying she does not know how the scarf came to be at the crime scene, and yes, she believes it is hers." Nate sat back in his chair, his fingers resting on the edge of the table. He seemed relaxed. Bored, even.

"You often wear scarves, don't you, Mrs. Brooks? Several people have identified it." He poked his finger at the photo. "You were wearing it yesterday."

"Yes, to both your question and your statement." *So far, so good.* I resisted the urge to add a tidbit about a scarf's versatility in accessorizing an outfit. Somehow, I doubted the gruff detective would be appreciative.

"So, you admit you were wearing this scarf yesterday."

Was he deliberately being obtuse? It's not like I'd use my own scarf to kill someone. I peeked at Nate before answering, my voice shaking. "Yes. I'm sure many people—" Nate placed his hand on my arm. I whispered to him, "He's right. Several people saw me wearing it."

With a slight nod, Nate removed his hand.

"You were saying, Mrs. Brooks?"

I looked back at the detective's pointed nose and spiked hair, wishing he didn't remind me so much of a vulture. "What I meant to say was that I ran into lots of people who could've seen me wearing the scarf. I discovered it was missing in the afternoon. I don't know when I lost it."

"Who else had access to it?"

"I don't know."

"Can we move on?" Nate shifted in his seat. "Mrs. Brooks lost her scarf but doesn't remember when or where. I assume that will be part of your investigation, and if my client remembers anything, we'll be happy to share it with you."

Detective Cram nodded, his spiky plumage bobbing.

"You already admitted to touching the victim." Lifting a corner of his mouth while riffling through his notes, he tapped his pen on the page. "Ah, yes. You claimed you were checking for a pulse. Please tell me about that."

I fumed at his sarcastic tone. "I didn't know Tiffanee was dead. I sure was hoping she wasn't, so I felt her wrist for a pulse."

"Did you touch anything else, move the body, perhaps?"

I clasped my hands in my lap and answered his question. "I didn't move the body, but I touched something."

Detective Cram steepled his fingers. "What was that?"

"Tiffanee's camera. I saw it lying on the ground and picked it up. I just remembered this afternoon." Something played in the back of my mind. Something still wasn't right.

"So, you admit to disturbing a crime scene." Detective Cram's voice boomed. "Did you remove anything?"

"No. I mean, I didn't know it was a crime scene. I thought Tiffanee had fallen, you know, accidentally. The embankment is steep. I nearly fell myself. Photographers often get lost in the scenery and forget to pay attention." My heart raced. Something about Tiffanee's camera lying on the ground wasn't right. The lens had pointed toward the sky, clouds reflected in the glass. That was it—no lens cap. It proved my theory correct. Tiffanee had been taking photos when she was murdered. Did that mean there were photos of the killer on her missing memory card? I flashed back over the scene, scanning the ground in my mind. Where was the lens cap?

"Mrs. Brooks?" The detective's pen tapped the table. "It was a simple question."

"I didn't remove anything." I leaned back, my mind swimming. Someone had not only stolen the memory card, but the lens cap was missing, too.

"We'll need to take your fingerprints."

"I understand." Even though I'd known this was coming, dread filled my chest with a new realization. *I'm the prime suspect.*

The moment I arrived back home, I sank into the comfort of my couch, flinging my arm over my face and mulling over Detective Cram's questions. How was it possible the day had turned out like this? After our meeting, Nate had gone to his office, promising to follow up on the lens cap.

"The police should have noticed the missing cap by now," I suggested to Nate. "I'm wondering if there's a missing camera bag, too. Tiffanee had some pricey gear, and I didn't see a bag at the scene." If I had to guess, I would say she not only carried a camera bag, but a fancy designer one.

It wasn't until I heard the click of Darcy's toenails on the wooden floor that I realized he hadn't greeted me at the door. He sat on the floor next to me as Alicia entered the room. She leaned over the arm of the couch. "I thought I heard you come in. You left your phone here. Emma has been trying to call you. I hope you don't mind, but I answered so she wouldn't worry."

I sat up with a start. In the day's turmoil, I'd forgotten to call Emma back. "Is she okay?"

"She's fine." Alicia waved me back to the kitchen.

I stood, and the heavenly aroma of something warm and cheesy wafted from the oven. My sister's specialty was a grown-up version of macaroni and cheese that was to die for. I hadn't eaten all day. Suddenly hungry, my mouth watered.

"Nate and Connor have a baseball game tonight." Alicia's mention of her husband and his second cousin once removed—or something like that—partially answered my unasked question of why she was cooking in my house. "I'm making dinner, and Rose is bringing wine."

"Sounds fantastic." I pictured the Crowley duo on the baseball diamond and smiled as I shuffled into my newly renovated kitchen. Inept at all things culinary, my modern appliances gleamed. If Alicia didn't come over now and then, they'd never get used. On the granite countertop, Alicia had left a pitcher of iced tea. I poured a tall glass, settled at the table, and lifted my phone to press Emma's name on my video chat speed dial.

Tearful blue eyes and blonde curls escaping a ponytail filled my screen.

"What's wrong, honey?" My voice caught.

"I'm okay. It's just that I wish you were here."

"You don't look okay." *Clearly, not okay.* When Emma hurt, I hurt—more than I should.

"I'm okay, really." She sniffed. "But what's the tea? Aunt Alicia says you found a dead body? Please tell me she was joking. That did *not* happen. I can't even."

"Unfortunately, Alicia wasn't joking."

"I don't get it. Someone from your camera club was murdered? Was it random? What if it had been you? I knew moving to Vermont was such a bad idea. You need to come home."

I looked up to find Alicia staring at me; her eyebrow arched as we listened to Emma ramble. She pointed toward the oven. "Dinner will be ready soon."

I nodded and returned my attention to my daughter, waiting out her babble. "I don't think it was random. And I'm pretty sure I've made no one *that* angry yet. That's all I know."

Emma's eyes clouded with concern. They were so much like Dan's, my heart ached. "I wish you'd never moved."

The jab was like a gut punch, knocking the wind from me. Emma and I had always been close. Without a doubt, my move had been impulsive. In my flurry of getting things done, I hadn't fully considered the impact it might have on her. In her last semester of college, she'd already landed her dream job as a nurse at a prominent Boston hospital. Facing an empty nest, it seemed like a good time to pursue my dream. Besides, the drive between us was less than three hours.

I dodged the subject. "You tried to call yesterday?"

"Ryan and I had a huge fight." Her eyes welled again. "He doesn't have time for me anymore. It's like he's ghosting me."

"Oh, honey, it's all new. You both need time to adjust to your new work schedules."

"He was supposed to meet me for lunch, and he never showed. I sat at the restaurant feeling like a complete loser."

I counted to five before answering, hoping she didn't notice my blotchy red cheeks. *How dare he!* "What did he say when you asked him about it?"

"He said he couldn't get away from the office. That I don't understand all the demands of his new job. As if I don't have a new job, too."

"Oh." I grasped for words to soothe my hurting daughter.

"And now this. A murderer. You're not safe."

"I'm fine. Alicia and Nate are here. I'm sure the police will figure it out soon." I almost choked on my lie.

"Could you at least think about coming home?" Emma asked.

"I'll think about it." I didn't remind her Vermont was my home.

"Okay, well, I better run. Ryan and I are going to attempt a dinner date. We'll see how it goes."

"Good luck," I blew Emma a kiss. "I'm sure you two can work through this." After exchanging *I love yous*, our call ended, and my screen went black.

"So, Emma doesn't know," Alicia stated without a hint of surprise in her voice.

"That I'm a suspect? Nope, and I plan to keep it that way." I wasn't about to tell my only daughter that if Detective Cram had his way, my next home would be in a jail cell.

39

Chapter Seven

"Yummy." Rose's round cheeks puffed as she swallowed. "This is absolutely, positively the best macaroni and cheese I've ever had."

Alicia smiled, her fork midway to her mouth. "I enjoy experimenting with recipes, incorporating my chèvre."

At least they agreed on something. I had never understood the odd dynamic between Rose and Alicia. They were more alike than either of them realized—both strong women who had built their businesses from nothing. Rose ran the popular village coffee shop, and Alicia was not only the proprietor of the village's busy market, but she was transforming the old Crowley dairy farm. With a barn full of goats she'd bought as a hobby, Alicia was learning about artisan goat cheese and soap.

Across the patio, Darcy lounged in the grass near my barn—my future photography studio. Behind the overgrown brush and weed-choked flower garden hid a rustic structure with good bones. At least that was how Nate's cousin Connor described it, assuring me its renovation wouldn't be too extensive. Someday, I, too, would run a business of my own.

If I don't wind up in jail first. I let out a shaky breath.

With each sip of wine, I relaxed a little more. It would take more wine than I wanted to think about to make me forget the reason for this dinner. Alicia had orchestrated the impromptu meal to perfection. Of course she had. As the sun dipped behind the rustling trees, the three of us dined on my stone patio. I couldn't help feeling we were acting out parts in a play, pretending this was any other beautiful spring evening. Alicia and Rose were persuasive in their roles, their performances nearly believable. I could almost convince myself there was no dead body. My scarf was not a murder weapon.

Almost.

I gulped the rest of my wine, setting my glass on the table. This was no play, even if it was a tragedy. One I wanted no role in.

"Good grief, you need a top off." Rose lifted the bottle to fill my glass. As she plunked the bottle on the table, a gunshot echoed from across the river.

I nearly jumped out of my chair, my pulse racing. "What was that? It sounded like a rifle—a huge rifle." As if sensing my distress, Darcy ambled over and sat next to me, resting his snout in my lap. The feel of his silky ear between my fingers soothed me.

Seemingly unconcerned, Rose raised her fork for another bite of gooey macaroni.

Twisting to face the river, Alicia scanned the horizon. With a shrug, she said, "No big deal. Just target practice."

"You mean this is normal?"

"You seriously haven't heard gunshots before now?" Rose asked.

I studied their passive expressions. "How can you be so cavalier about this? And you say Boston is dangerous."

Rose laughed. "In Boston, a gunshot means a drive-by or a murder or something. Here, it's just a bunch of shattered cans or clay ducks."

"That's true," Alicia said.

"It's like the Wild West of the North up here." I took another gulp of wine.

"Also true." Alicia studied me. "It never bothered you when Dan and Nate took rifles out for target practice."

I bit my lip, remembering how our husbands would line empty cans along the fence at the edge of the woods. Shooting had seemed out of character for Dan, and I'd always been surprised by how much he enjoyed it. "But…"

Alicia raised her glass. "Never mind all that. Here's to us and to Bobbie's beautiful new home."

We clinked glasses. I hoped this would feel like home someday.

I blocked out Emma's voice, imploring me to come back to Boston. At least I wasn't a murder suspect there. "I've been thinking." I hesitated before deciding to push forward. "And I need your help, so it's time we stop avoiding the elephant in the room."

Rose set her fork on the table. "Oh, thank goodness. I didn't know how much longer I could do this." Leaning toward me, her eyes searched mine. "People were jabbering in the coffee shop all day. Something about your scarf? What the heck is going on?"

I filled Rose in about my lost scarf and Detective Cram's accusations. "I think he enjoyed showing me the photo. There's something wrong with that man."

"You said it," Alicia said. "The Vermont State Police are a top-notch force, but Cram has always been laughable. When he was a newbie, he tried to arrest Lester Miller for jaywalking on Main Street. It's a state highway, after all."

I chortled at the image. My neighbor had lived on Main Street all his long life. It was easy to imagine the arrest hadn't gone well for the detective.

Rose brought us back to our conversation. "Are we talking about the scarf you lost yesterday? The one you thought you stuffed in your backpack? Wouldn't you have seen it on Tiffanee last night?"

I explained about Tiffanee's upturned collar. "She must have been lying on top of the rest of it."

Rose was silent and nodded thoughtfully.

"And this brings me to my problem. I'm afraid Detective Cram is looking for a quick win."

Rose gasped. "He can't do that, can he?"

"My scarf and now my fingerprints on the camera." I couldn't believe how dumb I'd been to touch it. But then, I hadn't known I was at a crime scene. Not yet, anyway. I took another swallow. The fruity wine tasted sour on my tongue.

"He can't arrest you. Nate won't let it happen." Alicia sounded so sure. I wanted to believe her.

My glance skipped between Rose and Alicia. "I'd like to talk this through, come up with alternative suspects. For starters, who wanted Tiffanee dead?"

Alicia snorted. "It might be easier to ask who didn't."

"I'm in," Rose said.

"We should probably let the police do their job," Alicia said, pragmatic as always.

I flashed her with a stern side-eye. "Detective Cram, you mean? We're only brainstorming."

"I guess it won't hurt to talk it out." Alicia stood to light the citronella torches.

"I'm not sure where to start. Did anything about that night seem off to you?"

"Not at our photo shoot," Alicia said. "What's bothering you?"

I explained about the missing lens cap and camera bag. "Let's say she wasn't carrying a bag, which is incredibly unlikely. She never would have gone out without a cap to protect her expensive lens."

"You think the killer took it?" Rose asked.

"That's what I'm wondering. Maybe the cap was on the ground somewhere, and I didn't see it. I'm doubtful. She would have put it in her bag or in one of her pockets. Nate is checking into it."

"Tiffanee always carried a canvas messenger bag," Rose said. "It was way more stylish than I'm making it sound, because we all know Tiffanee wouldn't be caught dead with an ugly bag." She clamped her hand over her mouth, but amusement lit her face.

I stifled a morbidly inappropriate laugh. "I can't believe you said that." A giggle escaped.

Alicia cleared her throat to end our mirth, but her wide grin told another story. "Tiffanee and that camera of hers." Having lit the torches, Alicia busied herself with refilling our wine glasses. "She had the entire village on edge. I bet that explains the lack of enthusiasm for our club."

"People don't like our club?" Why was this the first I was hearing of it? A heads-up might have been nice after everything I'd put into it.

Rose's voice softened. "It's not your fault. Tiffanee's stalking around was totally creepy."

Great. Just great. The camera club was supposed to be fun. All I wanted was to get involved in the community and get villagers excited about photography.

Alicia waved her hand. "Forget about it. It's not worth worrying about. And, I hate to say it, but Tiffanee's gone."

And now the village will be more accepting of my club. I filled in her unspoken thought, hoping the idea never crossed Detective Cram's mind. As far as motives went, it was weak, but I wasn't sure the detective would see it that way.

"Still no thoughts on where you lost your scarf?" Alicia asked.

"It must have been on the village green. I was taking photos there after hanging with Rose at her coffee shop."

Alicia looked thoughtful. "Who do you think picked it up, the killer or Tiffanee?"

I sputtered, choking on my wine. "I've been so focused on the killer I hadn't even considered Tiffanee taking it. We saw her on the village green, remember?" I glanced at Rose, who nodded. "Maybe she'd planned to bring it to our meeting?"

Rose wrinkled her nose. "Wearing it? That's kind of weird."

"Agreed," Alicia said. "Let's assume it wasn't Tiffanee. No offense, but your scarf is hardly her style."

I cleared my throat. "None taken."

Alicia plowed ahead. "Whoever killed Tiffanee must have been on the village green yesterday afternoon."

That didn't exactly narrow the suspects, but it was a starting point.

"What about her cell phone?" Rose asked. "Maybe her call history or calendar can help."

I couldn't believe I hadn't thought of that. "Smart thinking. I'll ask Nate if he's heard anything."

"The most obvious suspect is Travis," Alicia said, moving our discussion along.

At the mention of her ex-husband, Rose's mouth dropped open. "Seriously? You think Travis would kill his girlfriend?"

"It's always the boyfriend, isn't it? Or, perhaps, the ex-wife."

Rose gaped. "You've got to be kidding. Why would I kill Tiffanee?"

"I'm joking. But be truthful, you loathed that Travis and Tiffanee were together," Alicia said.

"Nuh-uh." Rose shook her head. "What I hated was that they were shacking up around Ethan."

"Subtle difference," Alicia said.

"Yeah, but you said it yourself. Who didn't want Tiffanee dead?"

"This is getting us nowhere." I turned to Rose. "I'm sorry, but I think we should consider Travis for now."

Rose huffed. "Fine. But it's not Travis I'm worried about. How would Ethan feel if his dad was a murderer?"

"It would be awful," I said.

Alicia stood and gathered our plates. "How about Harmony? She and Tiffany were besties in high school. From what I can tell, they aren't anymore. Where was she coming from when we crossed paths on the way to the bridge?"

"It was such a lovely night. Maybe Harmony was out for a walk," I said.

"Maybe." Alicia didn't seem convinced.

"Harmony? No, I don't see it." Rose paused. "But if she was coming from that direction, maybe she saw something."

Rose had a point. We didn't know yet when Tiffanee was killed. It had been after seeing her on the village green. What if Harmony saw something—or someone?

Alicia said, "I never could get a read on her. All that new age serenity. You may not think so, but she's definitely a suspect."

Harmony seemed like a long shot, but I was in no position to rule out potential suspects.

"If we're thinking of people who walk across the bridge, how about William?" Alicia asked. "He lives on the other side."

"Wouldn't he have been in his bookstore? He doesn't normally close until six and probably doesn't leave much before seven. That would make it nearly impossible." Like me, William was new to Stonebridge. Also like me, I thought it seemed improbable he knew anyone well enough to kill them.

"But he seems so nice—and handsome." Rose's cheeks flushed, matching the crimson flowers on her blouse. "You don't really think he killed Tiffanee, do you?"

Alicia shrugged. "What do we know about him?"

"All I'm saying is he doesn't seem like a killer." Rose crossed her arms in front of her chest.

"Doesn't Penny live next door to Tiffanee?" Rose sipped her wine. "She would have crossed the bridge on the way to the meeting. Maybe it was her."

Alicia nodded. "Penny makes an interesting suspect. She was the valedictorian of Connor's class. After high school, she took off. I figured she was college-bound, but I don't know for sure. At any rate, about a year ago, she reappeared, pregnant."

"Now she lives at home with her mom and her baby, Hope," Rose said. "That baby is such a cutie."

"What about the baby's father?" I asked.

Rose shrugged. "I've never heard anything about him."

I set my wine glass on the table and contemplated Penny as a suspect. She was an enigma. Hidden beneath her tattoos, piercings, and surly temperament, I detected a shyness about her. It made me wonder what she kept bottled inside.

"How about Jackson?" Rose asked. "He was at the photo shoot, right?"

I shook my head. "I'm pretty sure he was at his antiques shop until our meeting. And I never lost sight of him during our shoot. What is it with him and all his French phrases? He doesn't strike me as being from France."

"Maybe his family is French-Canadian like mine," Rose suggested.

"Maybe," Alicia said. "He studied in France, and I'm pretty sure he makes frequent buying trips there. Have you visited his shop? Think what you want, but the man has impeccable taste."

Rose winked. "In women, too."

I shuddered. Jackson and me, that was never going to happen.

"We need to get our club together," Rose said. "Maybe they can help, too."

"Rose is right," Alicia agreed. "Someone might have seen something."

It made sense. I warmed to the idea. "Maybe they'll know something that helps."

Rose pushed her chair back. "I'll let you think about it. I should get home. Morning comes fast when you run a coffee shop. And tomorrow is the season opening of the farmers' market."

Alicia groaned. "Don't remind me. The market will be mobbed. I still have a small batch of cheese to wrap, along with jams and soaps that need labeling."

I gave them each a hug and took the dishes from Alicia. "Go on. I'll clean up. I may not be much of a cook, but I'm a pro at washing dishes."

After they left, I set the plates on the table and sat back. Cleaning would wait. It always did. The cool evening air and the sounds of Darcy ambling around the yard soothed me. Above, there must have been a million twinkling stars in the cloudless, black sky. I'd always loved how the night sky made me feel small. It was a reminder that in the greater scheme of things, my troubles and worries were infinitesimal even when they didn't feel that way.

My mind drifted once again to Tiffanee, her lifeless body lying by the river. How long would it be before I was free of the image? I didn't know her well enough to miss her, and what I knew—it didn't help. Still, she hadn't deserved to be murdered.

Across the patio, my barn brought thoughts of my new business. It was the reason I'd moved to Vermont. But if Tiffanee's murder wasn't solved soon, there'd be no business. No one was going to book a photo shoot with a murder suspect.

I jumped to my feet, desperate to do something. While thinking about potential suspects, I walked into my kitchen and grabbed my laptop. I'd start with a simple chart—motive, means, opportunity. In the first column, I added Travis, William, Harmony, and Penny. I left the motive column blank. William and Harmony both had shops facing the village green. Access to my scarf gave them means. It wasn't much, but it was a start.

As much as I loathed the idea, I'd leave the real investigating to Detective Cram. But maybe if I kept my ears open and asked a few questions, I'd get lucky and find something to point him in a different direction. Surely, there was no harm in that.

Chapter Eight

After a fitful night of tossing and turning, I dressed hurriedly, thinking about the first steps of my plan. Eager to get my day started, I stood by my kitchen door, waiting impatiently for Darcy to return. He was in no hurry, and I'd swear he was purposely procrastinating.

"You'd best do your business right now," I said.

He looked up and gave me that tilty-headed look I always found cute. If I didn't know better, I'd swear he was asking, *or what?*

While I waited, I gave my coffee maker a quick glance. All those dials and knobs were all the convincing I needed to head next door. I walked back to my kitchen table and fired up my laptop. My chart had been such a good idea. Something about seeing everything in neat rows and columns made me feel like I had it all together. I didn't, but there was something to faking it. Finally, Darcy scratched at the door and I let him back in with a stern warning to be a good boy while I was out.

Stepping onto my front porch, I watched as Rose opened the door of her café and called a cheerful greeting to the droves of bleary-eyed caffeine-seekers waiting on the sidewalk. If her coffee didn't wake them, her lime green polka dots would. Only Rose could pull off a blouse like that.

The morning air sparkled with the upbeat excitement of the summer season's opening. I'd hoped for a chance to show Rose my chart, but I could tell it wasn't to be. Early birds already filled the wicker rockers on the Rosebud's wrap-around porch, where hanging baskets overflowed with colorful blooms. From across the street, voices called out greetings, and metal poles clanked as vendors set up their market tents. The sky was losing its golden glow and held the promise of another beautiful day in the mountains of Vermont.

I entered the café, scanning the room before beelining for a stool at the counter. The Righteous Sisters had wasted no time getting their daily gossip session underway. The trio of middle-aged women sat with their heads together, their faces lit by the glow of an electronic tablet. As I walked past, their titters silenced, and the heat of their collective glares singed my back. The ringleader, Lorraine Adams, shook her salt and pepper curls and tsked.

"That was certainly weird," I whispered to Rose as I slid onto the stool.

"They're reading the Stonebridge Scandal. The latest post is all about your scarf."

"What?" I gulped. "Who owns that page, anyway? It seems to have a ridiculous number of followers."

"It's a big mystery. Nobody knows who writes it, but pretty much all of Stonebridge follows it. You should probably ignore it today."

"That bad?" I slumped forward, leaning my elbows on the counter.

Rose's smile drooped, morphing into a scowl when Travis dropped onto the stool next to mine.

"What do you want?" Rose asked.

"Is that any way to say good mornin'?" Travis gave Rose a lopsided grin I suspected she'd once found charming, but she didn't appear to be having it. With his dark hair pulled back into a disheveled man bun and a face full of stubble, he looked like he'd just rolled out of bed.

"Is that any way to answer my question?"

The line of customers had eased, and Ethan strolled over to join us. "Hi, Mrs. Brooks. Hi, Dad. What can I get you?" He used his forearm to push his tousled, reddish-brown hair from his face. The style gave him a popular bad-boy look, but his sheepish smile gave away his friendly nature.

"Ethan, get Mrs. Brooks a cup of coffee, light and sweet. I'll take care of your dad." Rose issued the order without taking her eyes off Travis. She spun around, filling a heavy white café mug with steaming coffee before placing it on the counter with a thud.

Travis took a gulp, swallowing without a wince.

"Why are you here?" Rose folded her arms across her chest.

"The coffee." He raised his cup. "And, to remind you, I have Ethan tonight."

"No kidding. I seriously didn't need a reminder."

"Ah, Rosie, give a guy a break." He took another gulp. "Bet you're glad you can stop harping about keeping Tiffanee away from Ethan."

I spun on my stool, taking in the hard set of his jaw. If Travis meant for Rose to feel guilty, he'd missed his mark.

"Don't *Rosie* me." Rose fisted her hands on her hips. "I can't believe you're making it sound like I wanted her dead."

"Are you saying you didn't?"

Rose shook her head and stomped off, muttering over her shoulder, "I've got customers to wait on."

"Here you go, Mrs. Brooks." Ethan handed the cup to me before darting back to help his mom.

Travis swiveled to face me. "If I didn't know better, I'd think you lived here."

"I might say the same about you." I gave him an appraising stare. Either he was truly miserable, or he was putting on an award-winning act.

Travis tipped his head toward the table of tittering ladies. "Word has it you're to blame for this whole mess."

Rose rushed over, her lips barely moving when she spoke. "What is the matter with you?"

"All I'm saying is, Tiffanee mentioned how Bobbie didn't like any of her ideas."

I set my cup on the counter, heat rising to my cheeks. Tiffanee had complained to Travis? Who else had she talked to?

Rose threw her hands in the air. "What's your story? Where were you on Thursday night?"

My attention perked up, waiting for his answer.

"You must be kidding." Anger rose in his voice. "Why would I kill my girlfriend?"

"She wasn't exactly easy to get along with." Rose tipped her chin toward the church lady trio. Keeping her voice low, she said, "This village is full of gossips, and where do you think they do it? I hear things."

Before I could wonder what Rose might have heard, Lorraine called out, her voice dripping with syrup. "Rose, did you happen to see the Stonebridge Scandal this morning?"

I twisted to face the women. Lorraine's thin lips formed a harsh, judgmental slash. Her smear of candy-pink lipstick did little to soften them. I had met her once before to discuss photography for the upcoming Farmer's Breakfast. The meeting had gone well, but then, I hadn't been a murder suspect. I was counting on the opportunity to show off my talent, which I hoped would translate into future clients.

"I sure did," Rose answered Lorraine with a smile so icy it could chill the café. "But I don't put much stock in online gossip." She leaned over the counter, lowering her voice. "I'm going to cut Lorraine some slack on this one. She was Tiffanee's aunt and must be grieving."

I softened my gaze at the woman's pinched expression. I couldn't imagine how awful it would feel to have a murdered niece.

"The woman next to Lorraine, the brown-haired one with the outdated Princess Diana hairstyle, is Penny's mom, Bernadine. She must be the same age as you, but you'd never know it."

I nodded. "She works at William's bookstore. She's always been nice enough." Which was true, even if she wasn't overly welcoming.

Rose continued to whisper. "The third of the trio is Vickie Sue Miller. She's pretty harmless. If you catch her without Lorraine, she's even kind of nice."

I glanced at the woman with a long gray braid. She had a pleasant face. "Miller? As in Lester Miller, my next-door neighbor?"

Rose nodded. "Yeah, lots of Millers in Stonebridge. The branches of that family tree are so tangled, even they can't keep them straight."

Lorraine refused to be ignored. "We're not comfortable sitting here with a murderer."

The normal background hum of conversation silenced. Weekenders— recognizable by their eager-eyed familiarity and brand-new but perfectly crumpled hiking clothes—followed Lorraine's pointed finger. All attention seemed to be directed at me. If I had one wish, I'd be able to don an invisibility cloak.

Rose offered Lorraine another frosty smile. "I'm not keeping you here. You're free to leave."

Lorraine's mouth formed a small circle, and a blotch of magenta dotted each of her cheeks. "Well!"

I grabbed Rose's hand, heat rising up my neck. "It's okay. I don't want you to lose customers because of me."

"I'll decide what's okay. Cutting her slack doesn't extend to insulting my friends. Besides, it's not like there's anywhere else for them to hang out. I'm the only place in town that would allow them to sit half the day for the price of a coffee."

The weekenders continued to gawk while Lorraine stood, knocking her chair to the floor. A man seated at a nearby table leaned over to pick it up, shrugging, when Lorraine snatched it from him and set it upright with a bang.

As Lorraine stomped toward the door, her breath was hot on my neck. "Go back to where you came from. We never had a murder in Stonebridge until you arrived."

I jerked my head back with an involuntary shiver, noting the vengeful glimmer of her glare—a glimmer not remotely akin to grief. I clenched my jaw and held my tongue while the entourage marched out the door.

Without missing a beat, Rose turned back to Travis and picked up where she left off. "I'm waiting for an answer."

Stunned by my encounter with Lorraine, I'd forgotten what Rose's question was. Oh, right. Where he'd been on Thursday. Before he answered, the bell over the front door chimed, announcing a group of hippie wannabes.

Rose pointed a finger at her ex-husband. "You stay put. We're not done." She winked at me, then joined Ethan to wait on the customers.

The café clatter had returned to normal, closing in on me. As much as I wanted to hear Travis's answer, I needed to get out. I stood and leaned toward him. "I'm sorry for your loss." Then, with squared shoulders, I waved to Rose and sped out the door. If Lorraine Adams thought she could intimidate me, she was wrong—dead wrong. It was time to get my plan started.

53

Chapter Nine

The farmers' market teemed with shoppers. I dodged and wove through the massive hoard, pushing my way through the crowd while on the lookout for Alicia's tent. The more I thought about Lorraine and her friends, the more urgently I needed answers. If I was going to be accepted in Stonebridge, not to mention run a business, villagers needed to know I wasn't a murderer.

My frustration mounted as I worked my way through the crowd. Vermont was pulling out all the stops for opening day. The cerulean sky was cloudless. A bluebird day, the skiers would say. A cool breeze carried the bold, mouthwatering aromas from the market tents. On any other day, I would meander through the market, tasting and sampling while taking photos to capture its festive feel. I fought the urge to use my city-girl elbows to force my way through the swarm. Even so, I stepped on one woman's heel and tripped, crashing right into William.

I clutched his arm, steadying myself. "I'm so sorry. This place is crazy. It reminds me of the Boston Common. Are you okay?"

William laughed, and a red flush rose on his brown cheeks. Pointing to my empty tote, he said, "No worries, Bobbie. You seem to be in a hurry."

"I'm heading to my sister's tent."

"You'd better be quick. Her cheese is extremely popular. I was fortunate she hadn't sold out of my favorite herbed chèvre." He lifted his bag with a triumphant gleam.

"Good choice." I flashed a quick smile, thinking Rose was right. William was much too nice to be a murderer.

"I'll let you get to it," he said. "It was good to see you again."

"Likewise." I pivoted to find the banner for Jackson's tent right in front of me. *Maison des Souvenirs*, the sign read. House of Memories, if my schoolgirl French was correct. Jackson shifted, turning his back to me as I walked in his direction. He appeared busy at a nearby table, wiping dust from a stack of French country dishes that didn't look the least bit dusty.

"Hi, Jackson." I stepped under his tent and lifted a plate to admire its colorful floral design. My style tended to be more minimalistic, although Emma would simply call it boring. Nevertheless, I imagined how pretty the plate would look on an antique sideboard, with homemade cookies piled on top. I was unlikely to bake cookies anytime soon and carefully set the plate down.

Jackson edged toward me and whispered, "Why are you here?"

"Our club got off to a terrible start," I blurted.

Running his hand along the side of his head, Jackson said, "I read all about your scarf online."

The mention of my scarf made me flinch, and I wondered if it explained Jackson's less-than-friendly behavior. I drew in a breath, struggling to keep my voice even. "Social media is not exactly a credible source for news."

He shrugged. "If you say so."

"I was thinking it might be helpful to talk things through as a club. You know, put our heads together."

"You want another meeting?" Jackson asked.

"Tomorrow at four o'clock?"

He turned to dust another display. "*Oui.* Sure." I'd been dismissed. No arm patting, no close talking, and no offers to keep the lonely widow company. Surely, he wasn't taking the Stonebridge Scandal seriously.

So much for you can count on me, no matter what. For any other reason, I would have welcomed his lack of interest.

Wending my way through the throng of shoppers, I found Alicia's tent. As William had warned, it was inundated with customers. From behind a long table, covered with a simple homespun cloth and an artful display of jams, pickles, goat cheese, and crackers on rustic wooden boards, Alicia acknowledged me with a tip of her chin while offering samples to a woman with bleached-blonde hair pulled so tight, her eyebrows lifted with it. I was trying to remember where I'd seen the woman before when my sister gestured toward the back of the tent.

"I only have a minute." She grabbed a water bottle from her cooler. "Connor is better with the high-maintenance customers, anyway."

Tall and muscular like his cousin, Connor had a thick mop of brown hair and an affable smile that clearly charmed the woman who made holding a jam-topped cracker between blood-red fingernails look flirtatious.

"He's definitely a Crowley." Alicia grinned. "Spill it. Something is bugging you."

I got right to the point, telling her about my morning at the coffee shop, including my confrontation with Lorraine.

"I heard about that," she answered with a wave of her hand.

"How…?" It was futile to question Alicia's superpowers. "I made a chart."

"What kind of chart?" Alicia asked.

"You know, suspects, motives, opportunity,"

"Good idea." Alicia paused. "Something came to me last night while I was wrapping cheese. It has to do with Tiffanee's old beau."

I couldn't help laughing. "Old beau? I mean, I guess Travis was a little old for Tiffanee, but—"

"Not Travis. Heavens, he's only in his early forties. I'm pretty sure we've got a few years on him." Alicia waved her hand again. "I'm talking about one of her boyfriends from high school. She had several, but this one was around longer than most. I recognized him when he came into my store the other day."

An old boyfriend hardly seemed relevant. "He's probably just visiting family."

Alicia shook her head. "He's not from Stonebridge, and I haven't seen him around here for ten or fifteen years. When I saw him with Tiffanee, it took me back."

"Tiffanee was with him?" I frowned. "Did Travis know?"

"Not a clue. Maybe Rose can find out."

"Interesting. It could be a motive." It might be nothing, but the timing gave me pause. Tiffanee's old boyfriend surfaces from who knows where, and days later, she's murdered. I made a note to add both the mystery man and Travis's potential motive to my chart.

"Nate's asking around about the camera bag, but has heard nothing yet," Alicia said.

I nodded. "I really appreciate his help. Did you read the Stonebridge Scandal this morning? I hear it's all about how I strangled Tiffanee with my scarf. The entire village is eating it up."

"You're today's gossip. There'll be something new tomorrow. Don't worry about it." She stopped, her brows lifting as "The Wicked Witch Theme" played from my pocket, loud and clear.

"Fiona," I whispered, grabbing my phone. I couldn't help it; I always thought of our mother by her first name. Probably because she'd always seemed bigger than life—definitely not the meek, motherly type.

"Tag, you're it. I talked to Mom earlier this morning," Alicia said.

I pressed my lips and sent the call to voicemail while suppressing my tinge of jealousy over the way Alicia and my mother had always gotten along. "She's only going to lecture me about how I'm ruining my life by leaving Boston."

"That from the woman who took off for Florida only months after Dad died." Alicia chuckled. "You know she means well."

Deep down, I supposed she did, but she had a funny way of showing it. Gesturing toward the hungry mob that had gathered in front of Alicia's tent, eagerly noshing her samples, I said, "Looks like Connor needs your help. I'm heading to Penny's to invite her to our club meeting. Tomorrow at four."

"You're coming to Sunday dinner, aren't you? We can sneak away and talk afterward. We need to find out if Tiffanee was cheating on Travis. He'd be livid, but would he be livid enough to kill?"

Penny's house came into view as I emerged from the covered bridge. A single-story ranch-style home that sat on a large corner lot, it wore the forlorn appearance of neglect. Its overgrown grass and peeling paint stood in stark contrast with Tiffanee's neat lawn and inviting flower-lined walkway next door. If not for a stroller with a cheerful array of toys strewn on its tray, I might have thought the house abandoned.

I startled when the door opened, my fist raised, prepared to knock.

"Yes?" Bernadine stood inside the door for an awkward moment before showing recognition. "Oh, hello. Bobbie, is it?"

"Bobbie Brooks," I said as Bernadine tugged the elastic waist of her baggy trousers and smoothed the hem of her blouse. "Is Penny available?"

"I wonder why you didn't just call." Bernadine stepped back, holding the door open. "Come in, then."

I entered the tidy living room and shivered despite the warm afternoon. Except for the old-fashioned crochet doilies adorning the arms of the chairs and couch, the room was devoid of personal items. No toys scattered about. Bernadine closed the door, and I stepped aside, almost knocking a tote bag from a hook on the wall. I reached to catch it before it fell, my heart melting at the sight of the tiny pink jacket hanging next to it—the only sign an infant lived there.

"Follow me. Penny is in the kitchen feeding Hope, and I was about to put cookies in the oven." Bernadine's sneakers shuffled soundlessly as she led the way. "I don't know if we've met in person before."

"Maybe once at the bookstore?" *Not to mention this morning at Rose's coffee shop.*

Bernadine entered the kitchen and turned, clearing her throat. "That's right."

Like the living room, the kitchen was tidy. No crumbs allowed, it seemed. Penny sat at a scratched Formica table, cradling her baby, an empty bottle in her hand. Dressed in black slacks and a red polo shirt, she appeared ready for work at The Crow. She nodded without surprise when I entered, and her long bangs fell across her face.

When I peered longingly at Hope's wispy blonde waves and rosy little cheeks, I almost felt the soft snuggle of Emma's downy head. Dan and I'd always wanted a houseful of babies. After Emma was born, we'd tried, but after a string of miscarriages, I'd learned to feel grateful for the beautiful daughter I had.

"What's this about, then?" Bernadine slid a cookie sheet into the oven.

"I stopped by to invite Penny to a club meeting tomorrow afternoon. Four o'clock. The other members are planning to attend." I hoped it was true.

"Goodness, but this club is becoming demanding." Bernadine shut the oven door. "Penny already gave two nights this past week."

I nodded, acknowledging Bernadine, and a thought came to me. "How do you like working at the bookstore?" I asked.

Bernadine stopped, her spoon held aloft before she turned to face me. "What a peculiar question."

Was it? In Boston, asking someone how they liked their job was common enough. "I was only wondering."

Bernadine dug her spoon into her bowl of dough. "It's a job." She shrugged. "Seems like William's been awfully frazzled lately."

"Running a new store must be stressful for him," I offered.

"I suppose that's true," Bernadine said. "It seems like more than that lately. He even asked me to stay and close up. He's always done that himself."

"When was this?"

"Just last Thursday." Bernadine turned and busied herself with the cookies. "I couldn't do it, of course. I needed to come home to babysit Hope."

My heart skipped a beat. Tiffanee was murdered on Thursday night. "Why did he need you to stay late?"

"So he could leave early," Bernadine said. "I didn't think much of it at the time."

"Did he find someone else to close for him?"

"No. He closed the shop early. It seemed awfully urgent."

Very interesting. Opportunity. Although, I'd have preferred a motive, I couldn't wait to update my chart. "I'm thinking Tiffanee must have gone to the bridge early. Did you see her on your way home?"

"No," Bernadine answered while spooning dough onto her tray.

It was worth a try. I turned to Penny. "Maybe you saw what time she left her house?"

Penny shook her head.

"Didn't you tell me you saw Travis?" Bernadine asked her daughter.

"I heard Travis's truck. I didn't see him." Tilting her head, Penny moved her bangs to the side, showing off the peridot stud in her nose. I couldn't help admiring the way it sparkled.

"Do you remember what time that was?" I asked.

"Before five, I think. His truck is kind of loud. It woke Hope from her nap." She bounced her baby on her knee. "I heard the truck door slam, and then there was shouting before his truck took off again."

"Shouting? Tiffanee and Travis, you mean?" Whatever they were arguing about could be a motive. "Did you hear what they were saying?"

Penny shrugged. "Something about dinner? I'm not Tiffanee's keeper."

Dinner? That didn't sound like much of a motive. Still, it would seem all was not as harmonious as Tiffanee let on. She'd mentioned Travis waiting for her—right after her flowered muumuu insult. If Tiffanee had been getting out of Travis's truck, had he picked her up near the village green? In my head, I added another note to my chart. Travis—access to scarf? Penny stared at me with a quizzical expression.

I smoothed my ponytail. "How about it? I think a quick debrief might help us as a club."

The baking sheet full, Bernadine turned to face me. "Penny already talked to the police. In fact, I heard it was your scarf that killed Tiffanee."

Her words were like a slap. Before I could stop myself, I said, "You shouldn't believe everything you read online."

Bernadine waved her spoon. "Tiffanee was like a second daughter to me and a big sister to Penny. They were two peas in a pod. I don't want Penny involved in this."

My cheeks burned. From what I'd seen, two peas in a pod was a bit of a stretch, but I recognized Bernadine's concern. "It's not my intention to involve the club in a murder investigation."

My voice softened when I spoke to Penny. "Together, we may come up with something to help the police."

"I can't babysit," Bernadine said. "I have a Women's Guild meeting." She opened the oven door and peeked inside. The spicy-sweet scent of cinnamon filled the room.

"Not a problem," I said. "Hope is welcome, too. In fact, I'd love nothing more."

Before Bernadine could answer again, Penny spoke up. "Yeah, sure, I'll be there."

"Well then, I'll have Penny bring some cookies along." Bernadine pulled a hot tray from the oven. "I have more than enough for my meeting."

I showed myself to the door, thinking about what I'd learned. Tiffanee and Travis had argued. Travis had been on the village green, and William left work early. My chart was filling up.

Chapter Ten

On Sunday morning, I pulled up the winding, unpaved driveway to my sister's sprawling farmhouse and found Nate sitting on the front porch. He appeared comfortable in a pair of faded jeans and a baggy T-shirt, pushing the porch swing with the toe of his hiking boot. Two black Labrador retrievers lay placidly at his feet, completing the peaceful tableau. Their ears perked, and tails wagged when I parked and let Darcy out.

I closed the car door with my hip, and the dogs ran off toward the barn. "Darcy is one happy boy. He loves nothing more than playing with Harry and Sally."

Nate nodded, watching as the dogs dashed across the field. "Alicia threw me out of the kitchen." He laughed, unbothered by being banished to the porch. "You know how she gets."

"I do, and I don't imagine she'll want my help any more than yours."

He patted the seat next to him. "I'm sorry you were uncomfortable after church."

I hadn't been uncomfortable, not exactly. But the stares of several congregants had been like a warning—attending the coffee social after the service might be less than sociable, at least for me.

I dropped onto the swing next to my brother-in-law. "It was fine. I might even be getting used to it." I swallowed my lie. This couldn't be easy for Nate, either, defending the village murderer.

"The police will solve the case, and life will go back to normal," Nate said.

I bit my lip. *Normal? What would that look like?* An easy silence settled

"

between us, the slow sway of the swing lulling me to accept what Nate said was true. Almost. From where I sat, I admired the bucolic scene—the goats grazing in the pasture, the tire swing hanging from the ancient oak tree, and the dogs playing in the field.

This was Nate's childhood home and the home where he and Alicia had raised their twin boys, Liam and Aiden, who were only a year older than Emma. Connor had spent much of his childhood there, too. After his father had died and his mother had fallen apart, Nate had taken his young cousin under his wing, offering a safe space to hang out. Dan, Emma, and I had visited so frequently over the years, they'd given us our own bedroom, although Emma had always preferred bunking with the twins.

Pushing with the toe of my sneaker, I matched Nate's rhythm. "What did Detective Cram say about the missing lens cap?"

"He's holding everything close but seemed interested, even if he tried not to show it. I'm guessing he didn't find it at the scene, and I'm not sure he was aware it was missing. I told him your idea. Now it's up to him to run with it."

I rubbed the smooth silk of my scarf and wondered whether the detective would look into it. "Did you hear anything about Tiffanee's cell phone?"

"It was in her jacket pocket. The police have it, but it's locked. I haven't heard anything more." Nate gave a slight shrug. "Detective Cram shared one interesting piece of information."

I was afraid to ask and kept my mouth closed, waiting for Nate to continue.

"Your scarf didn't kill Tiffanee." He raised his hand, staving off my excitement.

This was good news, wasn't it?

"There were marks on Tiffanee's neck suggesting she struggled, but the bump to her head ultimately killed her."

I wasn't sure what I felt. Relief, I thought. Relief that my scarf didn't kill Tiffanee.

"Unfortunately, it changes nothing. I figured you'd want to know your scarf wasn't the murder weapon. Either way, have faith."

I studied his profile: so calm, so trusting, believing things always came out the way they should. As if that's the way life worked. In order to have the faith he seemed to have, I needed to trust Wyatt Cram. But how could I?

The screen door screeched open, interrupting my thoughts. Alicia appeared in the doorway. "Great, you're here. Dinner is almost ready, and Connor's inside setting the table."

I glanced over my shoulder at Alicia. Her ruffled apron softened her usual straight-leg jeans and plain blouse, giving it a girlish look. "I'll go help him."

Before I stood, Nate touched my arm. "I understand you're worried, but try not to think about it too much."

Clearly, my brother-in-law had never been a murder suspect.

I found Connor in the sun-filled dining room—one of many additions built to the rambling home over the years. Unlike the formal dining room in the Beacon Hill townhouse of my childhood, filled with Queen Anne style furniture and heavy velvet drapes, this room was alive with memories of countless family dinners and generations of aunts, uncles, cousins, and friends gathered around the oversized wooden table.

"Hey, Bobbie." Connor rushed around the table with a set of placemats.

"Hey, yourself." I nudged him with my elbow. "Which napkins today?" I opened a drawer of the rustic oak sideboard and thumbed through a stack of linens worn smooth by years of use.

"Your choice."

Napkins in a muted shade of dusty violet, reminiscent of the hedge of lilacs at the distant edge of the yard, caught my eye. The sweet scent of their faded blooms seemed to linger, wafting through the open windows. Following behind Connor, I placed a softly worn napkin at each setting.

"Just us today? Where's Mama June?" I asked, referring to Nate's mom who still lived in her old house part-time.

"She's staying with Uncle Luke in Albany for the next couple of weeks," Connor said, mentioning Nate's younger brother.

Not so long ago, family dinners had been boisterous events with children running through the house, playing tag or hide-and-seek. Over the years, the kids had grown, and the adults had aged. Most of Nate's siblings had scattered. Liam and Aiden—*the twins,* as everyone called them—had moved to New York City for their careers on Wall Street, and Emma had her own life in Boston. Sunday dinners rarely included more than immediate family, but Alicia carried on the tradition, always preparing enough food for unexpected guests.

"I was wondering." My voice was more tentative than I'd intended. "Have you heard about one of Tiffanee's old boyfriends hanging around Stonebridge lately?" I pulled white stoneware plates from the hutch.

"You must mean Hunter Harrison. It seems kind of weird he'd be hanging around."

So far, so good. Learning more about the mystery boyfriend might help solve the murder. "Did you know him?"

Connor hesitated, placing knives and forks alongside each plate. "I read what everyone was saying on The Scandal, but I know you didn't kill Tiffanee."

"Thanks. That means a lot to me." I couldn't help wondering if there was anyone who didn't read the Stonebridge Scandal.

"I doubt I can tell you much," he said. "Hunter wasn't from Stonebridge. He was friends with Harmony, you know, from her old town."

"But Tiffanee was dating him?" The more important question, of course, was whether any of it mattered now.

"Yeah, he was like a big jock in his town." Connor looked thoughtful. "Funny thing, about a month ago, me and a couple of buddies stopped at a bar in Bellows Falls after a baseball game. Hunter was there. He looked like a regular."

I filed that tidbit away. "Did Penny hang out with them, too?"

"Not really. She was in my grade. Tiffanee treated her like a pet. Harmony always seemed nice enough. Kind of protective, even. Do you think this has something to do with Tiffanee being killed?"

"I guess I'm trying to figure out why Hunter was here."

The oven door banged shut, and the savory scent of herbed roast beef wafted from the kitchen. I didn't want to be caught grilling Connor, so I changed the subject. "I'm really excited about having you work on my new studio."

Connor's expression brightened at the mention of my barn renovation. "The windows should come in any day. A buddy is helping me prepare everything."

Alicia entered the dining room with Nate on her heels, carrying a steaming platter of pot roast with all the trimmings. Surrounded by the scent of Alicia's delicious meal, all thoughts of murder vanished from my mind. Later, my sister and I would sneak away for a chat. I was excited to hear her thoughts about Tiffanee's mysterious old beau, who now had a name—Hunter Harrison.

Chapter Eleven

The camera club members arrived at my house within minutes of each other, even Jackson, whose curt *oui* the day before had left me feeling uncertain he'd attend. Together, Rose and Alicia climbed my porch steps, laughing. Rose flashed me a cheeky smile, her blue eyes sparkling, while Alicia squeezed my arm. Balancing Hope on one hip, Penny dug the promised plate of cookies from her stroller and handed it to me before lifting a diaper bag so large, I questioned if she was planning to move in.

Greeting my guests with a wagging tail, Darcy accepted dog biscuits from Alicia and Rose before I shooed him away.

"Off with you," I said. "No pestering the guests."

He licked his chops with calm defiance and ambled back to the kitchen where, satisfied with his treats, he'd resume his nap on his bed near the back door.

My guests shuffled quietly into my living room. Jackson gave Hope a dubious glance before palming several cookies and settling on the couch farthest from Penny. I waited as the club members filed past the cookies and iced tea like a well-trained kindergarten class.

Once they all found seats, I started. "Thanks so much for coming on short notice."

Jackson popped a cookie into his mouth, garbling his words. "Anything to help you out, *mon ami.*"

"So, you've said." His attitude changes were giving me whiplash.

Giving Penny a motherly smile, Alicia lifted Hope from her lap and shook a rattle in front of the baby's cheerful little face.

"I think we can all agree our photo outing didn't end well. Finding Tiffanee's body was certainly not what I'd planned."

"I can't imagine what it must have felt like." Rose held her hand to her heart and faced Penny. "Especially for you, Penny."

Penny looked at Rose through the veil of her bangs. "Me? Why me?" She pinched her lips, muffling the familiar clicking sound of her tongue ring.

Rose sat back without answering, and I continued. "Let's all take a minute to think back. Was there anything that felt normal at the time, but now it feels off? Or maybe it was something that happened earlier in the day."

Silence.

Jackson popped another cookie into his mouth; Rose offered an apologetic smile, and Penny rooted through her voluminous diaper bag.

"O-kay." I clasped my hands. "The police said Tiffanee died from the blow to her head. It must have happened sometime between five and when we arrived. She was on the village green late Thursday afternoon. I'm assuming she was home long enough to change clothes because she was wearing a different outfit at the river." I scanned the group. "How about you?"

Silence. Again.

Jackson washed down a mouthful of cookie with a gulp of iced tea. "As you know, *Maison des Souvenirs* is more than a mile down the road. Which means, of course, I wasn't in the area until our meeting. I couldn't have seen anything."

His answer wasn't unexpected, but something in his quick dismissal set me on edge. I made a mental note to add him to my chart. His alibi needed checking.

Alicia set Hope's toy on her lap and smoothed her denim skirt. "I was in the market until we met at the gazebo. But I saw Tiffanee on the village green that afternoon."

"Bobbie and I talked to her. She said she was meeting Travis." Rose scrunched her nose and smoothed her blouse, no doubt remembering Tiffanee's insult.

"Then he was probably the last person to see her alive," Jackson said.

"Only if he killed her." Rose's face reddened, turning her freckles an angry shade of russet. I suspected her defensiveness was for Ethan rather than Travis.

"What are we hoping to accomplish here?" Jackson asked.

"As I'm sure you're all aware," Alicia said, "the focus of Detective Cram's investigation seems to be Bobbie." She glanced at me before continuing. "Since we all know Bobbie didn't do it, we need to point our oblivious detective in a different direction."

Jackson wore a thoughtful expression. "What time did you say you left the village green?"

"Around five," I said.

"Our meeting was at seven. Which leaves you without an alibi for two hours." Jackson sat back with a self-satisfied grin.

Rose nearly jumped from her seat. "Jackson! You can't possibly think Bobbie was involved." The flush on her face deepened.

"I'm only pointing out the obvious."

I clasped my hands behind my back. "That's fair," I said, struggling to keep my voice from shaking. "Let's move on." I asked if anyone remembered seeing Tiffanee's camera bag.

"A camera bag?" Jackson asked.

"She used to always carry that khaki messenger bag," Rose said.

Penny tucked her bangs behind her ear. "I know the one. It was a designer crossbody thing she got on the internet. She paid a small fortune for that flippin' bag and couldn't stop bragging about it."

"I remember it, too," Alicia said.

"Did anyone see it Thursday night?" I asked.

Jackson took a swig of tea before setting the glass down. "So what? Perhaps she decided not to bring it."

"That's possible." I conceded the point, though I considered it unlikely.

Penny's voice was little more than a whisper. "Do you think the killer took it?"

"I don't know," I said. "There was no bag at the scene, at least none we noticed, and her lens cap was missing, as well."

Jackson nodded slowly, as if considering my words. Alicia sank back into the couch's cushions, still playing with Hope. The baby's dimples flashed with her giggles.

"I don't remember seeing it, but I wasn't near Tiffanee for long before the rescue squad herded us back up the hill," Alicia said.

"Also," I continued, "scuttlebutt around town mentioned Tiffanee's ex-boyfriend has been hanging around Stonebridge. Supposedly, this was recent."

Penny scoffed. "Which one?"

"I believe his name is Hunter Harrison," I said.

The tapping of Penny's tongue resumed as she took Hope from Alicia and settled her baby on her lap.

Jackson spoke, his cheek bulging with what appeared to be an entire cookie. "But Tiffanee was dating that old ski bum, Travis. That would give him a motive."

Where did Jackson get off calling Travis old?

"Old ski bum seems about right," Penny muttered.

"Hey." Rose's objection sounded more resigned than angry.

"No one knows anything about Hunter?" They met my question with silence.

"This is absurd." Jackson glowered at Penny. "Weren't you BFFs, or besties, or whatever the term *du jour* is? You must know something. Did you even care about your friend?"

Penny answered his glower with a scowl. "As if you would know."

"Let's not argue amongst ourselves. We're a club, and we should work together," Alicia said.

"Here, here," Rose said.

"We're a *photography* club," Jackson said. "What does that have to do with *this?*"

"In case you haven't noticed, the police have accused our leader of murder. As a club, I think we should help her." Rose didn't bother to disguise her annoyance.

"Shouldn't we leave that to the police?" Jackson asked.

Rose sat back with a huff. "Haven't you been listening?"

"I really don't think I can help." Penny's voice was soft. "Between work and taking care of Hope, I don't have any spare time. My mom is my main babysitter, and she already thinks I should quit this club."

Rose turned to Penny. "You work at The Crow. Maybe you could sort of—eavesdrop?"

Penny gave a reluctant nod.

"All I'm asking is that we keep our eyes and ears open. Someone killed Tiffanee, and there must have been a reason." I let out a slow breath. "If you remember anything, or hear anything, it could be helpful. This is for Tiffanee as much as for me."

"That sounds reasonable. I guess I can help," Jackson said with what seemed like a sudden change of heart.

It was time to wrap up the meeting—end it on a positive note. I cleared my throat. "I'm grateful for any help you can offer. Our next meeting will be all about photography." I smiled at Jackson, hoping to placate him. "Come prepared to critique each other's photos of the covered bridge and choose a location for our next photo shoot. Unless anyone has something to add, I think we're done." The room filled with a combination of nods and relieved sighs.

As everyone gathered their things and stood to leave, Darcy entered the room and started nibbling crumbs from the floor.

"Maybe I should borrow Darcy for the café," Rose said. "Canine vacuum cleaner."

Darcy wagged his tail as if he thought Rose's idea a good one.

I laughed. "Not sure the health inspector would approve."

With a shrug, Rose patted Darcy's broad head. "Sorry, Darce. I tried."

As Penny approached, I handed her the empty plate. "Tell your mom her cookies were delicious." They'd looked and smelled delicious, anyway.

"I'll let her know. She's always making cookies for something or other."

I made a goofy face at Hope while stroking her soft cheek with my finger. Rewarded with a dimple-cheeked smile, I couldn't help laughing. As my heart melted, I did all I could to resist my urge to hug that sweet baby.

Raising my gaze to Penny, I said, "You can bring Hope anytime. She's always welcome here."

From beneath her fringe of bangs, Penny's eyebrows raised. "Really? That would be great." Her lips curled with the hint of a smile, which she hid by busying herself with tucking the plate into her bag and trundling Hope out to the waiting stroller.

On their way out the door, Rose and Alicia stopped. "Let's touch base tomorrow," Alicia said, keeping her voice low.

Only Jackson lingered after the rest of the group left. "I know how upset you must be. Why don't I stay and keep you company for a while?"

Not happening.

I walked him to the door and pulled it open. "Thank you for your offer, but I have a lot to do tonight." I bit my lip. I'd find something to make it true. After seeing him out, I collapsed against the door and slid the deadbolt home. Anything would be better than his patronizing company. That's what I thought, anyway.

After a quick dinner on my patio, I pulled Darcy's leash from the hook near the kitchen door, hoping a walk would clear my mind. Darcy's head perked up, and he rewarded me with a wagging tail. Ambling toward the sidewalk, I paused for a quick peek at my neighbor's porch recliner. No Mr. Miller, no wave, no harumphing reply.

A few steps into our walk, my mind went back to the meeting. I hated to admit it, but I agreed with Jackson. If Rose had an old boyfriend sniffing at her door, I would know about it. It was hard to tell if Penny was lying, but I was certain she knew more than she was saying.

Then there was Jackson. He'd been a little too quick to distance himself while pointing out my lack of an alibi. After insisting we leave everything to the police, he'd finally agreed to help. His moods swung like a pendulum. He didn't seem like someone I could count on. As far as I could see, he had no connection to Tiffanee's death. My footsteps slowed.

"Huh." I stopped, gathering my thoughts.

Darcy raised his head with questioning eyes. "Sorry, boy." I quickened my pace, spinning back toward town. He'd be fine with a short walk after his morning cavorting with Harry and Sally. It was time to fill in my chart. Alicia and I had tried to sneak away after dinner, but hadn't managed more than a few stolen whispers. We'd agreed Hunter's reappearance in Stonebridge was more than a little fishy. So far, the only connection I had was Travis. But I couldn't shake the feeling Penny was hiding something, too.

Chapter Twelve

Twilight darkened to dusk, the sun's warm rays scarcely a memory above the forest pines. Lost in thoughts of lies and omissions, I had barely noticed the steady breeze that rustled through the leaves. I was relieved to be back home before dark. Clicking Darcy's leash open, I paused. A steady *bang, bang* sounded from behind my house. Darcy ambled to the front porch while I, distracted by the noise, strolled back to my driveway. From my vantage point on the sidewalk, the banging grew louder. The barn door swung on its hinges, hitting the side wall with steady blows.

I hesitated, sure I'd bolted the door. Connor had come by earlier, but it wasn't like him to be careless with the latch.

Before venturing forward, I checked on Darcy, who perched at the top of the porch stairs, looking content. Like Mr. Miller, my dog had a favorite spot from where he watched the village green and passersby.

Satisfied, I strode down my driveway. "Is someone there?"

The only answer was the sound of the creaky hinge.

I peeked inside the barn. The interior was dark and dreary. Dust motes dulled what little light entered through the one small window. I grasped the rusty handle and pulled the door closed. Something thumped. I swung the door open again and stepped inside, peering through the gloom. Nothing. Convincing myself I'd imagined the noise, I turned back toward the door just as it closed with a bang. I froze, swallowed in darkness.

Without thinking, I lunged for the door, pushed it open, and rushed outside. I took huge gulps of air to calm my racing heart. From inside my kitchen, a light glowed like a beacon, signaling safety. I went to close the door one last time, and a paint can caught my eye. Nudging it with my toe, I wedged the door and tiptoed back inside.

"Who's there?" A shuffling sound came from the back corner. I froze. Had I imagined it? There was only one way to find out. I scanned my cluttered barn and spied a rake leaning against the wall. With a tight grip on my weapon, I inched toward a pile of boxes—remnants of Dan's life I hadn't been able to part with.

I crouched low to hide, listening. The only sound was the rustling leaves on the evening breeze. Convinced I'd allowed my imagination to get the better of me, I chided myself. The last few days had been stressful. It was no wonder my mind was playing tricks.

Still hunched, I set the rake down and pivoted on my toes, preparing to stand. I'd barely found my footing when the tower of boxes fell, knocking me back to the floor. Stunned, I lay on the dirty, splintered wood, pinned by the weight of books, clothes, and assorted memorabilia. Beside me, a ragged sweatshirt fell. I inhaled Dan's familiar scent, and tears threatened. Struggling with my free arm, I grasped the sweatshirt and hugged it close. Blinking my tears away, I caught a shadowy view of dark shoes scampering out the door, kicking up a cloud of dust that blew in my face. I was alone.

Too dazed to move, I lay facing the open door. My shaking eventually subsided, but I couldn't muster the energy to get out from under the boxes.

"Bobbie? Are you in here?" Harmony stepped inside, Darcy at her heels, a soft floral scent following her like springtime rain.

"I need help," I called out, thankful someone—anyone—had arrived.

Harmony tiptoed quickly across the barn floor, lifting her flowing skirt above the dust. "I was walking by and thought I heard a crash. What happened?"

"Did you see anyone leaving my barn?" My gaze met Harmony's dark eyes in the dim light as she kneeled on the floor next to me.

"Someone else was here?" Harmony asked. "Let me help."

The weight lifted from my back and shoulders as Harmony moved Dan's belongings. Finally able to sit up, I rolled my neck, and Darcy licked my dusty face before burrowing his snout in the sweatshirt.

"Hey, boy." I ruffled his fur. I peeked at Harmony, my relief tinged with apprehension. "You just happened to be walking by? You didn't see anyone outside?"

"No, no one." Harmony removed the last box from my legs and stood. "Did someone push these boxes on top of you? Why would anyone do that?"

"Maybe the killer?"

Rose's voice came from the doorway. "What on earth are you doing in here?" She clasped a bottle of wine in one hand.

Harmony greeted Rose while I stood. "I should split. Are you okay?"

"Yep. All good. Thanks again." I clutched Dan's sweatshirt and watched Harmony disappear. *Had the crash really been loud enough to hear from the sidewalk?*

"Should I even ask what's going on?" Rose brushed dust from my arm. "I brought over a bottle of wine, but then I saw Darcy in your driveway. It's not normal for you to be out here in the dark. Were you looking for that sweatshirt?"

I hugged Dan's scent closely. "Someone was in here."

"Someone other than Harmony? I don't get it. Why were you on the floor?"

I explained about the banging door and the clattering sound.

"Someone pushed a pile of boxes on you? Let's go back to the house." Rose grasped my arm and guided me toward the door. She stopped outside to lift something from the ground.

"What is that?" I asked.

Rose shrugged, handing me an envelope. "I figured you dropped it."

The brightness of the white envelope glowed in the moonlight just enough to make out the block letters written on the front—BOBBIE.

"Someone left you a letter by your barn? This is getting weird." Rose chewed her lip. "Let's go inside."

Back in the brightly lit warmth of my kitchen, with the door locked and bolted, I placed the envelope on the island's countertop.

"Sit. First, a change of plan. I'm making tea. Then we can decide what to do about that." Rose jabbed her finger at the envelope.

"What do you think it is?" I sat on a stool and slumped over the counter, noticing a bright red welt on my forearm. It would, no doubt, be a lovely shade of purple by morning.

"You need to buy a heavy-duty lock for that door." Rose busied herself at the stove, waiting for the tea kettle to whistle. "Chamomile tonight?" She lifted a bag of loose tea from Wild Meadow Herbs, my favorite local herbalist. Without waiting for an answer, she scooped some into an infuser.

"Wait." I lifted Rose's wine bottle. "You brought wine. What was it for?"

"That can wait for another night."

I fixed Rose with a steady stare.

She pushed the mug toward me. "I just wanted to blow off steam. Heaven knows there will always be another night for griping about my troublesome ex."

I placed my head in my hands while the tea steeped. My cheekbone hurt.

"That's going to be a nasty bruise." Rose leaned across the island and touched her fingertip to my face. "Does it hurt?"

"Not much." I wrapped my hands around the mug. "It's the least of my worries."

If Rose needed to blow off steam, Travis must have been up to something. "I want to help."

"Don't be silly. It was a bad idea. How about you hang onto the bottle, and we'll drink it another night? I should be a good mom and find out what's eating Ethan. I'm sure it's his dad. Like, what else is new?" She pushed a curl from her forehead.

"Did you learn anything? Is that why you want to talk?"

"Anything that points to Travis as the killer, you mean?" Rose lifted an eyebrow.

"Penny told me Tiffanee and Travis were shouting at each other the evening she was killed. All she heard was something about dinner, but I wonder if it could have been about her old boyfriend."

"Dinner? It seems like a leap to connect that with her old boyfriend."

"Maybe," I said. "But I doubt Travis would appreciate Hunter hanging around with his girlfriend."

"Travis being jealous?" Rose shook her head. "I don't see it. Travis isn't passionate about anything other than snowboarding."

I sipped my tea, its warmth soothing my frazzled nerves. I wasn't ready to dismiss Travis quite yet. Rose was likely biased, unwilling to accept her ex-husband's passion for another woman—a younger woman. It wasn't hard to imagine Tiffanee as a bewitching vixen.

"Besides, it's not about that," Rose said. "I'll see what I can find out. Let's drop it, okay?"

I nodded, willing to let it go for now. Our attention transferred to the white envelope. I placed my finger on it, pointing at the bright red letters. "I don't get why someone would leave this on the ground near my barn. Why be in my barn at all?"

Rose stood quietly, sipping her tea.

"It doesn't make sense," I said. "I rarely go there. Connor is starting renovations, but right now, my barn is basically a junky shell."

Rose set her mug on the counter. "I've been thinking about that. What if someone wanted to leave it somewhere else, like in your mailbox or by your front door? Then you and Darcy came walking down the street? Mr. Miller wasn't on his porch. Everyone knows he goes inside early in the evening."

"They thought I was inside my house, too? Maybe I surprised them. But the barn was supposed to be locked."

"That rusty old lock?"

"If you're right, they weren't trying to hurt me." I held the mug under my nose, inhaling the fragrant steam.

"I'm only guessing. You could have been trapped under those boxes all night." Rose pointed at the envelope, her red-painted fingernail matching the bright lettering. "It could have been the killer who was in the barn with you. You didn't see them?"

Had I? Everything had been so dark—nothing more than a silhouette of dark legs and shoes scampering across the dusty floor. Had the intruder been large or small, male or female? I puffed my cheeks, lost in thought. The light had been too dim to tell. I shivered, shaking my head, my eyes drawn to the envelope. "Go ahead. Open it."

Chapter Thirteen

Rose leaned against the kitchen island, flipping the envelope in her hands. "You're sure you want me to open it?" She hesitated for a moment before tearing the flap. Inside was a piece of white paper. She unfolded it and placed it on the counter. In the same bright red block letters as the envelope, three words covered most of the page. FLATLANDER—BUTT OUT

I gasped, my cheeks burning.

Rose placed her hand on mine. "It's a warning. Everyone knows you've been asking questions, and someone doesn't like it. Maybe you're closer than you think."

"But every question I ask leads to more questions. I don't know anything."

"They must think you do," Rose said.

Pinning the note with my finger, I said, "It's a clue. *Flatlander*. It's from a native, but who?"

"It could be from someone who wants you to think it's from a native. Honestly, Bobbie, we Vermonters are a welcoming bunch. Your assumption is super insulting." Rose shook her head. "I'm going to call the police. Stop touching it."

"I didn't mean…" I couldn't finish my sentence. She was right. Rose and Nate were two of the friendliest people I knew. There were only a few villagers who'd been less than welcoming, and I could hardly blame them. They thought I was a murderer. I shifted gears. "I'd better call Nate. The thought of Detective Cram coming over here again makes me want to gag."

"This is good. Don't you see? This will get the police off your back."

Beneath her cloud of red curls and vibrant yellow tunic, Rose was a genius. A slow smile spread across my face. *When Detective Cram sees the note, he'll realize I'm innocent, and I'll be more than happy to stop investigating .*

I woke to Darcy's snout on my pillow. With a long, loud, dramatic yawn, he lifted his muzzle for a morning chat.

"Good morning to you, too," I mumbled. I petted his velvety ears and brushed a strand of hair from my face, wincing at the touch to my sore cheek. The events of the previous night rushed back in vivid detail. FLATLANDER, BUTT OUT, the note had read.

Rose had phoned the police while I called Nate. Because of a car accident in a neighboring town, Detective Cram was unable to respond right away. After determining my situation wasn't an emergency, the dispatcher promised to send him to my house in the morning. Nate, however, had rushed over, imploring me to leave the investigation to the police.

"I'll back off," I'd promised. "Just as soon as I'm no longer a suspect."

In the light of morning, remembering the note made me more angry than scared. I couldn't wait to wipe the sneer from Detective Cram's face with my fresh evidence.

"Okay, boy." I rolled out of bed and threw on the first clean pair of jeans and T-shirt I found in my closet. I slipped into a pair of flip-flops and braided my hair with one of my scarves, scrutinizing my reflection in the mirror. Multiple shades of red and purple stared back at me. I bent closer and dotted my cheekbone with a pale concealer. *Good enough.*

Letting Darcy out the back door, I scanned the patio. My gaze rested on the barn. In the daylight, there was nothing evil about it, only the vision of my new studio. Later, I would give it a thorough once-over. But first, coffee.

My sandals slapped the floor as I approached my coffee maker with a wary eye. Resting my elbows on the counter, I peered at the buttons and dials. I should have insisted the kitchen designer keep it simple—one button—on and off. Really, how hard could it be? I was contemplating my next move when Emma's jazzy ringtone broke the silence.

Saved from my indecision, I poked my phone, accepting the video chat.

My smile dropped as Emma came into view, her eyes puffy and red—an all-too-frequent sight these days.

"Mom, where were you?" Emma's voice was accusing. "I tried to call you last night."

"Long story. I'll tell you about it later. What's going on?"

"I think Ryan is going to break up with me, and I don't know what to do. I really, really wish you were here." She sniffled. While I was happy Emma felt she could come to me, this level of neediness was relatively new. During her college years, she'd had a tight group of friends. After graduation, her classmates had scattered, seeking new careers and new lives.

I dropped onto a stool at the counter, the red lettering of the unwelcome note screaming for attention. I wished I was in Boston, too. How wonderful it would be to sit at a sidewalk café with Emma, sun on my face and a steaming mug in hand. Instead, space-age appliances taunted me while I awaited a visit from the dreadful Detective Cram. I stood, shuffled back to the coffee maker, and squinted as I sought the words to assuage my daughter's hurt.

"Ryan might be cheating on me." Emma swiped her cheeks.

I jolted upright. "What makes you say that?"

"You know how he's been working late?" She gestured air quotes.

"Mm-hmm."

"We all know it's a euphemism for hanging out with his coworkers at a bar until all hours of the night."

"They're probably just blowing off steam," I suggested, remembering those first heady months out of college—the long days pretending to be an adult and the longer nights clinging to the last remnants of youth.

"No, but that's not all. I have a friend who told me she saw Ryan with his work buddies, and he was looking a little too cozy with one of them, a sexy brunette."

"What does Ryan say?"

"He says I'm making a big deal out of nothing, that my friend was imagining it. Ryan and I have been together forever. What will I do if we break up?"

"I don't know, honey." I turned my back on the offending machine, ignoring the mockery of all those mysterious dials.

"You sound distracted."

"I'm listening. I promise I am. It's just, well, you know me and my morning coffee. The kitchen designer talked me into a fancy coffee maker with a built-in grinder and who knows what else. She neglected to teach me how to use it." I shifted my screen to show Emma. "How is anyone supposed to make coffee with this thing?" A wave of chestnut hair fell over my eye, and I pushed it back, returning my attention to my daughter. "As for Ryan, it sounds like you two need a long heart-to-heart. If he's seeing someone else, that's not okay. You deserve better, and it's *you* who should break up with *him*."

Emma rubbed away the last of her tears before giggling. "Only you, Mom, would have trouble with a coffee machine. It's hardly rocket science."

My kitchen door creaked open, and Connor popped his head in. "Hi, Bobbie."

I waved Connor into the room.

"Do I hear Connor?" Emma's tone lightened.

"Hey there, city girl." Connor strode toward me. From over my shoulder, he waved at my screen, but not before I noticed Emma swipe at her eyes and smooth her hair back. Growing up, Emma had enjoyed playing with the Crowley twins, reserving her crush for their older cousin, who'd stop in occasionally to hang out. As I remembered it, Connor had always been friendly when he came to the farm, but with the seven-year age gap between them, he'd treated her like the little girl she was.

"How're things in Beantown?" Connor smiled at my screen.

"Oh, you know." She shrugged with a nonchalant air. "Work and more work. What are you up to?"

"Came by to see your mom's barn. I'm doing the renovation work."

"And here I thought the coffee angels sent you to rescue me from this dreaded contraption." I pointed toward my coffee machine.

Connor flashed an impish grin. "Sure, I can do that too. Where do you keep your coffee?"

Emma laughed. "You know you're pathetic, don't you?"

I grabbed a bag of coffee beans from the cupboard and walked back to my stool.

"Mocha Joe's." Connor read the bag's label. "Sweet! I'm making a big pot."

"The bigger the better." I plopped onto my stool to finish my conversation with Emma. The renewed sparkle in her expression was hard to miss. Too bad the boyfriend she'd been crying over just moments before wasn't more like Connor.

"Okay. Coffee is brewing," Connor said after pressing a button and facing me. "I'm heading out to the barn if it's all right with you. The buddy I told you about should be here soon. Nate told me about last night. I promise not to move anything."

"Sounds good."

"What about last night?" Emma asked as soon as Connor had left.

I clenched my jaw. As much as I wanted to, I couldn't keep this from my daughter. "Someone was in my barn last night, and they left me a note." I lifted the paper from the counter so Emma could read it.

Emma's mouth fell open. "Big yikes!"

"It's okay," I said with an unhealthy dose of false confidence. "The police are coming this morning to get it sorted."

"Wait," Emma said, staring into the screen with narrowed eyes. "Is that a bruise on your face?"

My finger went to my cheekbone, touching the tender spot. I thought the concealer had done a better job hiding it. Apparently not. "A box fell over, but I'm fine. Really."

"Mom! Enough is enough. Come home."

"I'll try to visit soon." Knowing my stubborn daughter, she wouldn't give up easily. "There's a lot going on right now, for all of us. I need to deal with this, and you've got your new job, not to mention figuring out what's going on with Ryan, even if it means ending things with him."

"Thinking about breaking up is kind of scary, you know? I hardly remember life before we started dating."

As much as I wished I could fix Emma's problems for her, I knew I couldn't. This was no scraped knee I could kiss and slap a bandage on. Like it or not, being an adult meant facing challenges. Sometimes, the right option was the most frightening one—one requiring a giant leap of faith.

Our call ended, and I sighed. Unfortunately, my leap of faith had landed me in the middle of a murder investigation. The bright red letters of the anonymous note caught my eye, and my lips widened with a slow smile. My troubles would be over soon. When Detective Cram arrived, I'd hand the note off to him, and he'd know I wasn't the killer.

Chapter Fourteen

As the kitchen filled with the heavenly aroma of fresh-brewed coffee, I grabbed my camera and hung its strap around my neck. The machine beeped, and I loaded a tray with the steaming pot, mugs, cream, and sugar, and carried it to the barn. A thrill of anticipation ran through me. This would be the first of many cups of coffee in my studio.

I peeked inside the open door with a feeling of relief. Gone was the eeriness of the previous night when the flying dust had clouded the dim gray light. Connor stood in the center of the room near the toppled boxes, scrutinizing the back wall. He turned to face me as I entered.

I set the tray on a box. "Help yourself."

Struck by the low angle of the sun streaming through the dirty window, I raised my camera to click several photos of my dusty barn. The light created an interesting stream of haze that was both challenging and fun to capture. Dirty footprints crisscrossed the lines made by the contrasting light and shadows across the floor. Remembering our upcoming challenge, I snapped several shots, moving around to create a series of compositions. At our meeting, I'd impose the three-by-three grid over each to illustrate how to use the rule of thirds in photo composition.

Connor's voice brought me back to the present. "The largest window will arrive in a day or two. You want it centered, correct?" He pointed to the back wall while sipping his coffee.

After lowering my camera, I poured myself a cup, adding sugar and a generous splash of cream, then angled my head to picture the expansive view of the river and natural light replacing the gloom. "Centered, definitely."

"Just making sure." Connor pulled a tattered piece of paper from his back pocket, unfolding it on the old workbench. He sipped from his mug while studying the plans and invited me to join him.

My barn—which was more like an old carriage house—wasn't cavernous like Alicia's dairy barn. It needed work, and lots of it. The picture window was the beginning. I also needed a darkroom, a dressing room or two, a bathroom, and a sturdy staircase leading to the loft. I cranked my neck, already imagining my desk and file cabinets in the old hayloft. It would have a sort of modern-rustic vibe. But first, the rickety ladder needed to go.

I considered the ceiling and its rustic boards. Skylights might be nice. I craved light, lots and lots of light.

Connor looked up from the blueprints. "Did you have time to look around? Was anything disturbed?"

In my excitement over the renovation, I'd forgotten about the intruder. "Not that I can tell. There are so many tracks in the dust, and they all seem to blend."

"I've been in and out a lot lately. It's kind of hard to tell one footprint from another."

I blew across my steaming mug. Even if the barn held no clues, I still had the note. And that would be enough to steer the police elsewhere, letting me get on with my new life.

"Let's talk about next steps," Connor said.

I pointed toward the ladder, full of ideas about the staircase's design. As I spoke, a shadow crossed the floor, and a tall, dark figure stood in the doorway.

I froze under Detective Cram's lurking presence. Lost in dreams of my studio renovation, I'd all but forgotten to expect him. My mouth opened and closed before I found my voice. "Detective Cram," I said. "Thank you for coming."

"You're not in your house." The detective's voice grated accusingly.

"Astute observation," Connor mumbled, his back to the doorway. I nearly spit out my coffee. I'd never loved him more than I did right then.

Recovering, I said, "No, I'm not. We are making plans for the renovation of my studio."

"You shouldn't be in here. It's a potential crime scene." Accompanied by the powerful scent of his brutish cologne, Detective Cram stepped inside. "If your story is to be believed."

Connor peered at me and raised an eyebrow, so like Nate, it felt uncanny. He leaned over the blueprint, running his finger along one side as if absorbed in his work, but I could tell his attention was with the churlish detective.

I held my breath and counted to myself before answering. "Please look around. We made sure not to move anything, including these boxes. They used to be in a neat pile."

Detective Cram sniffed, pinching his lips together. He strode to the far corner, then returned to the doorway and motioned toward the house. "I've seen all I need to see. Shall we?"

Before I left, Connor said, "I plan to install a new lock in the door. I'll hang the key on the hook inside your kitchen before I leave."

"That would be wonderful." One less thing to worry about. I turned to Detective Cram and led him to the kitchen.

Darcy sat by the door. A low, rumbling growl came from his throat as we approached.

"You need to do something about your dog." Detective Cram squeezed himself against the doorframe.

"Mmm." *As if that's going to happen.* I gave Darcy's head an affectionate pat. "Good boy," I whispered.

As soon as the detective sat on a stool, I handed him the envelope. "Here you are. It should be self-explanatory."

He pinched the corner, turning it to view both sides. "A plain white envelope with your name on the outside."

I pushed the folded note toward him. "This was inside."

After opening the note, he let out a loud snort. "Anyone could have written this."

"Indeed."

"Including yourself." The corners of Detective Cram's mouth lifted into a condescending smile.

My jaw dropped. "Why would I do that?"

"Elementary. To deflect suspicion away from yourself."

Was he kidding? Sherlock Holmes, he was not. I lifted a finger to my bruised cheek. "I suppose I punched myself to make my scheme more authentic." My voice became shrill as my frustration mounted. "Someone pushed a pile of boxes on me, pinning me to the ground."

"It's no wonder the boxes fell on you. Your barn is a mess, and it's a good thing no one was hurt, or else you'd be liable."

I stiffened, sitting upright. So much for putting the nightmare behind me. But I had his attention and wasn't about to let the opportunity slide. "Has the medical examiner determined a more exact time of death?"

Detective Cram glared at me. "All I can tell you is the time of death shouldn't matter to you, since you don't have an alibi." He thumbed through his notebook. "Ah, yes. At home, getting ready for your club meeting."

"If I'm interpreting this correctly, you're saying Tiffanee died between five and seven o'clock." As I spoke, the detective looked up from his notebook with a sharp expression that bolstered my confidence, and I continued. "Because, as you know, that was the time I was at home."

"Yes, well, the victim may not have died right away," Detective Cram said.

"Meaning the assault could have happened before then? But we know that's not true. She was on the village green." I didn't wait for a reply before forging ahead. "What about the fingerprints on the camera?"

Placing his palms on the counter, the detective stood. "Yours were the only prints we found."

This news didn't surprise me. The killer had, no doubt, wiped the camera clean. "What about Tiffanee's? The killer must have wiped them."

He shook his head, running his fingers through his spikes. "That doesn't rule you out."

I crossed my arms in front of me. "I wiped Tiffanee's prints but left my own, you mean?" It was ludicrous. How did he not see that?

"We have to consider everything," he said. "You could have been sloppy."

"Have you considered Jackson's alibi?" Remembering Jackson's behavior at our meeting, I wasn't ready to give up. I'd only seen dark pants and shoes the night before. They could have been Jackson's, even if it didn't feel right.

"It was as he said. There was a customer in his shop right before he locked up. Everything checks out." He tucked the note in a folder. "Unless you have some useful information, we're done here."

Motioning toward the door with a limp hand, I let out a long breath and stared at the empty spot where the note had been. At least he'd taken it with him. The lingering odor of aftershave was giving me a headache. I pressed a finger to the bridge of my nose, smoothing the deep grooves where worry made itself at home, and took my phone from my pocket to fire off a group text to Rose and Alicia.

I cannot believe Detective Cram!!! He thinks I made the whole thing up!!! Rose replied with a string of angry emojis.

And then, from Alicia: ***I have an idea.***

Chapter Fifteen

This was a bad idea, a terrible idea. From the driver's seat of my Subaru, I groaned, giving Alicia the side-eye. "Are you sure we should do this?" The streetlight illuminated my sister's face, pale beneath her black cap.

The lines near Alicia's eyes and mouth were set in the determined look I knew well. It was a look that told me nothing could sway her. "You said it yourself. Detective Cram isn't taking you seriously."

"True." I drew out the word, my fingers worrying the matching black knit cap in my lap, thankful she hadn't chosen balaclavas.

A quick glance in my rearview mirror reflected Rose, similarly topped, looking scarily bright-eyed. Beside her, Jackson reached to twist his cap for probably the hundredth time. I had yet to hear the story of how they'd roped him into our adventure.

"This is so exciting." Rose was bouncing in the back seat like a child on her way to a birthday party.

Jackson chimed in. "I only hope learning about Tiffanee will help us solve this."

My blinker clicked as I signaled my turn onto River Street. The streetlights of Main Street behind us, the road ahead was like a tunnel concealed beneath a dark canopy of leaves. In the distance, a muted glow, faint against the black sky, shone from a window in Penny and Bernadine's house at the far end of the street.

"Breaking into Tiffanee's house, though? Aren't her parents in town?" I chewed my fingernail. Alicia's scheme had seemed like a good idea earlier, when I'd been fuming over Wyatt Cram's dismissal of the warning note. With Tiffanee's funeral only two days away, Mr. and Mrs. Jacobsen would come back to Stonebridge, wouldn't they?

"If they're here, we'll see their car and leave," Alicia said as I pulled my car into a space behind the stone mill building.

Rose snorted. "I doubt they'll stay in their old house. They're more the bed-and-breakfast type. By that, I mean they'll probably stay in a luxury inn."

I swallowed, accepting that Alicia and Rose knew the Jacobsens. What I needed to think about was the more important things—like staying out of prison.

I flicked the headlights off, blanketing us in blackness. Parking at the old mill had been my idea, a way to keep my car hidden should someone drive by. In retrospect, I needn't have worried about being spotted from the road, making my cover story of a nighttime photo shoot seem silly. No way I'd go into the dilapidated mill building at night. Not even for intriguing photos. The jagged edges of broken windows staring back at me were spooky enough. I opened my door and let my eyes adjust to the darkness.

"Are you sure this is a good idea?" I repeated with a shudder.

"Nope. But what else can we do?" Alicia tucked her blonde hair into her cap. "Are we all ready?"

Rose took a springing leap from the back seat. "Let's do this!"

"What if we don't find a key?" We'd gone over this several times, but I couldn't help asking again.

"We will." Like always, Alicia's voice was so calm, so sure. *So annoying.*

I pushed my hair back, pulled the cap over my head, and exhaled slowly.

"If we don't find one, we're going home. I'm not adding breaking and entering to my string of potential charges."

"We'll find one." Alicia stepped to the ground.

I flinched at the car door's creaking in the otherwise still night. Clutching the handle, I was reluctant to leave the security of my car's hard metal sturdiness. I leaned against its side, pausing for a moment. Trees swayed at the edge of the forest. In the dim moonlight, their shadows loomed over me as though ready to pounce. The city never got this dark.

"Let's go." Jackson's voice was but a whisper in the dark.

I stepped forward, following Alicia with Rose at my side. Behind us, Jackson's plodding footsteps seemed unnecessarily loud. A field full of spring's fresh growth separated Tiffanee's cottage from the crumbling mill. High above the treetops, twinkling stars dotted the sky. Their stingy light did little to light the path before us.

Alicia gave me a gentle nudge. "We'd better stay in the field. I don't want to take a chance of being spotted on the road. Besides, the shortest distance is straight through."

It was too late to back out. We needed to find Tiffanee's killer. I rolled my shoulders and stepped forward.

"It is unbelievably dark out here." Rose's voice was spookily soft. "And uber creepy, like some sort of horror movie where zombies come out of nowhere."

Jackson let out a low-throated, growling noise before chuckling to himself.

"So not funny," I said. Fortunately, I never watched the kind of movie Rose had described. And yet, I scanned the surrounding woods. Wild animals were dangerous enough, but zombies? I shivered.

"It really is dark." Alicia seemed completely unperturbed.

"Dorothy, we're not in Boston anymore." My shaking voice didn't help my attempt at a joke.

"I think you meant Kansas," Jackson said.

"Never been there." I stopped walking. "I bet it's not as brightly lit as Boston."

Alicia huffed and tugged my arm. "Let's get going."

The impression of stillness was deceiving. Tall stalks bent and swayed, grazing my face and neck. Insects buzzed, and critters scurried beneath my feet. I was swatting a bug from my face when a shadow swooped from a nearby tree and headed straight toward my head. Ducking, I clamped a hand over my mouth to stifle my scream.

"Just a bat," Alicia said.

"What? Eww!" Rose's voice was shrill.

"You must be kidding me," Jackson said. "You've lived in Vermont all your life, and you're freaking out over a bat?"

"That doesn't mean I like them," Rose said.

"Shh. Keep your voices down," Alicia warned. "Be glad for bats; they eat mosquitoes."

I stood, thrashing at imaginary critters flying around my head. "There are more than enough mosquitoes to go around. The bats don't need to use my cheek as their serving platter."

At the sound of Jackson's snicker, I debated turning around once again.

"Laugh all you want, but I'm thinking I prefer jungles to be more urban." I slapped at the weeds.

"You can't possibly mean that." Rose's face was close to mine, her eyes shining with concern.

"No, I guess not." I'd moved to Vermont to get away from the harshness of the city, and bats aside, I was determined to see it through.

"We're here." Alicia beamed at our accomplishment. She spread the last bit of weeds open, revealing a tidy yard, once well cared for. A feeling of melancholy came over me as I took in the abandoned home with its windows staring blankly into the night. Terra-cotta pots lined the steps of the small wooden deck, their flowers wilted.

Jackson switched on his flashlight, sweeping a beam around the deck. "Do you think she used a fake rock or a key under the mat?"

"Keep your light low." I pointed toward the dim glow I'd seen earlier, confirming it came from a window in Penny's house next door. Thankfully, the curtains were closed.

I kicked a jagged stone with the toe of my boot. "I hope it's not a rock." Finding the fake one would take all night.

Alicia made a beeline to the doormat. She lifted it, shaking her head. "Drat, I had her as the doormat type."

"How about a planter?" I ran my gloved finger along the edge of a window box. Nothing. I lifted a flowerpot and looked beneath it. Again, nothing. While I dug into the dry soil of a planter near the grill, Jackson and Rose wandered through the yard, kicking at rocks. I stirred my finger around the pot and touched something hard and jagged.

"Bingo." I waved a dirt-encrusted key.

Alicia snatched it from my fingers, wiped it on her jeans, and inserted it into the lock. The door opened. "We're in." Her grin was triumphant.

Inside Tiffanee's tiny kitchen, the air was stagnant. On the deep windowsill, a thirsty plant sat next to a scented candle whose fruity scent did little to freshen the stale air. Embroidered tea towels hung from the handle of a dated oven. Alicia and I exchanged a glance as Jackson and Rose stepped inside. The room was neat and homey in an old-fashioned way that seemed unlike Tiffanee.

I lifted my chin and sniffed again. "Do you think the police have been here?"

"It's hard to tell. The place looks pretty neat." Alicia opened and closed drawers and cupboards. "I get it wasn't the crime scene, but they must have come here, don't you think?"

"Yes." I swept my flashlight over the floor. "What are you searching for?"

"I really don't know. Let's spread out. We're trying to learn who Tiffanee was and why someone killed her. Remember?"

"Shh." The banging drawers echoed in my ears. "Be careful of the windows on this side. The last thing we need is for Bernadine to see our lights."

"I told Penny about our plan," Rose said. "Hopefully, she'll keep her mom distracted. Bernadine seems like the neighborhood watch type."

"Smart thinking. Let's hope she's successful," I said.

"I'll head upstairs." Jackson disappeared through a doorway and skulked toward the front of the house, his flashlight trained on the floor.

While Alicia started a methodical search of the kitchen, I tiptoed to an adjoining room—Tiffanee's office, from the looks of it. Despite the pendant light fixture suggesting a dining room, a long credenza, a desk, and a filing cabinet lined the walls. An empty file drawer was ajar, folders strewn over the desk. I ran my fingers over the tabs, leafing through the files labeled Rosebud Café, Long Trail Booksellers, and Crowley Farm, but found nothing more than invoices and receipts.

"Tiffanee was your bookkeeper?" I called out to my sister.

"Mm-hmm," Alicia answered, but offered nothing further.

Interesting. Rose, William, and Alicia had all used Tiffanee's services. That was an angle I hadn't considered. Money was one of the main motives for murder.

"What if the murderer was one of her clients?" I asked.

"Possible," Alicia said. "But we've never had problems with her."

"Neither have I." Rose sidled past me, heading toward the entry hall.

I filed the thought away and opened the desk drawers, shining my flashlight over their contents. Pens, pencils, and miscellaneous office supplies. Nothing incriminating, but something wasn't right. I turned and scanned the room. Where was her computer?

Alicia appeared in the doorway. "Nothing of interest in the kitchen, unless this is helpful." She held a strip of photos from a photo booth.

"Tiffanee and Harmony. This looks old. Where did you find it?"

"Tucked in a junk drawer." Alicia shrugged, stashing the strip into the pocket of her sweatshirt.

I moved my flashlight over the top of the desk, landing on a photo printer. As I ran my fingers along the sides, I hit a memory card protruding from a slot near the back. I turned on the printer and jumped as it screeched to life, its beeps and dings amplified by the surrounding quiet.

"What have we here?" Alicia pointed at the memory card. "Is that what I think it is?"

"The missing memory card? I don't know yet, but it might shed some light on Tiffanee's covert camera habits." I opened the LCD screen and followed the prompt to view images. There were numerous shots of various village residents. "I wonder what these are about." I scrolled through the first few pictures. The subjects appeared unaware their photo was being taken.

"Can you make copies with your phone?"

I dug my phone from my pocket and snapped the first image, satisfied with the less-than-perfect results. Decent enough.

Alicia stood for a moment, watching over my shoulder. "It's working. Get as many as you can, and I'll go ransack the front room." She disappeared through another doorway.

I scrolled and snapped, irritated by the slowness of the printer.

"Lookie what I found." Rose's sing-song voice came from the entry hall. She leaned against the doorframe, holding a canvas messenger bag.

My jaw dropped as I abandoned the printer and took the bag from Rose. "The missing camera bag! It must be. Do you think it was here when the police searched the house?" I pointed at the jumble of file folders. "Assuming it was the police who messed up Tiffanee's files and took her computer."

Setting the bag on the floor, I rifled through its contents.

"Wouldn't they have taken it if it was?" Rose sat on the floor next to me, and Alicia entered to examine our find.

"What's inside?" Alicia asked.

Jackson's footsteps sounded on the stairs before he, too, entered the room. "Nothing unusual upstairs." He cleared his throat while dangling a lacy strip of fabric from his finger. "Except for maybe some obscenely sexy underwear."

"That's not unusual. Put those back!" Rose huffed.

I set a fifty-millimeter lens on the floor. "A nifty fifty. Tiffanee's wallet." I handed the wallet to Alicia. "And guess what else." I held up a lens cap, my heart hammering. "I bet this goes to the lens on Tiffanee's camera."

"Nothing weird in the wallet. Driver's license, credit cards, a picture of Hope, sixteen bucks." Alicia placed the wallet back in the bag and pointed at the lens cap. "Does that mean what I think it does?"

"No way Tiffanee left this at home. The lens she was using is more expensive than most people's cameras. Leaving it uncapped risks nasty scratches."

The four of us exchanged glances as the implication of our find hung heavily in the room.

"That means the killer—" Rose stopped, snapping her head toward the front of the house. She placed a finger on her lips. "Did you hear that? It sounds like someone just parked out front."

Chapter Sixteen

"We need to get out of here now." I jumped to my feet, and a wave of dizziness came over me. I ran to the printer and fumbled with the power button.

Alicia stuffed the lens cap back in the bag and stashed it under the desk. "Did you get the photos?"

"Only a few."

"Grab the card," Alicia said.

"But—" I hesitated. Taking the card would be stealing. What if it was the one that should have been at the crime scene? My fingers shook with indecision.

"Come on!" Alicia grabbed my arm.

With no time to think it through, I snatched the memory card and stashed it in my pocket. Thank goodness the printer had finally finished beeping and dinging, shutting off as a key rattled in the door.

Still clenching the lacy panties, Jackson raced toward the kitchen, colliding with Rose as they both tried to squeeze through the doorway.

"Seriously?" Rose squeaked before taking a step back and pushing Jackson through. "We need to get out of here."

Alicia and I caught up with them as the scraping in the lock continued. Jackson grabbed the kitchen doorknob and flung the door open with a force that caused Rose and him to tumble onto the deck. Recovering first, Rose stood and waved for us to follow. Jackson stood and made a run for the side of the house.

"Hey!" a male voice shouted. "Who's here?" His footsteps pounded toward the kitchen.

"Run!" I whispered to Alicia as we took off, slamming the door behind us.

We'd almost made it around the corner of the house when the back door opened, and a light illuminated the backyard. "Who's there?" a male voice called.

The four of us stood with our backs flat against the side wall. The sound of our panting would make anyone think we'd just run a marathon. Without making a sound, Alicia motioned toward the field, taking charge as she normally does. It was several yards away. Her expression was commanding when she held up one finger, then a second. A universal childhood game—we knew when Alicia raised her third finger, it was time to run. At her signal, the "Wicked Witch Theme" rang from the back pocket of my jeans, loud in the otherwise silent night. I ignored it and dashed toward the field, diving into the weeds.

After fumbling for my phone, I pulled it out and hissed into it. "This isn't a good time. Hang on." I could hear my mother's voice as I stashed her back in my pocket.

"You could have silenced your phone," Rose whispered.

"Shh." This wasn't the time to discuss my stupidity. I held my breath, listening for the sounds of movement. All I heard, though, was the muffled, yet forceful, voice of my mother.

The sound of heavy footsteps came from the wooden deck. I exhaled slowly, trying to calm my pounding heart. Silently, we crouched among the weeds, waiting for his next move, but heard nothing. When I felt I could kneel no longer, Tiffanee's back door shut with a resounding bang, and the porch light went out, casting the yard in darkness once again.

"He's back inside," Alicia said. "His voice sounded familiar. Did you see who he was?"

Rose sighed. "Yes. It was Travis."

I dug my phone from my pocket. "Sorry, Mother." In my relief over making our getaway, I failed to notice the ease with which I walked through the field. I swatted at the weeds once or twice while my mother's voice buffeted the airwaves.

"I've been thinking about that poor girl," Fiona said.

"Me too, but I can't talk right now. Can I call you back in the morning?"

"Yes, yes, of course. I wanted to say that when someone kills a woman, they're usually close to the victim. I know you can't help getting involved."

"Wh-what makes you say that?"

My mother let out a beleaguered sigh. "I know you, Bobbie Ann. You care too much. Look close to home. That's all I'm saying. And for heaven's sake, don't let Alicia talk you into something that puts you at risk."

Too late. I shot Alicia a fierce look I knew she couldn't see. As my screen went black, I noticed a spotlight shining from the corner of Bernadine and Penny's house. It hadn't been on before, had it? I grabbed Alicia's arm and pointed. "How long has that light been on?"

"We'd better get out of here."

We cracked the car doors open and slid inside, closing them as quietly as they allowed. In no time, I inched my car onto the street, headlights off. We barely made it to the corner of Main Street when sirens blared. I stopped and flicked on my headlights in time to see a police cruiser speeding in our direction.

"Duck," I said. As Alicia, Rose, and Jackson bowed their heads, I watched the cruiser screech around the corner and race past. When the lights had faded, I turned to peer out the back window. The cruiser came to a sudden halt behind Travis's truck.

I pulled onto Main Street and into my driveway.

"That was close." Alicia pulled her cap off, shaking her hair loose.

"Too close," I whispered, gulping air.

"I don't know about you, but that was more fun than I've had in ages." Rose giggled.

"I'd better get home before Nate wonders what's keeping me. We can look at what you found tomorrow." Alicia's voice softened. "It will be okay."

"Do you think Travis knows it was us?"

Jackson shrugged. "I guess we'll find out. I'm not worried. He isn't exactly a pillar of society, and it will be his word against ours."

"Hey." Rose gave up her protest. "Oh, never mind. When you're right, you're right."

I slumped in my seat, my fingers touching the stolen memory card, knowing it made me less than a pillar of society, too.

The next morning, my coffee pot gurgled, filling my kitchen with its warm, nutty aroma. Rattled from our escapades of the night before, I'd gone straight to bed after we'd said our goodbyes. It had been late—later than I was normally out—and the thought of viewing stolen photos wreaked havoc with my moral compass.

I lifted a stoneware mug from the shelf as the coffee maker gave one last hiss, signaling the brew was ready. With a feeling of accomplishment, I poured a cup, added cream and sugar, then ambled toward the kitchen table. Armed with caffeine courage, I was ready to start.

I opened my laptop and sipped from my mug while waiting for my computer to power on. Mmm, the kitchen designer had been right. That contraption made fantastic coffee. I swelled with a sense of pride at mastering it.

With another gulp, I fiddled with the memory card, flipping it between my fingers. Rose and Alicia had both mentioned how Tiffanee's surreptitious snapping habits had put villagers on edge. Nervous about what I might find, I inserted the card and imported the photos into my photography software. Images popped onto my screen, fuzzy at first. Mostly residents working, talking, or going about their day-to-day business. I sat back, waiting for the photos to finish loading.

"Hey, Bobbie," Connor called from the kitchen door. Darcy followed on his heels, his tail wagging. "I'm heading out to the barn and wanted to let you know I'm here."

"I made coffee. Help yourself."

"You made it yourself? No way." Connor grinned. "That's great. Thanks."

"No problem." I leaned over my laptop as Darcy placed his snout on the table and sniffed. He flicked his gaze between me and my computer. "Don't judge," I said. "You'd take the photos too."

Without moving his snout, he gave me a side-eyed stare. Then, apparently deciding to come off his high horse, he took a step back and plopped to the floor with a grunt.

The photos had loaded, and I opened the most recent image first, relieved it was almost two weeks old. Tiffanee's missing card should have photos from the afternoon at the covered bridge. So far, the images confirmed what I'd expected. No smoking guns. At least, not yet.

Clicking on the next image, I jolted. Harmony with a young man, his light hair shielding part of his profile. They appeared to be deep in conversation. The expression on Harmony's face was unreadable. It could have been anger, frustration, or something else entirely.

"Connor?" I turned to find him opening the kitchen door, steaming mug in hand. "Could you come here for a minute?"

"Sure thing." Connor walked over to peer at my screen.

"Do you know who this is?" I pointed to the young man in the photo.

Connor leaned forward. "That's Hunter. You know, the guy I told you about." He examined the photo again, a deep crease forming at the bridge of his nose. "Hey, where did this photo come from?"

My mind raced as I grasped for an answer. Clearly, sleuthing was not my thing.

"The photos belong to one of my club members." The lie tumbled from my mouth. "This is the first chance I've had to view them." It was a stretch, but there was a smidgen of truth to it. What would Connor think if he knew Alicia and I had broken into Tiffanee's house?

"Oh, okay then." Connor shifted his weight. "Are you all set? Your window arrived, and a crew is coming to help install it."

"Sounds good, and thanks for your help." I held my breath, doing all I could not to show relief when Connor left, the door banging behind him.

With him safely out of the room, I clicked on the next photo and whispered to Harmony's image. "Well, well. What have we here?" Harmony had been friends with Hunter before she moved to Stonebridge, so it shouldn't have seemed strange to see them together. It was possible the photo meant nothing. But there was something about the image that made the hair on my arms stand at attention. It didn't look like nothing.

Wrapping my hands around my warm mug, I stared at my screen, scrutinizing the photo from corner to corner. Where had I seen Hunter before? He seemed familiar. Fiona's words rang in my ears. *It's usually someone close.* After all her years working with victims of domestic abuse, she would know.

I recalled tagging along with my mother, visiting women's shelters, and playing games with the children while waiting for her to finish whatever business had brought us there. Back then, I hadn't fully appreciated her passion for the work she did, the endless fundraisers, charity events, and foundations she sat on the board of. Selfishly, I would've preferred her to be more like my friends' moms, sitting down to family dinners, eager to hear the minutiae of my day. As an adult, I'd often attended functions with my parents. I'd gained a better understanding of their dedication and was proud of my mother's tireless efforts and ability to use her position in society to affect change.

I doubted Tiffanee had been abused. At least, not by Travis. Rose and I were close enough that I think she'd have mentioned a violent streak if he'd had one. Even without the suspicion of abuse, I understood what my mother was trying to tell me. Statistically, most violence against women was perpetrated by a partner, either former or current. In Tiffanee's case, that meant Travis and Hunter, but I wasn't ready to rule out her friends.

Leaning on my elbow, I rested my chin in my hand. Outside, wispy puffs of cotton drifted across the sky. The whir of a saw wafted through the open window. I refocused my attention to continue viewing the photos. Several more images featured Harmony and Hunter. More images of villagers going about their business, including one of a man and a woman who appeared ready to get down to business of another kind. Sheesh, not only was Tiffanee a gifted photographer, but she had some incredible stalking skills. I took another look at the photo. Something about the woman seemed familiar. I flagged it for Alicia's review. She knew everyone.

Sipping my coffee, I slowly clicked past two images of Rose working in her café—nothing nefarious there. Even the Righteous Sisters weren't immune to Tiffanee's stalking. One image showed the three of them with their heads together, no doubt sharing a bit of juicy gossip. Lorraine's lips formed their usual judgmental slash.

Then, I came to a photo of me sitting at my favorite table in the coffee shop. With a shudder, I examined my outfit and hairstyle, trying to remember the day. Unlike Rose, my clothes were mostly nondescript. Only my scarves stood out. According to the metadata, the photo was about three weeks old. No wonder residents were uncomfortable.

The sky grew brighter as the morning wore on. I slumped over my computer, my second mug of coffee in hand, or was it my third? Only a few more images to survey. I clicked on the next one and gasped, jerking my head around to be sure Connor hadn't entered without me knowing it.

I leaned closer, my nose inches from the screen. Alicia and… Who was that man? His hand rested on her arm; Alicia's expression was unreadable. The shot was intimate. Impressive photography. I wished it wasn't of my married sister. Who was she with? I pulled away from the screen and flipped through images in my mind. Then, sitting back, I pointed at my computer.

I know who you are. It's been a long time.

My fingers shook as I grabbed my phone and typed a message to Alicia.

We need to talk.

Chapter Seventeen

Full of nervous energy, I rushed down my porch stairs and gave Mr. Miller a hasty wave without waiting for his grumpy reply. After sending Alicia my text, we'd agreed to meet at her farm. I had just enough time for a quick stop at the Rosebud, not that I needed more caffeine. Police sirens in the night were sure to get tongues wagging, and this was one time I was curious to hear the village gossip. The Rosebud Café would be the place to find out whether I needed damage control.

Nearly out of breath from running the short distance, I flung the door open and strode toward the counter, coming to an abrupt halt when Rose gave a slight nod toward a nearby table. Her warning came a beat too late to hightail it back out of there. Detective Cram was smiling—an honest-to-goodness-actual smile, no less—as he chatted with the Righteous Sisters. When our eyes met, the corners of his mouth twitched. I took the last few steps before sliding onto the only empty stool at the counter and burying my face in my hands.

"You've got to be kidding me," I whispered, peeking through my spread fingers. I had expected the Righteous Sisters, of course, but I would have thought Detective Cram had a murder to solve.

"Coffee?" Rose's attention flitted from me to the detective and back again.

"Decaf, please." I dared a quick sideways glance and groaned. The detective and Lorraine were laughing.

"Having a problem, darlin'?" Travis's voice came from my other side.

I spun on my stool, letting out a louder groan. "Don't you have somewhere you should be? Like a job, maybe?"

Travis scoffed. "I'm a bartender. What's your excuse?"

Before I could answer—which I had no intention of doing—Rose returned and set my coffee on the counter. She glared at Travis. "Everything okay here?"

Just dandy. With a noncommittal shrug, I thanked her for the coffee. Detective Cram swung toward me, his gossip session over. He headed my way, and I angled my back to him, meeting Travis's lopsided grin. *Yep, just dandy.*

The corners of Travis's lips hitched a little higher as he leaned toward me. "I'm off. To work." His grin widened even more when I cringed at his mocking tone. He stood and paused before leaning closer to whisper in my ear. "Which of your friends is the Wicked Witch?"

My head snapped, but Travis didn't wait for an answer. He was halfway to the door when the spicy scent of the detective's lurking presence tickled my nose.

"How fortunate to find you here, Mrs. Brooks."

Fortunate for whom? I drew a slow breath and swiveled to find the detective standing beside me, thumbs hooked in his belt loops and a predatory gleam in his eyes. He appeared far too pleased with himself.

My voice was surprisingly steady when I spoke. "What can I do for you?"

"Do you mind telling me where you were last night?" he asked.

"I was with my sister. Why?" I glared at him, refusing to be his prey. How much did he know?

He placed his hand on the counter and leaned over me. "Where was that?"

"At my house." True. She'd come to my house to change into her cat burglar outfit. "Again, why are you asking?"

"I saw a blue Subaru, just like yours, on River Street last night."

"A blue Subaru." I laughed. He was fishing, I was pretty sure. Travis must not have ratted us out. Buoyed by the thought, my shaking lessened. "Do you have any idea how many people in Stonebridge drive blue Subarus?"

The gleam left his eyes. He appeared flustered. Almost.

Rose stood watching, her hands on her hips. Her head bounced to our game of predator and prey.

Detective Cram gathered himself, straightening so that he loomed over me from high in his nest. "Were you on River Street last night?"

I almost jumped. Now I was in for it. There was no way I could lie to a police officer. I fumbled for an answer. *Deflect.* "I don't understand why you keep going on about River Street. Was there some sort of problem there?"

Detective Cram's face turned a deep shade of puce. It was easy to imagine steam billowing from his ears.

Rose stepped forward. "This is a coffee shop, not a police station, and I don't appreciate you using my café to interrogate my customers. As Bobbie mentioned, half of Stonebridge drives Subarus like hers. If you're insinuating something, I'd prefer you do it elsewhere."

My jaw dropped. Rose's gumption was something to behold. It wasn't every day I watched a feisty redhead stand up to a bully who towered over her.

Detective Cram opened and shut his mouth, looking every bit as stunned as I felt. He jabbed his finger toward my face. "You had better watch your step." With his chin jutted, he strode out of the coffee shop.

I blew a wisp of hair from my forehead and turned in astonishment to my friend. "That was amazing."

Rose waited until the door closed behind the detective before answering. "Nerve-wracking is what I think you meant to say."

"You said it. He had me worried for a minute."

Chairs scraped against the floor as the Righteous Sisters stood in unison. I felt the heat of Lorraine's glare crawl up my neck. If looks could kill, I would be dead a few times over. To my relief, the entourage marched out the door without a word.

Rose leaned forward with a conspiratorial grin. "Did you get a chance to look at Tiffanee's photos?"

"She's been a busy bee," I said. "Lots of photos of villagers, including both of us."

"That girl had some nerve. Was there anything suspicious?"

I wasn't ready to tell Rose about the photo of Alicia. "I'm not sure. I didn't know everyone in the pictures. Alicia is going to look at them." I nodded toward the table where the Righteous Sisters had been seated. "What's today's gossip?"

"The uzh. Just that Bernadine called the police. She thought someone had broken into Tiffanee's house, but with Travis there, they figured it was a false alarm."

I told Rose about her ex-husband's comment about my ringtone. "He definitely knew it was me but must not have told Detective Cram."

"He's not someone who'd go out of his way to help the police. I'm guessing he knew I was there, too, and didn't want to get me in trouble. For Ethan's sake."

"Any idea what he was doing there?"

"Ha! He's not likely to share his secrets with me. At least we know he wasn't returning the camera bag. Besides, Travis has a key."

"That doesn't explain why he was there," I said with a soft voice. "If Travis has a key, it's possible he's been in and out of the house several times." I waited for Rose to understand what I wasn't saying out loud—that Travis could have returned the bag earlier.

Rose grabbed a rag from beneath the counter and swiped at crumbs only she could see. "Good heavens, I just told off a statie."

"You sure did." I pictured Rose squaring off with Detective Cram and couldn't help the grin from spreading across my face. "You should have seen yourself."

Rose waved her hand at me. "Stop. Was my face as red as my blouse?"

"Nope. And not nearly as red as his, either."

Rose scrunched her nose. "I still say last night was the most fun I've had in a long time."

I laughed. "Oh man, if that's true, we desperately need to get you out more."

Chapter Eighteen

Darcy poked his head out the open window, his tongue flapping in the breeze and his tail thumping on the passenger seat as I drove up Alicia's long driveway. In his excitement to play with his doggy cousins, he barely gave me time to open the car door before bolting to the broad farmer's porch, where Harry and Sally lazed at Alicia's feet.

"Have fun," I called while watching the dogs dash out to the field, running and jumping in circles. "Have you ever seen a happier dog?" I asked Alicia while grabbing my backpack and giving the car door a hip check.

"Dogs, you mean. Harry and Sally love it when Darcy comes to play." Alicia poured a glass of iced tea and offered it to me. "I thought we could sit out here and enjoy the sunny afternoon while the dogs run around."

"Sounds good." There was something about sitting on the old porch, its view of the mountains and forest framing the fields of hay. It always calmed me.

"I take it you studied Tiffanee's photos." Alicia rubbed her hands together, looking eager to dig in.

"I did, but first, I need to tell you about my encounter with Detective Cram." I set my laptop on the porch floor and sat in a rocker.

"Tell me he didn't recognize us last night."

I raised my palms.

"Shoot, he did?"

"Not exactly, but he thinks he did. My car, anyway. And I maybe, umm… might have told him I was with you last night."

"Pfft. Everyone in Stonebridge drives a Subaru. Or a pickup truck."

"That's what I told him." I told Alicia about Rose and the detective's face-off.

"I can picture it. Rose can get downright fiery if she's poked the wrong way. She's like a mama bear, protecting her cubs." Alicia sipped her iced tea.

"Travis knows it was me. He teased me about the Wicked Witch."

"Leave it to Mom to have horrendous timing. Seriously, though, you need to change that ringtone."

Gathering my thoughts, I took in the peaceful scene before me—the barn and the mountains beyond. I didn't understand how Alicia could be so cavalier. And yes, I admitted to myself, she was right about the ringtone. It wasn't that I actually thought our mother was a witch.

Alicia broke the silence. "What was on Tiffanee's memory card? It wasn't *the* missing card, was it?"

"No, I don't think so." I pulled out my laptop and explained about the photos of Hunter and Harmony, various villagers, and the couple I wanted her to look at. "Without thinking, I showed the one of Hunter to Connor."

"Please tell me you didn't."

"I think it's okay. I told him the photos were from our club. He seemed to believe me."

"Your detective skills need work," Alicia said.

"Sneaking around has never been my strength. I'd think you know me well enough by now."

Alicia gave me a crooked smile. "What was with your text?"

"Right." I opened the photos. When I found the one of Alicia with her old boyfriend, I pivoted the screen.

Alicia's expression remained impassive—the perfect poker face. Her sneaking skills far outshone mine. My sister studied the image, her head tilting ever so slightly. Then, facing me, she said, "I've already seen it."

"What? When?" The photo certainly looked incriminating.

"Tiffanee snapped the picture back in March, but she showed it to me about a month ago. I'm guessing the little witch also had photos of me pushing him away, but I bet she deleted those." She pointed at the screen. "I hadn't seen Matthew in years."

I remained silent, waiting for Alicia to continue.

"Remember when I told you that everyone was fed up with Tiffanee skulking around the village? This is why. It's what she does. Did, I mean."

"Why? Why did she do that?"

"Because she was a nasty piece of work," Alicia said. "I don't know. Blackmail? She thought Nate would be interested in seeing the photo. I can't even guess what she hoped to gain. A small-town lawyer and a farmer, it's not like we have lots of money to throw around. No matter, I'd already told Nate all about it."

I believed her. It wasn't like her to keep secrets from her husband.

"I was at The Crow waiting for our takeout order when I ran into him. He was with some friends on a ski weekend. You remember him, right?"

"You dated him in college."

"Believe me. Nate has nothing to worry about. I broke up with him long before I met Nate and never looked back."

"You've got to admit it looks kind of cozy."

Alicia leaned over again. "It does, doesn't it? His hand was there for a second at most before I batted it away. Kudos to Tiffanee for catching it."

I sat back and sipped my tea. A niggling thought played in my mind. "Are we thinking about this all wrong?"

"Go on."

"Maybe the murder had nothing to do with Travis or Hunter or any convoluted love triangle. Could she have blackmailed the wrong person?"

"Let's see the other photos."

I handed my laptop to Alicia. It had been silly for me to worry she was having an affair. She and Nate were rock solid.

While Alicia studied the images, I gazed at the open field dotted with wild daisies and dandelions. The goats bleated over near the barn while the rambunctious dogs continued to chase each other around the field, nipping and yipping. To have that kind of energy. But then, Darcy could zonk out later.

Alicia interrupted my reverie. "I'm not sure what to make of these pictures of Harmony and Hunter."

"I'm never sure what to make of Harmony," I said. "No one can be as serene as she seems all the time."

"Mmm." Alicia seemed to agree. With a mischievous sparkle in her eyes, she spun the screen to face me. "Tiffanee even took a photo of you. Do you feel like a villager now?"

I reached for the laptop. Ignoring her cheeky comment, I clicked on the touchpad. "Did you see the one I flagged?"

"Oh." Alicia's lips parted. "Oh, my."

"So, you know who they are?" I asked.

"I do. He's married. To someone else. And his wife is about to have a baby."

"Do you know the woman? That's some rock she's sporting on her ring finger. She looks familiar, but I can't think why."

"You've probably seen her around. She's a weekender," Alicia said. "Her husband is some big mucky-muck on Wall Street. They own a gorgeous home on Stratton Mountain." Alicia paused. "Come to think of it, she was sampling my blackberry jam at the farmers' market when you showed up."

"Right." I remembered. In her designer clothes and slicked-back ponytail, she'd stuck out like a sore thumb. I also recalled the way she'd flirted with Connor, making me shudder. "Do you think Tiffanee would blackmail either of them?"

"I'm thinking yes. Especially her." Alicia pointed at the woman. Moving her finger to the man, she said, "He's such a nice guy. It's hard to imagine him killing anyone, let alone being with her. What a cougar. She's at least my age. Although, with all the makeup and procedures, she pulls off a much younger look."

"Having an affair when your wife is about to have a baby? Not only does that make him *not* a nice guy, but it gives him a pretty big motive."

"You're right. Of course, you are. I'd think her motive might be bigger, but I can't picture her actually getting her hands dirty."

"That makes me wonder about Harmony and Hunter," I said.

Alicia's eyebrows knitted together.

"As far as I know, Harmony doesn't have a boyfriend, so I guess I kind of dismissed the photos of her." I nearly bounced from my seat, warming to my idea. "But I was forgetting about Hunter. What if he has a girlfriend—or wife? Maybe Tiffanee was blackmailing him, too. Maybe that's why he's been hanging around Stonebridge."

"It could be the reason Tiffanee is dead." Alicia finished my thought.

Tiffanee was known for skulking about the village with her camera. This whole thing—her death—it had to be about her photos. Snippets of people going about their daily lives, all caught on camera. But why? I slumped back in my seat, deflating. "What about the camera bag?"

"What about it?" Alicia asked.

"The killer must have taken it back to the house." I took the memory card from my computer and tucked it into my backpack.

"And since the lens cap was in it, we know Tiffanee was carrying it that night."

"Who has access to Tiffanee's house?" I asked. "We know Travis has a key. I think we can assume Penny and Bernadine do, too. You know, longtime friends and next-door neighbors. How about Harmony or Hunter?"

"It didn't take much to figure out the flowerpot thing. I'm sure they could do the same."

I groaned. "So, it's possible the man in that photo returned the bag?"

"More than possible," Alicia said. "He's a locksmith. Although these days, he's more into security systems than locks, but I'd say he knows his way into someone's home."

"Seriously? You didn't think to mention that earlier?"

"Earlier? As in thirty seconds ago?" Alicia tipped her head sideways. "You did good. These photos give us lots to think about. I'm not ruling out Travis yet, but blackmail is looking good for this murder."

I considered her words. "Detective Cram told me Jackson's alibi checked out, so I guess we can rule him out. What about William? Can we rule him out, too?" For Rose's sake, I wanted to eliminate him from our list.

Alicia shook her head. "He's a long shot, but he stays on the list. We need to find out why he closed his shop early. It's an odd coincidence. And don't forget, he lives on the other side of the bridge. He would have crossed it around the time when Tiffanee was killed. That gives him loads of opportunity."

"I've already got that." I opened my chart. "So far, we have Travis, William, Harmony, Penny, Hunter, and the Righteous Sisters. I need to add the cougar and the cheating guy—"

"Parker. His name is Parker Young. Hers is Kendall Lee." Alicia chuckled. "The Righteous Sisters?"

"Thanks." I added Kendall and Parker to my suspect list. "And yes, the Righteous Sisters. Tiffanee took pictures of them, too."

"You and Rose really need to stop calling them that. The Women's Guild does a lot of good for our church."

"Oh." I looked up from my computer. "That title isn't for the Women's Guild. Just Lorraine and her select crew. Anyway, I've already crossed off Jackson. You know, alibi and all."

"All right, what are our next steps?" My pragmatic sister always liked having a plan.

"Even with the new photos, I'm still mostly focused on Travis and Hunter." I closed my laptop and looked at my sister. "They're closest. And I can't get over the whole timing thing. What was Hunter doing here?"

"Okay. Your task is to find out more about Hunter. Harmony is probably the person to start with. Maybe William has seen him around, too. I'll talk to Parker and Kendall. They're both regulars at the market."

Alicia stood, gathering our empty glasses. "I'd better get dinner started. You're welcome to stay."

I pictured the contents of my refrigerator. It was tempting to stay for one of Alicia's home-cooked meals. "No, but thanks. I'm dying to get home to see how Connor is doing with my studio. And I've been meaning to research how to set up a business website—assuming I won't be in jail and I'll even need one."

"Of course your business needs one." Alicia twirled around and walked toward her door. "We'll see you tomorrow morning at Tiffanee's funeral?"

"I'll be there." There couldn't possibly be a gloomier way to start a day. That didn't mean I wasn't interested to see who turned up.

Chapter Nineteen

The following afternoon, I stepped out of my black dress and splashed water on my face, grateful Tiffanee's funeral was behind me. Between the oppressive humidity and my own tears, I was a soggy mess. Pulling crumpled tissues from my pockets, I scrutinized my reflection in the mirror. Most of the puffiness was gone, thank goodness. Finally, I could think about the morning without crying.

"But Bobbie, you hardly knew her," Alicia had whispered as soon as my tears started flowing.

I'd only managed a weak nod in response. Not only had I not known Tiffanee well, I hadn't particularly liked her. But funerals are sad, and despite my best efforts to suppress my emotions, I've always been someone with ever-ready tears.

As I'd expected, the entire village had shown up, including most suspects. Travis had certainly looked miserable. Not that I could blame him. His relationship with Tiffanee's parents appeared strained. They didn't seem the warm, fuzzy type. To be fair, grief didn't always bring out the best in people.

Across the graveside circle, a man I'd only recognized from Tiffanee's photo stood beside a young woman who was well into her pregnancy. *Parker the Cheater*. It's not like I'd expected him to wear guilt on his sleeve, but I saw no sign of his indiscretion. None at all.

Then there had been Hunter, spying from a nearby hilltop. If Harmony hadn't kept looking in his direction, I might have missed him. His shadowy figure on the hillside gave me the heebie-jeebies, as Rose would say. I couldn't imagine his reason for skulking at a distance.

Alicia had passed on one piece of useful information. Kendall had stopped in my sister's market late the night before. She claimed she hadn't been in town on the day Tiffanee was murdered. Like most weekenders, she and her husband usually drove to their Vermont home on Fridays and left on Sundays. I'd noted her alibi on my chart.

Shaking my thoughts away, I stepped into a short denim skirt and a sleeveless linen tunic in a cool shade of creamy yellow. A strappy pair of leather sandals and a floral scarf wrapped around a messy bun completed my outfit. The air was thick with humidity, but I felt human again.

Before stuffing my phone in my pocket, I scrolled through the photos I'd copied from Tiffanee's memory card. My task was to find out more about Hunter. The image of Hunter and Harmony was proof of her recent connection with the mystery boyfriend. I'd start with her, then question William. It seemed unlikely I'd find a connection there, but if he'd crossed the bridge that afternoon, he could have seen something.

I pushed a frizzy curl from my forehead, grabbed my backpack, and headed out the door.

Harmony's studio was dark, and the "Closed" sign hung in the window. She had canceled morning yoga classes for Tiffanee's funeral. It looked like she'd closed up shop for the rest of the day. Questioning the yogi would have to wait. That left William. Determined to find answers, I strode next door and entered Long Trail Booksellers.

A refreshing blast of air conditioning greeted me. My body relaxed to the dry air and the soft sound of easy-listening music. Customers milled about, browsing, while I gravitated toward an artful display of new releases, their colorful covers impossible to resist. I lifted a paperback from the table and flipped it over to read the back.

"Can I help you?" Bernadine stood behind the cash register.

I turned from the display and joined her at the counter. "I hope Penny told you how much our club enjoyed your cookies. We devoured them like a pack of hungry wolves." I laughed. "Thanks again for sending them."

Bernadine's pallid cheeks flushed. "I am so glad to hear that." She smoothed the hem of her faded plaid blouse.

"I stopped by to see Will—" Before I finished my request, William strode out of his office and stopped.

"Is there something I can help you with?" He remained planted in the doorway, gripping an open notebook.

"I hope I'm not intruding." I gave him a slight smile. "I have a couple of questions for you."

"What about?"

I glanced at Bernadine, who watched with undisguised interest. "Would you prefer we talk in your office?"

"Here is fine." He stepped to the counter.

"I heard you closed the shop early on Thursday." No sense beating around the bush.

"Something came up. I didn't have the staff to stay open." His glance flitted briefly to Bernadine.

"I guess I'm curious about your reason for closing early."

His shoulders stiffened slightly, but his expression remained impassive. "It was a personal matter," he said. "One that had no bearing on Ms. Jacobsen's death, if that's what you're insinuating."

It was clear he wouldn't say more. I hadn't come to question him as a suspect, anyway. It was Hunter I was interested in. I pulled my phone from my pocket. "Is it possible you saw this man on your way home?"

"Bobbie, really." He sighed as I handed him my phone. He gave the photo of Hunter a hasty glance, then drawing the image closer, his heavy brows furrowed.

I held my breath, waiting. I had almost forgotten Bernadine when she moved closer to peek at the photo.

"Who is this?" He pored over the image. "He looks familiar, but I can't think where I might have seen him. If it was here, Bernadine might know." He passed my phone to his clerk.

Bernadine peered at the photo. Her lips formed a tight line when she handed the phone back to me and pulled a water bottle from her tote bag.

"Well?" I asked.

"I don't remember," William said. "So many people come in and out of this store."

"But maybe you crossed paths with him? Possibly on Thursday night?" If Hunter had killed Tiffanee, he would have been near the bridge. William might have been in the area at the right time.

"It's possible." He raised his palms. "Like I told you before, I was rushing to another commitment. I'm sure I've seen him somewhere."

I nodded, rubbing the tail of my scarf. "How about you, Bernadine?"

"I know him. Hunter Harrison." She enunciated each syllable of his name like she was spitting the taste from her mouth.

"Have you seen him around?"

Bernadine gave her head a vigorous shake. "The last time I saw him, he was a teenager. He's changed a bit. And not for the better."

"But you'd heard he was hanging around Stonebridge?"

She sniffed. "I might have heard something about that."

"Anything you can tell me?" Talking with Bernadine gave me the same feeling as editing a fuzzy photo. Most were lost causes, but I couldn't resist the challenge of bringing the details into clearer focus.

William turned back toward his office. "Are we done here?"

"Of course." I thanked him before shifting my attention back to his stodgy assistant. "Anything?"

Bernadine fidgeted with the cap of her water bottle before meeting my gaze. She sighed. "Truth be told, Hunter was a bad influence on Tiffanee, and, well, Penny always admired her like a big sister. I might have heard him mentioned once or twice. They were only rumors, mind, and I don't take stock of rumors."

"I understand." I bit back a snarky comment, finding no trace of irony in the expression of one of the village's biggest gossips.

"It was a shame about losing your scarf," Bernadine said. "I never understood the purpose of wearing one, but the pink and purple flowers were quite pretty, anyway."

I froze. "You remembered my scarf?"

"You left it on the bench right outside." Bernadine pointed out the window. "I saw it flapping in the wind and thought to pick it up for you, but when I left work, it was already gone."

I looked outside to where Bernadine's finger pointed, thinking back. Before meeting Rose across the village green, I'd stopped at the bookstore and bought a new thriller. It had been breezy, and I remembered how my scarf kept slapping my face. I pictured myself untying it and setting it aside to peruse my new book. I must have neglected to tuck it into my bag prior to taking a stroll with my camera. A glance across the green confirmed a majestic oak tree blocked the view between park benches.

I smiled at Bernadine. One mystery solved. Who had taken it, though, and what had they planned to do with it?

Thanking Bernadine for her help, I turned to look at the bookcase full of new releases. The mysteries, I knew, were on the opposite side. As I slipped around the bookcase, Vickie Sue Miller, the third Righteous Sister, crept toward Bernadine.

"What did she want?" Vickie Sue's whisper was barely audible from where I stood.

"Phooey. She's playing detective." Bernadine didn't bother to keep her voice low.

"If she's asking questions, does that mean she didn't kill Tiffanee?" Vickie Sue was no longer whispering, but her voice was soft.

"Maybe that's what she wants everyone to think."

I pushed a few books aside and peeked through the gap in time to see Vickie Sue's whole body shiver.

"I don't like it," Vickie Sue said. "Lorraine is convinced she's the killer, but I'm scared. I can't sleep at night."

"Don't be silly," I heard Bernadine say. "Why would anyone want to hurt you?"

"I never told anyone this, but I saw Tiffanee and Harmony arguing that afternoon. You know, when Tiffanee died?" Vickie Sue was whispering again. I leaned against the shelves, peering through the open gap. "They were arguing about a hunter, which made no sense at all because hunting season is over, isn't it? I'm afraid they saw me."

Was there anyone Tiffanee hadn't argued with? Lost in the thought, my foot slipped on the carpet. I grasped the shelf and sent books crashing to the floor. Heart pounding, I jumped back from the now much larger gap in the shelf. As I stooped to gather the pile, Bernadine appeared at the edge of the bookcase, her shadow falling over the scattered books. Beside her, Vickie Sue cowered.

"So many books to choose from. I'm afraid I couldn't decide." My voice croaked as an armload of books clattered back to the floor. I grasped a book and held it up. "I hear this one is good. What do you think?"

Bernadine scowled, and Vickie Sue's mouth dropped open. "I think you're involved in enough clubs for now."

I rubbed the tail of my scarf while glancing at the book's cover—*The Thursday Murder Club* by Richard Osman. "Maybe you're right. Another time, perhaps."

"Leave the books where they are. You've already made a big enough mess. Is there anything else I can help you with?"

I shook my head, stood, and left the books on the floor. Then, casting a weak smile in Vickie Sue's direction, I scurried to the door.

There was a faint breeze outside, but it did little to cool my blazing cheeks. *Way to go, Bobbie Ann.* I trudged to the nearest bench, the one where, according to Bernadine, I had lost my scarf. I collapsed onto it and made a visual sweep of the green.

According to Vickie Sue, Harmony and Tiffanee had been arguing about a hunter. Obviously, the argument had been about Hunter, not *a hunter*, and Harmony had some explaining to do. Also, William had recognized him. I doubted he'd been perusing the latest book selection, especially if Bernadine hadn't seen him as she claimed. They must have crossed paths somewhere in the village. It was a hop, skip, and a jump to assume it had been Thursday evening near the bridge. But it was possible. The more I thought about it, the more I could convince myself it must be true. Hunter had to be involved in Tiffanee's death. I just needed more information to prove it.

Chapter Twenty

The Mad Crow Tavern sat at the end of the village green, spanning the entire bottom floor of Stonebridge's original roadhouse. I was a few minutes early for my dinner plans with Alicia and Nate. As I entered, a large open room boasting sturdy log beams and rough-hewn walls opened before me. Soft light glowed from wall sconces designed to mimic gas lanterns. I scanned the dining room; diners filled most of the rustic log tables and chairs. There was no sign of my dinner companions.

A microphone screeched. "Testing, testing…" A low, husky voice vibrated through the speakers, filling me with a tingle of excitement. It had been eons since I'd enjoyed live music—a night on the village. I patted my backpack, already anticipating photos of musicians and dancing.

After leaving my name with the hostess, I walked past the central fireplace, surrounded by leather couches and a scattering of high tops, to wait near the bar. Harmony sat on a tall stool, talking with Penny, who stood behind the bar wiping glasses. I stepped forward to greet them and paused as I recognized the man on the stool beside Harmony. At last, I was about to meet Hunter.

Harmony swiveled and greeted me.

Retrieving my camera from my bag, I lifted it and focused. "Smile," I said.

Harmony and Hunter leaned into each other the way people often do when someone points a camera their way.

"I came looking for you earlier," I said, hanging my camera around my neck. "I guess I shouldn't have been surprised you closed shop for the day."

"It seemed right to cancel classes. Was there something you needed?"

"It can wait." I wanted a more private place to interrogate Harmony. I fixed my gaze on the boyishly handsome man seated next to her. As talented as Tiffanee had been, her photos hadn't done him justice. The man exuded a magnetic charm.

"I'm Hunter." He extended his hand with a friendly and natural confidence. His shaggy mop of light-blond waves framed his face, and he appeared relaxed in his well-worn black leather jacket over a white T-shirt and faded jeans.

I grasped his hand in greeting, sure I'd seen him before. "I'm Bobbie."

His dimples flashed. With a grip that was tighter than necessary, he held my hand for what felt like a moment or two too long. His grin, which had been charming a moment before, was leering. I suppressed a shiver while plying my hand from his grasp and sliding it into my back pocket.

To my relief, the hostess appeared at my side. "I can seat you now."

"Enjoy your evening," I said, doing my best to hide my discomfort. I followed the hostess, not daring to glance back.

"I hope this is all right." The young woman placed menus on a table near the bar. "We're busy tonight."

"It's fine." *Perfect, actually.* I couldn't have wished for a better vantage point for spying on Hunter and Harmony.

I settled in my seat, scanning the room again, and spotted Nate with Alicia, head and shoulders above the crowd. His jovial voice cut through the restaurant clatter as he strode toward our table, greeting friends and acquaintances along the way.

With a playful eye roll, Alicia sat next to me. "That husband of mine knows no enemies." She glanced behind her before leaning toward me. "I talked to Parker."

"And?" In my excitement, I was careful to keep my voice low.

"When I showed him the photo, he truly seemed surprised. He claims Tiffanee hadn't shown it to him."

"He could be lying," I said. "If he's been cheating on his wife, he's probably gotten pretty good at it." I had no empathy for cheats.

"I haven't ruled him out." She cast another quick glance at Nate and mimed zipping her lips.

"And the cougar?" I really needed to stop calling her that. It wasn't kind, not to mention misogynistic. No one batted an eye at an older man with a much younger woman.

"Shh." Alicia tipped her head toward Nate and the couple he was chatting with. I recognized Kendall right away. She wore her blonde hair down. Soft curls framed her face, making it appear less severe. When she turned to look in our direction, her eyes narrowed, and her brow furrowed with the best scowl Botox would allow. On impossibly high heels, she sashayed in our direction.

"Alicia," she said in a low voice, articulating every letter of my sister's name so that it sounded like Ah-lee-see-ah.

Alicia seemed unperturbed by the way the woman held her head, peering down her long, thin nose. "Kendall, have you met my sister, Bobbie?"

"I can't say I've had the pleasure." Kendall leveled me with a critical stare that left me certain she'd found me wanting. I didn't have a chance to answer before she turned and said, "Ah, it looks like our husbands are wrapping up their little tête-à-tête. Enjoy your dinner."

Okay...

Alicia leaned toward me and spoke quickly. "Even though she's not our killer, she knew about the photo and wants it back. I told her I don't have it."

"It's Wednesday," I pointed out. "Since it's obvious she's here on a weekday, I'm going to put a question mark next to her alibi."

"You're right. I'll probe a little deeper." Alicia held her finger to her lip and assumed a neutral expression just as Nate pulled out the chair next to her.

"Looks like we're going to have music tonight." He took his seat and turned to Alicia, a glimmer in his eyes. "I can't wait to take you for a twirl on the dance floor."

"If I'm able to get up again. Fitting a full day of chores in after the funeral wore me out." Alicia's grumble didn't fool me.

"I talked to mother this afternoon," I said. "She's threatening to come visit."

The corner of Alicia's mouth lifted. "That would be awesome. It would be nice to have her spend more time here."

"Can you imagine her here with everything that's going on?" I asked.

"She'd probably have some choice words for Detective Cram." Alicia snorted. "That would be one way of getting him off your back."

Fiona Sullivan berating Wyatt Cram was something I wouldn't mind seeing. If only I took after my mother, just a bit.

Nate laughed. "We should all be thankful that hasn't happened. Your mother is great, but I don't think lecturing a state policeman is a great strategy." He paused. "Here comes Penny for our cocktail order."

"What can I getcha to drink?" Penny drew a notepad from her apron pocket. The tapping of her tongue ring sounded from behind her pinched lips.

I angled my menu so only Penny could see as I tipped my head toward the bar. "What's going on over there?"

With a barely perceptible shake of her head, she mouthed, "Later."

I nodded understanding and said, "I'll have a glass of chardonnay, please." As I set my menu on the table, I spied Jackson emerging from the growing mob near the hostess station.

Our eyes met. "*Bonsoir,*" he said after reaching our table.

Alicia looked up from her menu with a tight smile.

"May I join you?" He pulled out a chair and seated himself without waiting for an answer. It hadn't been a question.

"Please do," Nate said. "The more, the merrier."

While Jackson gave Penny his order, a ruckus broke out at the bar. Penny snapped toward the commotion and hurriedly scribbled on her pad before rushing away. Hunter was red-faced, pulling his arm from Harmony's grasp. Leaning in my chair, I strained to hear the argument.

"Stop telling me what I can't do. I want to—" A group of jabbering diners passed our table, garbling the rest of Hunter's sentence.

Bits and pieces of the conversation were all I could hear. It might as well have been gibberish, but I couldn't tear myself away. I shifted sideways and leaned closer. My chair no longer felt steady, but it couldn't be helped.

Hunter's voice rose. "It's only right." He was slurring his words, and I couldn't help noticing his line of empty beer bottles.

"Not tonight," Penny joined the argument from behind the bar. "I'm working—" Laughter from a nearby table drowned the rest of her sentence.

Hunter slammed his hand on the bar. "Tomorrow morning."

Harmony studied Penny, who shook her head.

The people at the laughing table seemed to be enjoying themselves, and my aggravation mounted. Trying to hear over them, I leaned even farther. Hunter scrubbed his hand over his face. Harmony seemed to have lost her battle to keep him calm. "When?" he shouted. After that, the only bits I caught were, "You can't keep hop—" and, "I'm coming over."

Through her fringe of hair, Penny pinned Hunter with an angry glare. Her voice was low but clear. "It's a lie." She lifted the bar tray and headed toward us, ignoring Hunter's answering sputters.

I jerked, not wanting to be caught eavesdropping—again. My chair wobbled, and I shifted, grasping for something, anything, desperately attempting to regain my balance. My chair teetered more, and I reached, my fingers touching the table, grabbing—almost. And then...

"Bobbie!" Alicia's voice called out as I crashed to the floor.

Chapter Twenty-One

Stunned, I lay on my back as if still seated in the chair, my knees pointing toward the ceiling. It had been a rough day for eavesdropping.

Time slowed to a standstill. Muffled footsteps surrounded me. I closed my eyes and reopened them to find Penny and Jackson standing over me. A fringe of hair shielded most of Penny's face, but her lips formed a round O. Nate ran around the table to join Jackson, and Penny stepped back. Both men grasped my arms and lifted me to my feet. Alicia bustled around over to right my chair, easing me into it.

"Are you okay?" Alicia asked.

I nodded, my cheeks burning. "I'll tell you later." Time returned to normal as diners, no longer interested in the commotion, resumed their conversations. I couldn't help noticing Hunter watching me from his seat at the bar. I brushed a wispy strand of hair from my face and turned back to my dinner companions.

"Well, okay." Penny stepped forward with her tray and plunked our drinks on the table. Business as usual. Despite the warm afternoon, I ordered the tavern's delicious Cheddar Ale Soup, already imagining its smooth, creamy taste.

As soon as Penny rushed off, Jackson picked up the conversation where he must have left off. "As I was saying, the Farmer's Breakfast is this weekend. Are you planning to attend?"

With a stifled groan, I smiled at Jackson and pretended interest. "I'm doing the photography." I rubbed my sore neck, trying to divert my attention from the scene at the bar. Hunter's voice rose again. Harmony and Penny appeared to be making a futile attempt at keeping him calm. Snippets of their argument drifted across the dining room. Just words. I wasn't close enough to make it out, and my dignity couldn't handle another fall.

"Speaking of photography, how is your studio renovation coming?" Alicia asked.

"Fantastic." I perked up. "It's truly amazing how much Connor has accomplished. You should come over to see—" I stopped mid-sentence as Hunter's angry voice echoed throughout the tavern.

"You can't keep me away," he shouted before stomping out the door.

All eyes turned toward the bar where Harmony sat with her head in her hands, and Penny placed dinner plates on a tray, ignoring the disturbance.

"I wonder what that was all about," Jackson said.

"Beats me," Alicia said in a low voice. "Did you see how Hunter was skulking around Tiffanee's funeral?"

"That was weird," I said. "Obviously, he has something to do with this whole mess. That man needs to be stopped."

The next morning, I found myself on a yoga mat contorting in ways my body didn't want to contort. Rose had finally worn me down, talking me into going to yoga class with her. True to her word, she'd appeared on my doorstep at seven sharp, in all her Lycra-clad glory. Seriously, there should be a law against exercising before coffee.

"Take a full breath in and a full breath out." The yoga instructor's voice was soft, almost timid. But where was Harmony? According to Rose, she usually taught on Thursday mornings. I'd been hoping to catch her after class. Instead, her friend, Iris Svensen, was instructing. Remembering the empty barstool not long after Hunter had stormed out of the restaurant made me wonder if something had happened.

I peered at the back of Rose's head while reaching one arm toward the ceiling and grasping my shin with the other—triangle pose. My hamstrings were screaming. I held the position, trying to ignore the wobbles warning of another incident like the night before. *Breathe.* No way I was falling flat on my back again. I envied my friend, who made the convoluted position look easy.

The night at The Crow had been fun—unexpectedly so. Harmony had left shortly after Hunter, and the rest of the evening had passed quietly. As promised, Nate had taken Alicia onto the dance floor as soon as the music began. I'd pulled my camera out and taken several photos. While living in Boston, I'd never listened to bluegrass. But in Vermont, the folksy music complemented the mist-capped mountains and flower-covered fields by the river.

Despite my hesitation, I'd danced to several songs with Jackson, mostly as part of a group with Alicia, Nate, and Iris, who'd arrived at The Crow looking for Harmony. Dan had never truly enjoyed dancing, but I'd always found the movement freeing. Begrudgingly, I admitted to myself the yoga stretches felt good, too. Therapeutic, somehow.

I gazed at Iris over my fingertips while transitioning to another pose—Warrior Two, apparently. She had a sweet cherubic face, framed by a short blonde bob so golden it glowed.

Snippets of last night's argument fought for my attention. "Too late…," "I have a right…," "Tomorrow morning…" I peered between my legs in my incredibly awkward downward-facing dog pose, and it hit me. Something was supposed to happen in the morning. I didn't know what, but that must have been where Harmony was. I made a mental note to call Penny after class. Hopefully, she could shed some light on their conversation at the bar.

Upside down, I peeked over at Rose, envying the way her plump body formed the perfect forward fold. I silently mouthed the words, "How much longer?"

Rose answered by pursing her lips into a silent *shush*.

"We're going to set up for *Savasana*. If there is a final pose you want to do, now is the time. We must all listen to our own bodies." Iris raised her arm over her head and grasped her lifted foot from behind. *Once upon a time, back in my dancing days.* I let out an envious sigh.

What my body wanted was a cup of coffee. But as luck had it, no one else heard the same message. Rose was already lying flat on her back with a serene smile. Reluctantly, I lowered myself to my mat. I knew what *Savasana* was. It was when I was supposed to empty my mind of thoughts, like that was going to happen. I blew my overgrown bangs from my face and craned my neck to look toward the door, wondering how quickly I could escape the studio. Remembering Hunter's tight grip, I had an overwhelming urge to find Harmony. The back of my neck prickled, warning me something was wrong.

After a quick *Namaste*, I jumped up and rolled my mat with record speed.

"Bobbie." Iris's voice stopped me. "I want to apologize for last night."

I stood, lifting my mat, confused by Iris's concerned expression.

Iris blushed, her normally porcelain cheeks a delicate shade of pink. "I didn't mean to ruin your date. I promise I didn't ask Jackson to leave with me."

"No worries." I ignored the gleeful sparkle in Rose's eyes. "We weren't on a date." *As if.* It wasn't until the check arrived that I noticed he was gone.

"I'm so relieved," Iris said. "I didn't want to cause problems between you two."

"None caused." I gave her my most reassuring smile and another thought came to me. Iris and Harmony were roommates. "Was Harmony not feeling well this morning?"

Iris tucked a strand of hair behind her ear. "I'm not sure. She seemed upset when I got home last night, and then, when I woke up this morning, she wasn't in her room. When I didn't find her here, either, I figured she'd want me to take over her class. I hope you enjoyed it."

"I did. Thanks." I couldn't help the shiver slithering down my spine.

Rose pinched my arm as we headed toward the door. "A date with Jackson? Do tell."

"Absolutely, positively, not a date." I gave my head a vigorous shake. "We danced, that's all."

"Sounds like a date."

I groaned. "For a minute, I felt like my life was almost normal again. I knew I shouldn't have danced with him."

"Hey, girl, don't mind me. I'm only teasing. It's good you were feeling normal again, you know? Even a minute is progress. You'll get there."

We stepped from the studio into the soft morning light. Lost in my thoughts, I bumped into Rose when she came to an abrupt stop. "Something feels weird." Her voice was barely a whisper.

I looked to where she pointed. At the far corner of the village green, a crowd gathered. Through the crush of lookie-loos, I saw the flashing lights of police cars. Rose and I crossed the green side by side, a shared feeling of unease buzzing between us. As we neared the corner, mumbling and murmuring grew louder, like bees around their hive. Something had happened—something terrible.

Shrill sirens and the bellow of a fire engine's horn pierced the air. Words sounded through the confusion. Words like *dead*, and *body*, and *river*.

The color drained from Rose's face, and her hand grasped my arm, her long nails digging into my skin. "Did you hear that? Another dead body. It can't be."

"Harmony," I whispered. My stomach knotted.

"Harmony?" Rose echoed. "What about her?"

"She was arguing with Hunter last night and didn't make her usual yoga class this morning."

"True…"

"Hunter hurt her. I know it."

Rose raced to keep pace with me as I stepped forward into the crowd. I had no idea where I was headed, but I needed to find Harmony. When I neared the edge of the village green, I noticed Alicia and Bernadine huddled with a group of women, their faces ashen. They wore garden gloves and held flats of budding flowers and rusty watering cans—a tranquil scene incongruous with the tension crackling in the air.

"A second victim," one woman said, her hands shaking as she rubbed her arms.

Another nodded, clutching her friend. "Same place as the last time."

I gasped. *That can't be—it can't.*

An ambulance screeched around the corner of Main Street, turning onto Bridge Street toward the river. I quickened my pace and met Alicia's solemn gaze through the horde.

"I need to find Harmony." My voice was breathless as I arrived next to my sister and her garden club friends.

Alicia's brow furrowed. "Harmony? Why?"

"He hurt her. I know he did." I gasped for air. "Have you seen her?" I moved toward the barricade in the street, but Alicia's arm shot out to block my path.

"What in the world are you talking about?"

"She was with him. Last night. You saw them." I struggled to move around Alicia's arm.

"Listen to me," Alicia said. "You're not making sense. I don't know what you think you've heard, but you can't go over there."

Deflated, I frowned and took in the flashing lights and rescue vehicles blocking the road. My shoulders slumped in defeat. "What happened?"

"Someone was walking by the river and found a dead body."

Hot tears welled. "Poor Harmony."

"Why do you keep mentioning Harmony?"

"The victim. It's Harmony, isn't it?"

Alicia spoke softly. "No."

"No?" I tilted my face to the sky, about to utter my thanks when I remembered—another dead body by the river. I struggled to form the question. "Who?"

"Hunter Harrison. Shot in the chest."

Chapter Twenty-Two

My knees buckled as the village spun around me. It may have been a stretch, but I'd been so sure Hunter was the killer.

"What's going on with you?" Alicia grabbed my arm to steady me.

I didn't answer. The buzzing grew louder, and I stared, the milling crowd little more than a blur. Unable to take it all in, I clamped my hands over my ears. I was only vaguely aware of being held upright and my feet moving across the grass.

"Bobbie, say something." Rose's voice sounded far away.

As my vision cleared, I found myself seated on a park bench, with Rose kneeling in front of me.

She squeezed my hand. "Holy moly! You scared us for a minute."

I swallowed, lifting my eyes to meet Alicia's. "Hunter was supposed to be the killer."

Alicia gave a small shake of her head. "Apparently not."

Collapsing against the bench, I let out a slow breath. I wanted to go home, to lie on my couch and listen to soft folk music while thumbing through old photo albums—to remember my life as it was before all this happened.

"I need to go."

Rose's gaze lifted to Alicia before returning to me. "Are you sure you're okay?"

"I'm fine. Just dizzy for a minute, but I'm all right now. I promise." I stood; my shakiness was gone.

"Maybe I should come with you." Rose held my arm.

I shook my head, giving Rose an anemic smile. "I'll call you later."

"If you need anything, text me," Alicia said. "I'll be right here and can easily run over. We have loads of flowers to plant."

"I'll stop by later," Rose said.

"Sounds good. I won't be going anywhere." Stonebridge had a murderer who had killed not once, but twice. I remembered the warning note, the red block letters. How foolish I'd been to brush it off, to assume I wasn't in danger. The killer was getting desperate. No one was safe.

Spinning around, I elbowed my way through the jam along the sidewalk, walking parallel to the roadblocks and emergency vehicles, until I found a clearing to cross the street. As I stepped off the curb, I glimpsed Harmony, heading toward the melee. Her normally sleek hair was dull and mussed, falling across her face in long, tangled strands.

I called to her. "Over here." With tears of relief welling in my eyes, I waved my arms to get her attention, only to be ignored.

Quickening my pace, I jogged the way I'd come, calling Harmony's name a second time. Finally, she paused and looked up with a vacant expression, black smudges rimming her eyes. She turned and vanished into the growing crowd of onlookers.

It made no sense to go back there, back to the confusion and chaos. Preparing to cross Main Street once again, I spied Kendall through the crowd. With her blonde hair slicked back into a high ponytail, black tights, and running shoes, she looked like she'd come to the village green for a jog. Weird, considering Stratton had state-of-the-art facilities. I'd have pegged her as a gym bunny—not that I actually knew her. Weirder still, it seemed that everywhere I went lately, I ran into her.

For a minute, I thought about walking over to question her about her alibi. The more I thought about it, the more I was certain she'd lied. But I didn't have it in me. I wanted to go home. Brushing the idea away, I strode across the street and raised my hand to greet my crotchety next-door neighbor, who leaned against his porch railing while watching the commotion.

The rest of the morning passed by in a blur. I'd spent much of it snuggled on my couch with Darcy. He normally napped the morning away and didn't seem to mind me curling up next to him. But then, he probably thought he was getting away with something, being allowed on the furniture.

After peeling myself from my cozy refuge, I settled at my kitchen table to pore over Tiffanee's photos again. The Tiffanee-Hunter-Travis love triangle motive only worked if Travis was the killer. I wasn't convinced. That left blackmail. But if Tiffanee had been blackmailing Hunter, why was he dead?

Loud rapping disturbed my thoughts. "Mrs. Brooks." Detective Cram's muffled voice was barely audible through Darcy's barks.

I shut my laptop and yanked the memory card from its slot, tucking it into my pocket before trudging to greet my unwelcome visitor.

"Hello." I held Darcy's collar and pulled the door open, blocking the entrance.

"I think you know why I'm here." The detective stepped forward, pushing past me.

"I hope it's not to tell me you found my scarf at the scene."

"Not this time." He scoffed as he strode toward the kitchen.

I followed behind, Darcy at my heels. Not only had the surly detective figured out Darcy was all bark, but he was much too comfortable in my home.

"Is it true someone killed Hunter?"

"As if you aren't aware." He seated himself at the table.

I slipped onto a chair across from him and pushed my laptop aside.

"Tell me about your relationship with the deceased." He clicked his pen.

I sat up, my back rigid, but remained silent.

"I asked you a question."

"You haven't told me who the deceased is."

The corner of his mouth lifted. This was one standoff I could easily wait out. I folded my hands in my lap.

"I think you already know the victim is Hunter Harrison."

"The rumor was for real, then." Tiffanee's old boyfriend was dead.

"You knew him?"

"I met him at The Crow last night." I shuddered, remembering his tight grip and smug grin.

"How did that come about?" He scribbled on his pad.

"Hunter was sitting at the bar with Harmony Santos. He introduced himself when I went over to say hello."

"Were you with anyone else?"

"Not at the time. The hostess seated me right after I met him, and then I ate dinner with the Crowleys." I paused. "Oh, and Jackson Gilbert."

Detective Cram stopped writing and looked up with a knowing smirk.

My arms folded across my chest. No doubt the gossip mill had already spun several versions of the story. I was thankful it hadn't made it to the Stonebridge Scandal—not that I knew of, anyway.

"What can you tell me about your conversation with Mr. Harrison?"

"Not much. He introduced himself and shook my hand." I blew out a breath. "Then I went to my table."

"This was the first and only time you spoke with him?"

"That's correct." I got the feeling he was hinting at something, but I couldn't fathom what it was.

"Why would you say, and I quote—" He flipped through pages in his notebook. "That man needs to be stopped."

My mind raced. Had I said that? My stomach knotted. *Right. Jackson.* This wasn't the first time I'd suspected him of being Detective Cram's source. If I hadn't already ruled him out as the killer, I'd think he was setting me up. Instead, I wondered what his mission was.

"I don't remember my exact words."

"What has me baffled," Detective Cram said, "is why you would say that about someone you had just met. Are you sure you hadn't met before?"

"Positive."

"Did you or did you not say he should be stopped?"

"Stopping someone and killing them are two completely different things. I thought he was the killer."

Detective Cram gave me a sharp look. "The killer? Based on what evidence?"

"Umm, well…that is…" I couldn't seem to form a coherent thought. "He was kind of creepy, you know? And then there was the timing."

"The timing." He glared. "I suggest you leave the police work to me. Now, back to last night. You weren't involved in the argument before Mr. Harrison left the restaurant?" His voice betrayed a liberal dose of skepticism. *Oh, honestly.*

"As I said, I was seated at my table eating dinner."

"Did he leave with anyone?"

"I didn't watch his every move, but I'm pretty sure he left alone." Remembering Nate's instructions to only answer questions asked, I didn't mention Harmony, who had left shortly after. I wasn't sure she'd chased after him, but it seemed likely.

"Where were you this morning between, say, midnight and eight o'clock?"

"That's a large window of time. Was that when he was shot?"

"Answer the question."

I flashed what I hoped was my most vicious stink-eye—something I'd never been very good at. "I was home well before midnight."

"Can anyone verify that?"

"Alicia and Nate walked home with me. They'd parked their car in front of my house."

"After that, can anyone verify you didn't leave your house?" The detective tapped his pen on the table.

I reached down to pat Darcy's head and chuckled. "Only Darcy."

Without the slightest flicker of acknowledgment, the detective forged on. "And this morning?"

So much for levity. I should have known better. "This morning, Rose came to my house at seven, and we walked across the green to the yoga studio for the seven-thirty class. Class ended at nine."

"Do you own a rifle?" Detective Cram asked.

"Like for hunting?"

He cocked his head to one side. "Yes, like for hunting. Or any other purpose."

"No."

The detective snapped his notebook shut and jammed it into his pocket.

CHAPTER TWENTY-TWO

"That will be all." He paused. "For now. I am sure we will meet again."

"No doubt." I led him to the door. It was clear I was now a suspect in not one, but two murders.

Later, I stepped onto my front porch and waved to Mr. Miller, knowing it was a futile gesture. He had yet to offer a friendly response, but right then, his grumpy harumph was comforting in its normalcy.

I dropped onto the porch swing and set a glass of iced tea on a side table next to me. The commotion on the green had died down, and the village was back to normal. A parade of white license plates from neighboring states processed down Main Street to get an early jump on the weekend. Darcy nosed around the sidewalk before ambling onto the porch and settling in his favorite spot at the top of the stairs. I leaned to stroke his head while glancing at my phone. One missed video chat from Emma. I dreaded her reaction to the news of another murder as I pushed the call button.

"Hi, Mom." Emma's answer was immediate. "I already read about it on that Scandal page. Like, what is going on there?"

Emma followed the Stonebridge Scandal? I sighed. "I can hardly believe it myself."

"You need to get out of Vermont. It's getting too dangerous."

"I wish I could." The truth in my words washed over me as soon as they escaped my mouth. Why not, though? I desperately needed a change of scenery, and Detective Cram hadn't told me not to leave town. Could he even do that? I wasn't under arrest. Not yet, anyway.

"I'm not taking no for an answer." Emma pushed a curl back.

"Well, maybe." *Could I?* "Only for a day or two."

"That would be awesome. I'm working tomorrow and Saturday, but I'm off Sunday and Monday. Aunt Alicia has a meeting with a vendor near Haymarket, so she might come too."

I couldn't help feeling excited at the idea of a trip to Boston. It had been a long time—too long. Restaurants, boutiques, and window shopping—I missed strolling through the city. If I took off first thing on Sunday morning, I'd miss church. I moaned, remembering the Farmer's Breakfast. "I'm taking photos at the church festival on Sunday." I crumpled, pulling my scarf across my face.

"Then how about Monday? I'm not working until Tuesday night."

Monday. Four more days—three and a half, really. Not so long. I sat up, my heart thumping. "Monday, then."

"Perfect." Emma's face brightened in that way she shared with Dan, and my breath caught.

"You look happy," I said. "Things with Ryan are good?"

"Better, I think. We had a long talk, and Ryan told me my friend was wrong. He and the sexy brunette are just coworkers."

I closed my mouth, aiming for a neutral expression. I hated myself for it, but after what Emma's friend had witnessed, I didn't believe for a second that the sexy brunette was merely a coworker.

"Anyway," Emma said, "I guess I owe him the benefit of the doubt, even if I loathe the idea of him working with some hottie."

"Aren't doctors hotties, too? They are on *Grey's Anatomy*."

"I guess." Emma shrugged. "Let's plan to have dinner out on Monday. We can invite Ryan and Aunt Alicia."

"Sounds like fun." And then I could see for myself what was going on with my daughter's less-than-trustworthy boyfriend.

"Great! I'll check with Ryan and make reservations. North End sound good?"

"Absolutely." My stomach grumbled at the mention of Boston's Little Italy.

"Okay, well, I'm working tonight, so I'd better run. Monday's going to be awesome."

"I'll text you when I leave, bright and early. Let's meet for lunch on Newbury Street."

"Perfect. Love you." Emma gave one last smile before hanging up.

As I set my phone down and reached for my iced tea, Darcy let out a low rumble from his perch at the top of the stairs. When I looked up, Kendall's foot was poised on the bottom step as though she was preparing to join me, but thought better of it. Something about her sandal caught my eye, something more than its red sole. I'd seen plenty of those in Boston. In fact,

I owned a pair of Louboutins myself—not that I'd worn them since moving to Vermont.

I raised my gaze to meet Kendall's questioning expression. Once again, she'd pulled her hair into a tight ponytail. That's when I remembered where I'd first seen her. She was Rose's prickly customer, the one sitting on the village green the afternoon Tiffanee was murdered.

Chapter Twenty-Three

I took in Kendall's startled expression, feeling as confused as she looked. The only person I knew Darcy to growl at was Detective Cram. He seemed wary of our guest, which made two of us. Everything about her seemed slightly over-the-top. Fake eyelashes, fake fingernails, fake tan, fake smile.

No longer in workout clothes, Kendall now sported a red polka-dot sundress with a cropped cardigan. Her outfit was fetching—for someone headed to a country club luncheon. Despite being on my own front porch, I felt decidedly underdressed.

"Darcy, come," I said, calling him to my side. Seemingly hesitant to take his eyes off our unexpected guest, he gave me a side-eyed glance to tell me he was working.

"Now," I said, letting him know I was his boss.

He stood and gave Kendall a warning sniff before turning slowly to join me. As he sat on the floor beside me, I leaned close to his ear to tell him what a good job he'd done.

"Is it safe to come up now?" Kendall's voice was sugary-sweet.

I rubbed the ridge of fur along Darcy's neck and nodded with a tight smile. Darcy might growl, but he was no attack dog.

When she reached the porch, Kendall grasped the porch railing with one hand while the other rested on her slim hip. "I hear you're in charge of the local camera club."

"That's right. Are you interested in joining?"

She huffed a laugh. "Lordy, no. But I heard the girl who died… She was in your club?"

"Right again." I didn't mean to sound curt, but couldn't seem to help myself.

Kendall's fake smile widened. "I don't suppose you know what happened to her photos?"

Bingo. Sweetness aside, Kendall looked like someone who was used to getting what she wanted. Would she have killed Tiffanee if Tiffanee had refused her wishes? As Alicia had suggested, I doubted Kendall was someone who'd get her hands dirty, let alone risk ruining her pricey high-heeled shoes. I couldn't even imagine navigating the steep, rocky hill while wearing them.

"The photos could be anywhere," I said. True. Tiffanee's photos were on her memory card, on my computer, on my phone, in the cloud, and who knew where else. It wasn't like the old days when all it took was tearing up a photo and destroying the negative. "Is there a particular photo you're interested in?"

"Oh well, not really." Kendall's tone was breezy, belying her tight expression and assessing stare. Her finger tapped on the railing as she sized me up, a ray of sunshine making her ring sparkle. That was one serious diamond.

"I think I might have one you'd be interested in." I wished I could bite back the words as soon as they flew from my mouth. With all the photos I'd clicked that afternoon, I was reasonably certain I'd find one showing her in the background. Even so, I wasn't sure I wanted to go there.

"Oh?" Kendall acted only mildly interested, which I suspected was another fake.

"I was on the village green the afternoon of Tiffanee's death," I said, gauging her reaction as I added, "Taking photos."

And there it was. I hadn't even had to lie. Kendall's face turned a ghostly white. "I see." Then, ostensibly deciding to play it cool, she flashed a smile that didn't quite reach her eyes. "Alrighty then." She stepped down the stairs. "I'll see you around."

Hugging my knees to my chest while swaying on the swing, I watched the bob of Kendall's ponytail as she strode across the street to the village green.

I couldn't shake the feeling I'd just played a round of poker and wondered whether I'd won or lost—and when the next hand would be dealt.

A day had passed since Hunter's death and my conversation with Kendall. I sat in the coffee shop, enjoying the warmth of the sun on my face. I couldn't help wondering what Kendall's next move might be, but it was my upcoming trip to Boston that I thought about most. Knowing I'd be away for a couple of days provided the much-needed motivation to do some research for my studio. Sitting at my favorite table in Rose's café to do it was a decadent treat.

I opened my laptop, letting my gaze slide across the street. Friday afternoon, the village green was teeming with weekenders. My mind flooded with memories of picnics with Dan and Emma under the leafy canopy of a large maple tree. Never had I imagined wanting to escape Vermont, though.

I turned back to my laptop and opened an article about studio lighting. Strobe light, continuous light, flashgun, and rim light. "Oh, my." I rested my chin in my hand. So many decisions to make, not to mention the cost. My savings were quickly depleting, and I needed to earn money soon.

"Oh, my?" Jackson dropped into the opposite chair with a whoosh.

"Hi." My lack of enthusiasm wasn't intentional, but I knew I needed to be more careful around him. I turned and stared out the window again, sitting on my hands.

Immune to my indifference, Jackson leaned back. "Did you see the Stonebridge Scandal this morning?"

That caught my attention. "No, why?"

"Just wondered."

I snapped the lid of my laptop and leaned forward. "Thanks, by the way, for telling Detective Cram that I said Hunter should be stopped."

A red flush crept up his neck, but Rose's appearance saved him from answering. Her eyes darted from me to Jackson and back again before she set my latte on the table. "Here you go."

"I'll have one of those, too." Jackson didn't so much as glance at Rose.

Rose shrugged, then strode back to the counter.

"You *did* see the Stonebridge Scandal, then." He circled back to our conversation. The flush had spread to his bald head.

"Oh, no," I groaned. Surely, whoever wrote that heinous page hadn't quoted me.

"You weren't expecting me to lie to the police."

"Of course not." But why did it seem he was offering information the detective couldn't have known to ask for? I shifted in my seat before continuing. "Wanting to stop someone and wanting to murder them are two very different things. Surely you understand that."

"That's for the police to decide."

Of all the patronizing things to say. "I thought we were supposed to be working together on this." I opened my laptop and feigned studiousness. "You should go wait for your latte."

Jackson ran his hand along the side of his head, smoothing his nonexistent hair. "*Très bien.* I can see you're in a mood." He stood, muttering as he walked away. "Probably one of those female maladies."

I let out a long breath, my relief only momentary, as I felt a presence behind me. Slowly, I lifted my head and met the hard glare of Lorraine Adams.

Before I could recompose my expression into something pleasant, Lorraine battled forward, her thin bubble-gum pink lips set in a rigid line that barely moved when she spoke. "Can I assume you're still planning to take photos at the Farmer's Breakfast on Sunday, as you promised?"

"I'm looking forward to it." I rallied a weak smile.

"Just see to it you're there on time. It starts as soon as church service ends and not a minute later." She spat her words with a shake of her permed poodle curls before tramping out the door.

The bell jingled, and I let out another sigh. It seemed Lorraine had forgotten I was volunteering my time and talent. Not that I'd remind her. I needed to stay on her good side, assuming she had one. Unable to concentrate on studio lighting, I shut my laptop and leaned back, sipping my coffee.

Two people were dead, and Hunter hadn't been the killer. I needed to find the connection between Tiffanee and Hunter. Who'd wanted them both dead? *If only I'd known him better.* I shuddered at the thought.

Connor's comment about running into Hunter at a bar in Bellows Falls came back to me. While watching Rose work, an idea took form. As if sensing my attention, she lifted her chin and tucked her rag behind the counter.

"Hey, girl." She plopped into Jackson's abandoned chair. "What in the world did you say to poor Jackson? He sure was grumbling when he picked up his latte." Beneath her topknot of unruly curls, her eyes sparkled.

"Poor Jackson?" My jaw dropped. Why did no one else recognize how insufferable he was? "Never mind." I waved off the topic. "I have an idea."

"Yeah? Should I be excited or scared?"

"Let's go for excited." I told Rose about my scheme, doing my best to make it sound like an adventure.

"Wait, you want to do what?" Rose asked when I finished. Her cheeks flushed. Excited or horrified, I couldn't tell.

"It sounds like fun, right?"

"Yeah, like your idea of a fun night is all about chilling in a dive bar." She lifted an eyebrow. "You'd better explain."

"I need to check out Hunter's world. We're missing something. Learning more about him might help."

"You know which bar is part of Hunter's world?"

"No, but Connor does. Worst case, we'll enjoy a glass of wine. What could be the harm?"

"I think *enjoy* might be overstating it." Rose snorted. "Should we ask Alicia to come along? Or Jackson?"

Remembering Jackson's comment about female maladies, I winced. "Let's keep it just girls for tonight. I'll text Alicia." I relaxed into a broad grin. "So, you're in? Not only will we find out more about Hunter, but it will be fun to dress up and have a night away from Stonebridge."

Rose twirled a curl around her finger. "Girl, you had me at dressing up, but a night away from this village might be what I need most. Who knows, we might meet some cute guys."

I laughed. "Not interested."

"I'll dress accordingly." She clapped her hands together. "This is going to be so much fun."

I was preparing to leave when the door opened, bringing with it a gust of air and the quick stamping sound of sneakers on the wooden floor. We both looked up as Ethan rushed behind the counter, Travis on his heels.

"Ethan," Rose called. "You're late."

Ethan stopped, spinning to face his mom. "Not now. I'll be back in a minute, okay?"

Rose gave him a quick nod as Travis ambled over.

"Don't you two look thick as thieves?"

Rose puffed out an exasperated breath. "What do you want?"

"Just waiting for Ethan." He turned his attention to me. "You're up to no good. I trust you're not planning to burgle any houses tonight."

I bit my tongue, remembering his tremendous favor, even if I didn't understand it. As far as I knew, Detective Cram was still in the dark about our adventure at Tiffanee's.

"Go sit at the counter. I'll be over in a minute." Rose turned her back to him.

"Not so fast," Travis said. "Since it seems Jessica Fletcher is still at it, I figured she'd like to know the police have cleared me." He gave me a lopsided grin.

My mouth fell open.

"That's right. I got called in to work on Thursday. And since Penny heard Tiffanee outside less than ten minutes before I arrived at the bar, I couldn't have done it." He raised his stubbled chin in triumph. "You know what that means, right? You can erase me from your suspect list."

Chapter Twenty-Four

When we drove into Bellows Falls later in the evening, a vintage 1950s-looking mural welcomed us, proclaiming the village *a friendly place to hang your hat.* The road ahead curved gently, leading us toward a clock tower that jutted into the sky against a mountainous backdrop. Although the old mill town was a little rough-and-tumble, its edgy-hip vibe charmed me.

"I still can't believe Travis's bombshell," I said while listening to the mechanical voice of my GPS.

"To be honest, I'm relieved," Rose said. "I would have been totally shocked if it was him, anyway."

"Yeah." I turned down a side street that led to another and another. "Now that the love triangle theory is dead, I guess it's a good thing we're going on this mission."

"For sure. This is going to be so much fun."

My GPS instructed another turn before announcing our arrival. I parked my SUV amidst a band of motorcycles outside a dilapidated brick building and eyed the sticky note on my dashboard, double-checking the address Connor had given me. With great effort, I resisted the urge to return to the main drag, where we'd passed a cute Italian restaurant.

"Whoa. I'm not sure about this. I wish Alicia could've come." Shooting the building with a dubious glance, I asked, "Do you think the graffiti is part of the décor?"

Rose's nose crinkled. "What? Not quaint enough for you? Stick with bottled beer. It's safer."

As promised, Rose had dressed for a night out. Her skin-tight jeans, ripped at the knees, were the perfect complement to her black leather biker boots. A riot of red curls tumbled seductively around her face, framing heavily lined eyes. I couldn't help feeling like the dowdy older sister.

Rose pulled down the passenger-side mirror and applied a thick smear of deep crimson lipstick to her full lips. She gave me a wink, then slid the tube into her purse.

"I'm completely out of my element." I smoothed my cotton peasant top.

"Weird, right? I love your braid and hoop earrings. You look great." Rose squinted, then dug around in her purse. She pulled out a pot of lip gloss and handed it to me. "This will be perfect for you. It goes with that retro hippie vibe you've got going on."

Retro hippie vibe? I accepted her offering. It may have been before my time, but glittery pale pink gloss brought images of miniskirts and white go-go boots. I shrugged, admitting to myself, the gloss was pretty in a psychedelic-sixties sort of way.

"Perfect. Let's go before you lose your nerve."

"I think I already have." I stepped from the car, closing the door with my hip.

"So, what's the plan?" Rose headed to the door.

I hadn't given as much thought to our plan as I should have. "I'm thinking we're maybe a little old to pull off being Hunter's long-lost friends."

"Speak for yourself." Rose puckered her Kewpie doll lips.

With a chortle, I continued. "Anyway, Hunter was an auto mechanic, right? Someone gave me his name about fixing my car."

"That's good. We think he's still alive, then?"

"Exactly."

"Then what?" Rose asked.

"I didn't write a script. Just improvise."

"Wing it. Not a problem. I wasn't the queen of the thespians in high school for nothing." Rose swung the door open.

Inside, the air was heavy and smelled of decades of sweat and spilled beer, stale and sticky. It took me back to my college days—fake IDs in bars too seedy and dark for anyone to notice. I blinked, adjusting to the dim light. Dang, I felt old.

A pool table, which seemed to be the major draw, occupied most of the lounge. A group of leather-clad men who inarguably belonged to the motorcycles outside stood around the table, watching a woman with a frazzled mane of badly bleached hair lean forward, squinting at the ball. She paused, her cue ready to strike, and stared at Rose and me over her tented fingers. Next to her, a man who I suspected used the same hair stylist, leaned on his pool cue and sized us up, his bleached mohawk bobbing with the motion of his chin.

I froze, fighting the urge to step back, right out the door.

"Oh, hey there." Rose waved to the group at the table. "Don't let us interrupt." Thumbs hooked in her front pockets, she sauntered toward the bar with a relaxed, friendly smile, owning the room.

I managed a meek wave and followed my room-owning friend, slipping onto a stool as I grasped the tacky wood counter. At the far end, a grizzly gray beard caught my attention. Human or beast, I couldn't tell, but the mug of beer he slumped over provided my best clue.

With a nod toward Grizzly Beard, Rose spoke to the bartender. "He's alive, right?" She hoisted herself onto the stool.

The young bartender's slouch cap bobbed as his lips curled. "What can I getcha?"

"I'll take a Switchback Ale," Rose said. "In the bottle."

"Make that two, please." I glanced at Rose, thankful she'd come along on this adventure. I never could've done it alone.

Rose swiveled, giving the room a casual once-over. The bartender plunked the bottles on the counter. He appeared about to speak when a call for another round came from the group at the pool table.

I took a long sip of my cold beer, my shoulders relaxing. When was the last time I'd had anything other than wine? I should do this more often. Ignoring the gumminess of the bar, I leaned on my elbows.

The bartender arranged drinks on a tray. "You ladies new around here?"

"Nope." Rose leaned on the bar like she had a juicy secret to tell.

CHAPTER TWENTY-FOUR

"I'm Corey. I don't remember seeing you in here before."

"Hi Corey, I'm Bobbie." I raised my beer bottle in greeting.

"Yeah? Bobby, like a guy?" He chuckled.

"Riiiight." I drew out my response. I'd only heard that one about a thousand times before.

"I'm Daisy," Rose said.

Holding my bottle to my lips, I suppressed a laugh. There wasn't a trace of guile in my friend's sparkling eyes. She was good at this game.

"Well then, Bobby, Daisy, what brings you here?"

Rose's smile widened. "You mean other than the ambience?"

"I'm guessing you're not here for that." He winked at her, then slung his rag over his shoulder and nodded toward the raucous crowd at the pool table. The clamor of their cheering and arguing filled the tavern.

"For starters, we were driving through town and thought it might be fun to stop for a beer." Rose leaned closer, her silky blouse's deep V flaunting her generous décolletage.

"I get that." Corey snaked his eyes over her again before lifting a beer-laden tray and carrying it to the pool table.

"Who *are* you?" I whispered. This was a side of Rose I'd never seen before.

A flush rose on her cheeks. "This is such a hoot. A change of scenery was such a great idea."

Corey returned, taking up his position behind the bar. "For starters, you thought you might stop in for a beer. Then what?"

Rose spun to face me, the stool creaking. "What did you say the mechanic's name was? The one we should ask for?"

I pretended to think about it. "Hunter? I'm pretty sure his name is Hunter." The bartender frowned, and I took another quick sip of beer to mask my nerves.

Rose pressed forward. "Do you know an auto mechanic named Hunter?"

"I did." Corey's tone was flat. He placed his hands on the bar.

I squirmed as heads turned our way. The lights above the bar felt brighter, somehow. Glaring, like spotlights pinning me to the stool.

"Oh?" Rose tipped her head, the picture of curiosity. "You did, or you do?"

"Did. He's dead."

The room fell silent.

I rubbed my sweaty palms on my jeans before lifting my beer and taking another large swig. This was where a script might have been helpful.

A burly man with a shaved head and faded black T-shirt swaggered over to the bar. "Who are you ladies looking for?" His bulging muscles appeared menacing, but he sounded more curious than threatening.

"My friend here was given the name of a mechanic to fix her car," Rose said with a bewitching smile.

How is Rose so amazingly cool?

"Hunter, did you say?" Burly Muscle Man grasped the back of Rose's stool and leaned over her. Tattoos smothered both of his arms, fading up the sleeves of his shirt, and his breath smelled of beer and stale cigarettes.

"That's right." Rose peered at him, her face mere inches from his.

The scene was mesmerizing. Rose was acting flirtatious—seductive even. This was going to make for an interesting conversation later.

"Who did you say gave you his name?" Corey leaned across the bar so that his nose almost touched Rose's.

"I didn't." Rose turned to me, subtly backing away from Corey.

"Harmony." I blurted the first name to pop into my mind. I was not-so-surprisingly uncool.

"Harmony, huh?" The burly guy's tattoos moved with his muscles as he leaned closer to Rose. "I know her."

I set my beer on the counter, my hands gripping the bottle. His smile had contorted into a grimace. My protective instincts on full alert, I stiffened. Rose didn't flinch.

"His death must have been sudden," I said.

"You could say that." Corey stood upright.

Burly Man nodded. "Yesterday. A bullet in the chest."

Rose and I exchanged a glance, feigning shock. But if I were to make a bet, I'd say my expression looked more like fear—and was very real.

"Oh, no." Rose put on a good show of looking surprised. "He was the guy who was shot in Stonebridge? I can't believe it."

"I'm so sorry," I stammered, watching my friend, amazed at how easily the lie had rolled off her tongue. She hadn't been kidding when she'd claimed a crown for her acting abilities.

"Another round?" Corey asked.

"Please." I slid my empty bottle toward him. "And whatever he's having." I tipped my head toward Mr. Burly. A peace gesture.

Silently, we waited until Corey placed the next round on the bar.

Lifting his bottle in thanks, the man said, "Yeah, Hunter never should have gone to Stonebridge. I warned him Tiffanee was bad news."

Corey chuckled. "No kidding, dude. He should have known better. You know Hunter, always chasing after the chicks."

Why was that scenario so easy to believe? At the mention of Hunter, I wiped my hand on my leg, in what was becoming an automatic reaction.

"Yeah, but this wasn't about chasing chicks." Burly Man's voice grew gruff.

"Cute chicks in Stonebridge." Corey gave us an approving glance. "Harmony, you said. Are you from Stonebridge, then?"

I waited for Rose to answer. Before she had the chance, the burly biker stood, letting go of Rose's stool. "No way, man. Hunter wasn't chasing chicks. He was looking for Penny."

Chapter Twenty-Five

L ater, I lit my tiki torches and settled on my patio, surrounded by chirping crickets and the sound of Darcy sniffing in the yard. Rose opened a bottle of wine, and we relaxed beneath the twinkle of a million stars. It was time to deconstruct our evening in Bellows Falls.

"Can we talk for a minute about how you almost picked up a bad-boy biker?" We had hardly spoken during the thirty-minute ride back to Stonebridge, both of us lost in our own thoughts.

Rose's eyes danced. "First, let's talk about how you froze like a deer in the headlights when he mentioned Penny."

"It made the hair on my arms stand at attention."

"I could tell," Rose said.

"Remind me if I ever decide to put myself back out there, I'm bringing you along. But somewhere different—classier. Much classier."

"You mean it? That would be so much fun." Then, shooting me a sidelong glance, Rose added, "And, so you know, you totally sound like a huge snob right now."

"Ha! Snob, no. Geriatric, yes. I'm way too old for dive bars. Besides, I was kidding. I'm not planning to put myself out there. It was rhetorical."

"I never get it when people say that." Rose sipped her wine.

"Anyway, if you could get your mind off the tattooed muscles of Mr. Dreamy, weren't you even a little surprised by what he told us?"

"Mr. Dreamy." Rose puffed her cheeks. "No more bad boys for me."

My voice softened. "I'm sorry. Is Travis still giving you problems?"

"Always. That man is going to be the death of me. I mean, I know things are rough for him right now, but he needs to figure out where his head is at. He's got Ethan all kinds of upset."

"Ethan did seem uncharacteristically sullen this afternoon."

"According to Travis, Ethan keeps going on about Tiffanee. Somehow, that's all my fault." Rose shifted in her seat. "I know it's crazy, but Travis has always done a number on my head."

"Speaking of Travis," I said, "Do you know why he never told Detective Cram about seeing us at Tiffanee's house?"

"Pfft. It's not like he'd go out of his way to help the police."

"Works for me," I said, sotto voce.

"Forget about him. I had so much fun tonight. You did, too, right?"

I stroked the tail of my scarf. *Fun* wasn't exactly the description I'd use, but watching Rose in a different setting had certainly been amusing. "Before we move to more important things, I've got to say, Mr. Burly might not be your type, but he sure thought you were smoking hot. You don't have to like him to feel flattered."

Rose's cheeks flushed. "I have to admit, it felt kind of good. Oh yeah, this girl's still got it." She crinkled her nose. "I'm serious. No more bad boys. Next time, I'm going for someone more like—"

"William," I said, finishing Rose's sentence. I couldn't help noticing the way she blushed whenever someone mentioned his name. The dreamy look in her eyes. William was smart and handsome and nice, and he would be great for Rose. For the sake of my friend's potential love life, I needed to solve these murders and clear William for good.

Blushing, Rose lifted her wine glass. "But you had fun, didn't you? You really should get back out there. And if we did it together, we'd be one hot duo."

"Not happening." The thought of meeting a new man, of pushing aside my love for Dan, was too scary to contemplate. Life with him was my happily ever after—until he'd been taken away. I wasn't sure which scared me more, forgetting my husband or spending the rest of my life alone.

Rose grasped my hand, giving it a gentle squeeze. "Give it time. Dan was a good guy, and I totally get not being ready to let go. I feel like it's been eons since I've been on a real date, and I'm pretty terrified just thinking about it."

I studied Rose. Did she mean that? She was so outgoing, so bubbly, so confident. If she was terrified, there was no hope for me—not that it mattered.

"Let's get back to the subject—Penny," Rose said.

"I definitely didn't see that coming." With the subject of dating forgotten, I relaxed.

"At our meeting, she acted like she knew nothing about Hunter. I really don't see how that can be true."

Even if Penny hadn't lied, she hadn't been forthcoming either. "She's definitely too close to this."

"I thought about it on the way home, and it kind of makes sense. Don't you think? I mean, obviously, Hope has a dad."

"Not anymore. If our assumption is correct, that is." How had I not seen it—the resemblance between Hunter and Hope? The white-blonde hair and dimples. When I first saw the photo of Hunter, I was sure there was something familiar.

"Maybe that's why Hunter was hanging around," Rose said, interrupting my thoughts.

"Getting my head wrapped around Penny as a killer is nearly impossible. Although," I paused, grasping for a piece of the puzzle. "Penny could easily have snuck the camera bag into Tiffanee's house. She lives right next door."

"It's not like she's the picture of innocence. I mean, I know all the piercings and tattoos are the thing these days, but no way Bernadine approves." Rose sipped her wine. "Good grief, listen to me. When did I get so old?"

"Her appearance is some sort of rebellion, isn't it?"

"I'll say. Or maybe it's a declaration of independence. Believe me, she looked nothing like that when she left Stonebridge. I bet she wasn't planning to come back, either."

I sat back. "Rebellion is one thing. It's an enormous leap from there to murdering two people. And I can't help thinking Tiffanee's photos play into all this somehow." I told Rose about Kendall's visit. "You remember her from last Thursday, right? She told Alicia she wasn't in town."

"For sure. She was such a monster over her mocha latte not being creamy enough." Rose huffed. "I'll have you know my lattes are the creamiest in all of New England."

I laughed. "You don't have to convince me. They're perfection."

Appeased, Rose asked, "You think Tiffanee was blackmailing her?"

"Most likely. It was strange the way she asked about Tiffanee's photos. Beneath her nonchalance, she was definitely scheming."

Rose snorted. "That lady has a lot to lose. But do you seriously see her killing someone? What's her connection to Hunter?"

I let out a long sigh. "You're probably right."

"How about Harmony?" Rose asked. "It's totally bugging me the way she wasn't at yoga."

"Connor told me she was protective of Penny," I said.

"That's it! She was protecting Penny from Hunter. I bet he was a dirtbag."

"I met him." I stared into the darkness, lost in thought. "He had a certain charm, but wow, did he ever give me the creeps. In fairness, I thought he was the murderer."

Rose nodded. "And don't forget what the biker dude said. Hunter came to Stonebridge looking for Penny."

"I'll talk to Harmony tomorrow," I said. "There's something up with her."

Wind chimes tinkled as I entered Harmony's yoga studio the next morning. After my conversation with Rose, I had more questions than answers. Before Tiffanee's death, something had been going on between our village yogi and Hunter, and I had the photos to prove it.

Haunting music played in the background while I roamed between display tables laden with all things new age. It wasn't really my thing, but a display of mantra bracelets caught my eye. I stopped to read their small engravings. They were beautiful in their simplicity. *ONE DAY AT A TIME*, one band read.

"Hmm," I said to the empty room.

"You'd be amazed at their positive energy." Harmony floated into the shop. "Truly powerful, if you find one that speaks to you."

I placed the bracelet back where it belonged. "That's not why I'm here."

"I didn't think so. Your aura has a reddish glow. I'm sensing anger." She raised her hand, halting my protest before it started. "Red isn't all bad. It's the color of passion. Anyway, what can I do for you?"

Red aura—pfft. I shook off the thought and dug my phone from my pocket. Scrolling through my photos, I stopped at one of Harmony and Hunter. "What can you tell me about this?"

Harmony's finger touched my screen. She handed the phone back to me and dropped her arms to her side, staring out the window. "Tiffanee, I assume. She was clever with her camera, wasn't she?"

"Can you tell me why Hunter was here in Stonebridge?"

Harmony weaved through the shop to her sales counter, smoothing and straightening items along the way. "It's all so complicated."

"Try me."

"There's that anger again. Amethyst is good for that."

My cheeks burned—probably red like my aura. "You haven't answered my question. Why was Hunter here?"

"As I mentioned, it's complicated. I've known him most of my life. It's been a difficult journey for him, and he wasn't always a nice person." Harmony paused, pointing a finger at the image on my phone. "I warned him not to get involved with Tiffanee."

"Involved how?" I asked. "We think Tiffanee was blackmailing people with her photos. Was Hunter involved with that?" I could picture it—Hunter as Tiffanee's strong-arm.

"I can't believe he'd do that. His reason for being here is not my story to tell."

"The story of Penny and Hope, you mean?"

Harmony's chin dipped in a slight nod. "Hunter was here to meet Hope. Tiffanee never should have gotten involved. Penny would have told him eventually."

"That gives Penny a motive," I said with a sigh. It was a possibility I'd been avoiding.

Harmony's eyes flashed. "Surely you don't think she'd kill her baby's father?"

"I don't want to," I said. "How long have you known Hunter was Hope's father?"

Harmony glided around the counter, her steps silent on the tile floor, her soft scent floating with her. "Penny told me before Hope was born. She'd planned to tell Hunter eventually. She never would have killed anyone over it."

I considered Harmony's words, wanting to believe her.

"Tiffanee was blackmailing people?" Harmony asked. "I had a feeling she was up to something, but I can't believe Hunter was involved."

"She's been secretly taking photos," I said. "Some caught people in compromising situations. You have to admit, the one I just showed you caught you and Hunter in a private moment."

"May I see it again?" Her eyebrows knitted together while studying the photo I handed her. "Where did you get this?"

"Umm." I stalled. I wasn't about to tell Harmony about stealing Tiffanee's photos.

The door flew open, and Iris breezed into the shop, halting our conversation. She smiled at me. "Hi Bobbie. It's nice to see you again." Then, turning to Harmony, she asked, "Are you ready for lunch?"

An expression washed over Harmony's face like a cloud clearing. It wasn't relief, exactly, but she visibly relaxed while smiling at her friend. She held the door open and flipped the closed sign.

As we stepped onto the sidewalk, Harmony turned to me. "I'm not sure what I can tell you. Unfortunately, Tiffanee wasn't a happy person. She had a murky aura. While I didn't agree with her interference over Hope, I thought she meant well. I shouldn't be surprised to hear she was blackmailing people. I had a feeling there was something clandestine going on between Hunter and her. But truly, Hunter never clued me in. Part of me thought they were getting back together. If only that had been true."

I followed behind the two women, mulling over the yogi's words. As Harmony stepped from the curb, she lifted her skirt, and a memory flooded back: my cheek pressed to the dusty barn floor, dark shoes scampering away,

Harmony's flowing skirt coming to my rescue. The intruder—it hadn't been Harmony.

"Bobbie," Harmony's voice interrupted my thoughts. "If you'd like to come back, I'll show you some crystals. Their positive energy can help you."

Chapter Twenty-Six

When I entered the Rosebud Café later that afternoon, the Righteous Sisters were at their usual table. I felt their stares, like prickles on my neck, and slinked past, pretending not to notice. The last thing I wanted was another run-in with Lorraine. I slid onto a stool and said a quick hello to the man seated next to me as Rose rushed over and plunked a plate on the counter.

"White chocolate-wild berry scone. Simply to-die-for. I saved you one." She gave me a playful wink. "How did it go with Harmony?"

I couldn't help my ecstatic eye roll when I took a bite of the scone. I held up three fingers while swallowing. "Three things," I said. "First, Harmony confirmed Hunter was here because of Hope. Second, she wasn't the intruder in my barn. Third is the biggie. Hunter was probably helping Tiffanee with her blackmail." I could barely hide my excitement.

"Wait. Harmony told you that? She knew about the blackmail?"

"Not exactly," I said after swallowing another bite. "What she actually said was that she couldn't believe Hunter would be involved."

"You lost me," Rose deadpanned.

I waved a hand. "She and Hunter were old friends. Of course, she'd defend him. But she admitted he and Tiffanee were up to something. What else could it be?"

Rose leaned on the counter, her eyes widening. "That would explain the connection between Tiffanee's and Hunter's deaths."

"Right?" My suspect list just got stronger.

"So, why can't Harmony be the intruder?"

I explained about Harmony's flowing skirt when she entered the barn not matching the dark legs and shoes of the intruder. "Have you ever known Harmony to wear dark shoes?"

Rose shook her head. "Mostly Birkenstocks, I'd say. Even in the winter, only with socks."

"Oh yeah, the fourth thing. Supposedly, I have a red aura and need some sort of crystals to help me manage my anger."

"Crystals?" Rose crinkled her nose, stifling a giggle. "Too woo-woo for you?"

"Insulting, more like. Regardless, I'm crossing Harmony off the suspect list." I nodded toward the Righteous Sisters. "So, what's new in the Stonebridge Scandal?"

Rose straightened. "You could read it for yourself, you know."

"No way. I refuse to follow that page."

"Except you do—through me."

"It's not the same thing," I said. "Why do I feel you're avoiding telling me? Out with it."

Rose seemed hesitant. "It was about the rifle, about how someone carried it away from the bridge after Hunter was shot, with no one seeing them."

"Cool." Hallelujah. The post wasn't about me.

"They're thinking the killer must live nearby," Rose said. "They would have walked through the woods behind Main Street."

Rose stood still while I worked through the scenario where the killer walked through the woods, behind the church, behind Lester Miller's house. Understanding hit me.

"Through the woods to my house, you mean?"

"Try not to get upset about it. It's just a bunch of wagging tongues." Rose's voice was soft with concern. "Wait here. I'll get you a latte."

I leaned on the counter, my head in my hands. This wasn't happening. I didn't own a rifle. I didn't even know how to shoot one. There had to be lots of other ways to sneak the rifle away. Both William and Penny lived on the other side of the bridge. It wouldn't have been difficult to creep across with a rifle in the early morning. Harmony had come from that direction, too, looking like she'd fought a battle. Where had she been all morning, and what had she been doing?

A frothy latte appeared under my nose. I wrapped my hands around the white mug, taking a breath of warm comfort before lifting it to my lips.

"Monday can't come soon enough." I sipped my coffee. "But before that, I have a new idea." Ignoring Rose's skeptical expression, I continued. "We still have two potential victims of blackmail, and I'm thinking I might accidentally on purpose lose the key to my barn. I predict a locksmith in my near future."

If I didn't know better, I might've thought Darcy was a vicious attack dog. His barking echoed from inside the barn, drowning out the sound of Parker's tools scraping against my lock.

"What kind of dog do you have in there?" Parker asked. When I'd called him about my *missing* key, he'd claimed he was swamped. His next availability wasn't for another day or two. It was only a barn, after all. That was when I came up with the brilliant idea of adding Darcy to my scheme. I'd figured, like most Vermonters I knew, he'd be a softy for a dog.

"He's a yellow lab," I said.

Parker looked up at me and chuckled. "Lots of bark without the bite, then."

I sniffed. "He's very protective of me." My defensiveness was irrational, considering Parker wasn't wrong.

"I'm sure." He chuckled again and twisted the doorknob, stepping back.

Darcy bounded from the barn and headed toward Parker, but not before tossing his head with what looked suspiciously like an eye roll. Possible or not, his disdain for my plan was obvious. Parker was more than prepared for my dog's excessive exuberance and held out a dog biscuit. Darcy's barking turned to sniffing, then to tail wagging. So much for protection.

"Do you always carry treats?" I asked.

"Always," Parker said with a nod. "You have no idea how many dogs I deal with in a day."

Darcy took his biscuit and ran to the patio to enjoy it.

"Well, I guess you're all set." Lifting his baseball cap, he ran his fingers through curly brown hair.

"I was wondering," I said, looking down slightly to meet his eyes. About five feet, seven inches tall, if I were to guess, he was slightly shorter than me. "I'm thinking of getting a security system."

"For your barn?" He asked. "Break-ins aren't common in the village."

"That's what I've heard. But with the recent murders, I'm thinking I'll feel safer with something more than a regular lock. Besides, this isn't a barn. It'll soon be my photography studio."

Parker's eyes narrowed. "I see." He peeked inside the barn. "You're Alicia's sister. The photography club lady."

"That's right," I said. "I bet you've done lots of security systems in the homes on Stratton."

Parker worked his jaw as though chewing on a piece of bad-tasting information. "You didn't really lose your key, did you?"

"I, uh…"

"You and your sister need to back off." He clenched his fists. "I mean it. I don't know nothing about the dead lady or her photos."

"You were at her funeral," I said.

"That's because of my wife." His fists opened and closed. "She knew her."

I took a step back, thinking he was about to swing one of those fists.

"I mean it." His voice grew louder as he spoke. "Just butt out."

I flinched. Butt out? My mind flashed back to the block letters of the note, and for a frightening moment, I realized we were alone. And as the sun fell behind the trees and the sky darkened, what was to keep him from pushing me through the open door of my barn and…? I couldn't finish my thought.

When he stooped to pick up his tools, I took another step back, preparing to run for it.

"My assistant will send you an invoice." He pinned me with one last glare before stomping up my driveway and speeding away in his truck.

"I can't believe he said that." Alicia's whisper did nothing to hide her incredulity. On Sunday morning, we followed Nate and Connor into the church, staying a few steps behind.

"Right?" I whispered back. "He told us to butt out. Just like in the note."

After Parker had left my house the previous evening, a string of text messages had flown between Alicia, Rose, and me. But this was our first opportunity to talk.

It was a gray, overcast morning, and a damp fog replaced the warm sunshine of the last few days. Dressed in a comfortable skirt and T-shirt, I'd arrived at the church early. Lorraine had asked—no, demanded—I be ready the moment church service ended, but I knew the real work took place before an event.

While volunteers buzzed around the lawn, adorning long tables with buckets of wildflowers, I'd stayed out of their way, using my telephoto lens to snap photos. The crew was impressive, operating with the precision of a well-trained regiment with Lorraine as their commanding drill sergeant. No one stopped working until the church bells rang, echoing in the morning mist. Tucking my camera into my backpack, I caught sight of my sister.

Nate stopped and turned before entering the church. "What are you two up to?"

"Not a thing," Alicia said. "Let's go inside."

Nate grasped my elbow as we climbed the stairs to the sanctuary. "You haven't heard anything more from the police?"

"No," I answered. "Thankfully."

"Good. Be sure to call me if you do. I still don't like that you spoke with Detective Cram alone."

We shuffled into a pew near the back. "Do you expect him to visit me again?" *Please let me get through the rest of the day and into my car tomorrow morning.* I gazed at the altar. *Amen.*

"I don't think so. I get the impression he's casting a wider net."

The congregation stood. I was dying to ask more, but the organ hit the opening chords. My off-key singing voice wavered, and my mind wandered as I tried to guess who the new suspects could be.

The pastor's voice was but a background hum to my thoughts. Normally, I found her words uplifting, but I couldn't stop thinking about the possibility I was safe from Detective Cram's crosshairs. Lost in my dreams of a carefree trip to Boston and lunch with Emma at a sidewalk café, I almost missed the cue signaling the end of the service. I made a quick exit, my camera ready as villagers poured from the church.

Chapter Twenty-Seven

The Farmer's Breakfast was a Stonebridge tradition, dating back over two hundred years. Alicia explained about the village holding the annual event to celebrate the planted fields. There were fewer farmers—fewer farms—than there had been years ago, but the village wasn't about to abandon a perfectly good festival. Tradition held fast in southern Vermont.

I ducked through the swarm of pancake-seekers, snapping photos as villagers chatted. Plates laden with pillowy hotcakes and sausages drifted by me, and the sweet scent of maple syrup hung in the air. Luckily, the rain held off, and the gray light turned out to be a blessing. A quick glance at my screen confirmed it was the perfect complement for the occasion, eliminating the harsh shadows that accentuated wrinkles and baggy eyes.

"Hey, girl." Rose appeared at my side, raising a plate piled with pancakes and bacon. "Looks like you need something to eat."

I let my camera hang at my waist, and a grin spread across my face. "For me?" It surprised me to find Rose away from her café.

"Who else?" Rose handed me the plate. "I figured with the whole village here, Ethan and his friend could hold down the fort for an hour or so." She answered my unspoken question. Standing on tiptoe, she scanned the crowd. "Who have you seen so far?"

"Who *haven't* I seen?" I shoveled a forkful into my mouth. "So good." The sticky sweetness of maple syrup filled me with a sense of pride for my newly adopted state when I licked a dribble from the corner of my lips. This was not the maple-flavored corn syrup of my youth.

Rose nudged me and pointed to a table where Jackson sat with Harmony and Iris, his plate nearly spilling over. "You should have been nicer to Jackson." She snickered. "Looks to me like he's interested in Iris now."

"We can only hope." I surveyed the crowd and groaned. "Uh-oh."

Travis approached us, his man-bun as disheveled as ever. It had likely been several days since his face met a razor.

"If it isn't the dastardly duo," Travis said with a devilish smile.

Rose huffed, crossing her arms in front of her.

"The entire village is here. Isn't there someone else you could pester?" I asked.

He smirked. "And miss the opportunity for an update from Nancy Drew?"

Rose looked over Travis's shoulder, a blush rising on her cheeks. I followed her gaze to where William stood, appearing hesitant.

"Go." Rose pushed Travis's arm. "The buffet is over there."

Slowly, Travis turned to look over his shoulder. Astonished understanding washed over his face. When he faced Rose again, her blush deepened.

"Be a good guy and go bother someone else. *Sherlock Holmes* has nothing to tell you."

Travis grumbled something incoherent before lumbering away.

Taking Travis's place, William joined us with a smile. "Good morning, ladies."

"Hi, William." I tried to hide my wince at the tight pinch Rose gave my arm. The meaning of her painful cue was clear. "You've met my friend, Rose, haven't you?"

He nodded, his attention on Rose. "I've been to your coffee shop once or twice since moving here, but I'm afraid we've never been formally introduced. I'm pleased to meet you."

Rose beamed with a radiant smile. "Me too."

I hadn't thought it possible, but Rose's flush deepened. *Oh boy.* I skimmed from William's friendly, self-assured smile to Rose, who must have left the confident Daisy behind at the biker bar. It had been a lifetime since I'd felt the kind of jitters Rose seemed to be feeling. The thought left me momentarily breathless. If I wasn't so happy for my friend, I might have felt envious.

"Don't let me keep you," I said. "I should get back to taking photos."

"Have you eaten?" Rose asked him, her blush deepening.

"Not yet. Would you care to join me?"

Rose squeezed my arm, excitement written in the sparkle of her eyes. Watching them walk away, I couldn't help feeling a pang at how cute they looked together. William's lean physique and gentlemanly manner complemented Rose's softer curves and liveliness. They joined the line at the buffet table, William smiling while Rose chattered, acting more like herself.

Before lifting my camera, I said a silent prayer that I wouldn't regret playing matchmaker. *Amen.*

As I composed my next shot, I nearly jumped at the sound of Alicia's voice. "Rose had better be careful. I have it on good authority Detective Cram is looking William's way."

"Oh no," I moaned, letting my camera fall on its strap. "But he seems so nice."

"Maybe he's a psychopath," Alicia deadpanned.

"Maybe who's a psychopath?" Nate appeared from nowhere.

Alicia merely nodded toward William.

Nate scoffed. "Let's not get carried away."

"You never know," Alicia murmured.

Nate's laugh was good-natured. "Why don't we get something to eat before all the food is gone?"

"You go ahead. I'll be right with you." She brushed his arm as he turned to leave, then fixed her gaze on me. "Guess who's here?" Alicia nodded toward Parker.

As though sensing my sister's stare, he looked our way, making my pulse quicken. He wore a faded plaid shirt over a broad, muscular chest I hadn't noticed the day before. A baseball cap shaded his eyes, but not enough to shield his glare.

"I wonder what he's thinking right now," Alicia said.

"Umm, that he wants to kill us?"

"Parker," Alicia called to him with a wave. "Got a second?"

Even from a distance, I saw his expression harden. He hesitated before giving a slight tip of his chin. After a few words with his wife, he sauntered over.

He's a cool one.

"What do you want?" His voice was none too friendly.

"Did my sister tell you about a visit from a friend of yours? She was quite interested in getting her hands on a photo you claim to know nothing about."

Parker's eyes widened. "We're done here. This is the last time I'm going to say it. Back off." He plodded away, his retreat far less casual than his approach had been.

"He's lying," I said.

"For sure," Alicia answered. "As is Kendall."

"I'm not sure what the detective might have on William, but we both know he's been wrong so far. My money is on Parker." My whole body shivered. "I'm thinking we need to take his threat seriously."

"It would seem so." Alicia arched an eyebrow while watching Parker rejoin his wife. "I need to think about this. In the meantime, I'd better join Nate."

As she took off for the buffet, I lifted my camera and aimed my lens at Rose. She radiated with happiness. Surely, William wasn't a psychopath. I vowed to search for him on the internet when I got home. If he had a shady past, Rose needed to know. Confident she was safe enough while the breakfast was going on, I turned back to the task at hand.

Weaving among the crowd, I snapped photos of cheerful villagers. At several of the tables, friends and family jumped together for group shots. I couldn't help laughing along with their antics. The breakfast was winding down. Volunteers cleaned the tables and prepared for the annual plant swap. Harmony was helping Iris arrange a profusion of greenery on a table when she met my gaze. After a quick wave, she went back to her task, and I wondered at her words from the day before. She'd warned Hunter about getting involved with Tiffanee.

I sensed, rather than saw, Alicia back at my side, her fresh, soapy scent announcing her arrival.

"Looks like you're getting some good pictures."

CHAPTER TWENTY-SEVEN

"I think so," I said. "Even Lorraine won't have anything to complain about."

Penny walked by, pushing Hope in her stroller. Beside her, a woman with choppy shoulder-length hair in a shocking shade of pink gestured animatedly with her arms as she spoke. Whatever story she was telling made Penny laugh.

"Who is that with Penny?" I asked.

"Are you telling me you haven't been to the library since moving here? She's our village librarian, Mackenzie Miller."

"Another Miller." I sighed, observing Penny with her friend. "They look close."

"That's what I hear," Alicia said. "They make a cute couple."

"They do." I couldn't help agreeing. Mackenzie bent over the stroller and scooped Hope into her arms. "Penny seems happy." Not at all like the surly young woman I'd grown used to.

"I can imagine the conniption Bernadine had when Penny started dating a woman. But Mackenzie is awesome. Penny could do much worse."

I nodded. *Like Hunter.*

As if reading my mind, Alicia lowered her voice. "I have to admit, I'm still processing your news about Hunter being Hope's father."

"Have you come up with any ideas that might tie it to the murders?"

"I haven't had much time to think about it." Then, changing the subject, she asked, "You're heading to Boston in the morning?"

"Definitely." I couldn't help my relieved sigh. The day was almost over, and the next, I'd be with Emma.

Alicia nodded. "I'm heading out early. You can drop Darcy off at the farm before you leave. He'll have fun with Harry and Sally, and Nate's cool with having one more dog underfoot."

"Great. Darcy won't even notice I'm gone."

We stood for a moment, watching the crowd. When my eyes landed on Penny and Mackenzie, my heart warmed. I doubted Penny could have looked that happy with Hunter.

Nate sauntered over, taking Alicia's hand in his. He gestured toward the tables laden with plants and flowers. "Is it time to choose more flowers we don't need?"

Alicia slapped his arm, laughing. "Nate will see you tomorrow morning. If he's not home, let Darcy into the house. He knows the place."

"I'll see you in Boston," I answered with a smile I was sure spread all the way across my face. Ready to call it a day, I lifted my camera and felt a tentative tap on my shoulder. Turning, I came face-to-face with Bernadine.

"I wanted to thank you for being here today, taking pictures of our event," Bernadine said. "I, I mean, we especially appreciated you coming early to take pictures of us setting up."

"My pleasure." And I meant it. Photography was what I loved to do, the reason I had moved to Vermont and was renovating my barn. Soon, I'd have my very own clients—paying ones. "I had a lot of fun today." I lifted my camera one last time. "Say cheese."

Bernadine raised her hands, laughing, as I snapped. It felt like progress.

The plant swap was in full swing, but the mob had thinned. Rose and William had left, presumably for their respective businesses. I packed my gear, my mind jumping forward to tomorrow's escape from Stonebridge. But first, I needed to research William. If the police were looking into him, there must be a reason. And I was going to find out what it was.

Chapter Twenty-Eight

Back in my kitchen, Alicia's words about William rang in my ears. I pictured Rose's flushed cheeks and the telltale twinkle in her eyes. She was undeniably smitten. I hoped there was nothing in William's past that would ruin their budding romance. The thought filled me with foreboding. The last thing I wanted was to see Rose hurt.

I let Darcy out the back door and walked to my table, firing up my laptop. What would Google tell me? I drummed my fingers on the edge of my keyboard, thinking about where to start. William Johnson was a common name, so it took several searches before I could find relevant information. No sooner had a newspaper article loaded on my screen than someone knocked on my door. As I strode through the hallway, a tall, shadowy figure appeared through the sidelights.

I groaned. Detective Cram.

Cracking the door open, I couldn't help feeling snappish. A visit from the detective was the last thing I needed. "What now?"

"I have a few follow-up questions." He pushed the door open and stepped into my foyer.

"Fine, but you'll need to make yourself comfortable because I'm calling Nate.

"Suit yourself." He pushed past me and strode toward my kitchen.

I followed behind and shot a quick SOS text to Nate. Fortunately, my sister's gregarious husband was not one to leave a party early and was still at the plant swap two doors down. He texted he'd be right over.

"Nate is on his way." I shuffled to my refrigerator. "Iced tea?"

"Not for me." As Detective Cram pulled out a chair, his phone rang. "I need to take this." He whirled around and walked from the room.

Careful not to make a sound, I tiptoed to where he'd left a file folder on the table. A corner of what appeared to be a copy of an email stuck out. Ignoring my better judgment, I set my tea on the table and pulled the paper from the folder. My breath hitched. It was an email from Tiffanee to William.

I know about your drug dealing at the high school.

That was all it said. I grabbed my phone and snapped a quick photo, but as I tucked my phone back into my pocket, my elbow hit my glass of iced tea. I jerked, jamming the page back into the folder with one hand while trying to grasp my glass with the other. Too late. Tea gushed over the table, threatening to soak the file folder and everything in it. I swiped at the pile with my forearm, sending pages scattering to the floor.

The sound of footsteps grew louder before coming to a halt in the doorway. "What do you think you're doing?" Detective Cram threw his arms in the air, accentuating his exasperated tone.

I grabbed a towel. "I'm so sorry. My tea spilled, and I didn't want your papers to get ruined." Kneeling on the floor, I gathered pages while sneaking peeks.

"I'll do that. You wipe your spill before it gets worse."

Being bossed around in my own kitchen stung, but I followed his orders and handed him the jumbled pile of papers before cleaning the icy mess. On my knees, I was doing all I could to ignore the detective's towering stance when the kitchen door opened, and Nate strode into the room, Darcy at his heels.

Nate came to a quick stop. "What's going on?"

"Your client made a complete mess of my papers." Detective Cram's face was red, and his flared nostrils made him look like a caricature of a fire-breathing dragon. He stood and slammed his folder on the table. With a vigorous swipe at his leg, he brushed dust and fur from his trousers.

"Bobbie?" Nate sounded like a parent questioning a petulant child.

My face burned, and I didn't dare look up. "It was an accident." My answer was childish and not completely true, but it was all I could offer.

Closing the door behind him, Nate shifted his attention to the detective. "What's this about?" He strode to the table with his hand extended.

The temperature in the room seemed to cool slightly as they shook hands. "I have follow-up questions for Mrs. Brooks."

I carried my empty glass and wet towel to the sink.

"Let's get on with it, then." Nate motioned for me to join them at the table.

I dropped into the empty chair next to him. Although embarrassed, I couldn't forget what I'd seen in the folder. William had been dealing drugs at the high school? Was that why—?

"Mrs. Brooks." Detective Cram glowered. "Let's revisit the evening before Mr. Harrison's death. You witnessed an argument at the bar of The Mad Crow Tavern."

I gave a reluctant nod. I'd witnessed it, but didn't know what it meant.

"Tell me what you heard."

"Not a lot." Thinking about William would have to wait. I tucked a wisp of hair behind my ear. "It sounded like Hunter was angry. I think there was something he wanted to do that night. Then he mentioned something about the next morning. I didn't hear what it was."

"Do you know what it was he wanted to do?"

After my trip to Bellows Falls, I had a few ideas, but nothing I wanted to share with the detective. I shook my head.

"Who was he arguing with?"

"Harmony, mostly. And Penny."

For a few moments, the only sound was a scratching pen. "Was Ms. Santos angry as well?"

Nate raised his hand. "You're asking Bobbie to speculate about someone's emotions."

Detective Cram shifted in his chair before rephrasing his question, asking whether Harmony appeared angry to me.

Wait? Harmony is the new suspect? I shook my head. I'd already ruled her out. "No. If anything, I got the impression she was trying to calm Hunter."

"But she missed her usual yoga class the next morning." He clicked his pen.

"Last Thursday was the first time I attended class. It was my understanding she usually taught it."

"What can you tell me about Mr. Johnson's relationship with Ms. Jacobsen?"

Aha! William *was* a suspect. "I think she was his bookkeeper?"

"And his relationship with Mr. Harrison?"

"I don't think they even knew each other." Did they? It occurred to me I knew very little about either of them.

"Very well." Detective Cram shut his notebook and stood.

"Are we through?" Nate stood as well.

"For now," Detective Cram said.

I held my breath with dreaded anticipation. This was when the detective would tell me not to leave town. Except he didn't. It wasn't until he and Nate closed the door behind them that I let out a premature sigh of relief.

The door swung open again, and Nate poked his head into my kitchen. "I'm going to want details of the spilled tea incident." He furrowed his brows in his sternest fatherly expression before closing the door again.

I slumped back into my chair. William and Harmony. Were they the new suspects? I already knew it wasn't Harmony. She'd been neither angry nor threatening toward Hunter, and she certainly didn't kill him.

William could be a different story. A drug dealer? I pulled my phone from my pocket and reread the email. No two ways about it, Tiffanee had been blackmailing William. Or at least attempting to. I returned to my laptop to read the article.

"Oh no, this is bad," I said out loud. As Tiffanee's email had intimated, William had been accused of dealing drugs at the school where he'd taught. The article didn't say if he'd been fired from his teaching job. But buying a bookstore seemed like a ludicrous plan. If William had been hoping to lie low, our mostly White village seemed an odd place for an African American to hide out. If discovered, he'd probably lose a second livelihood.

Was it worth killing for? *Yep. Quite likely.*

I sighed. If Hunter had been involved in Tiffanee's game, that would explain his death, too. I jerked. Or maybe it was my photo of Hunter.

Maybe when I'd shown William the picture, he'd thought Hunter could place him at Tiffanee's murder. I blew my bangs from my forehead. *Another secret worth protecting.*

A breeze blew through the window. I patted Darcy's broad head, wishing I could put all this behind me. What I really wanted was a long, hot soak in my tub with a cup of tea and a good mystery—a fictional one.

Darcy wagged his tail, his eyes begging. He'd been stuck indoors for most of the day, and a walk would do me good, too. I was only one night away from dinner in Boston. A break from murderous thoughts couldn't come soon enough. Assuming, of course, Emma's potentially wayward boyfriend didn't raise my hackles too much.

The evening air was damp and chilly. Darcy was at attention, watching something on the village green, when I bent to click the leash to his collar. As I straightened, I followed his gaze to where Kendall and Parker seemed to be having a heated discussion. Frozen, I watched Kendall stamp her foot, and Parker raise his hand as though telling her to back off. I couldn't help wondering if our earlier encounter at the Farmer's Breakfast had set their argument in motion. Not wanting to get caught staring, I led Darcy down the porch stairs and set a quick pace for our walk.

The Farmer's Breakfast had gone better than expected. It had been fun, even. Still, I was relieved the event was behind me. When I came back from Boston, I'd sort through the images and edit the best ones before emailing them to Lorraine. I felt certain she'd been pleased to be the star of my morning photos. I also felt certain she'd never admit it.

Leading Darcy down Main Street, I took a right onto River Street and breathed in the thick, humid air. We sped past the old mill building and Tiffanee's house, which seemed forlorn with the overgrown grass and flowers shriveled in their pots. A lamp glowed in the window of Penny's house, but I focused on the road ahead of me, hoping to pass by without being noticed.

Only a dim light remained on the horizon, the sky a deep violet gray. As I rounded the corner, the covered bridge loomed in front of me, cloaked in a thickening fog. Shadows shrouded the interior. From the opposite end, a figure approached, little more than a silhouette. I stiffened, recognizing the erect posture.

My stomach knotted, and I frantically surveyed my surroundings. I needed somewhere to hide, if only long enough for him to pass by. I peered down the rocky embankment and shivered. The footing looked precarious, and it was even darker beneath the bridge. My fingers sought the comforting silk of my scarf when my eyes met his.

William looked surprised. "Bobbie?"

"Hi." I could barely hear my voice above the roaring rush of the river below. Darcy stopped, sniffing William's leg.

"Is everything all right?"

Words eluded me, and my mouth opened and closed like a fish out of water.

William's smile vanished. "I take it you heard the police have been questioning me. That didn't take long."

My voice caught. "I need to get home."

His hand reached out to grab my arm, but I jumped back, suppressing a shriek.

"I came here to leave it all behind me." He clenched his fist, then let it drop to his side.

Words refused to leave my lips. I shook my head, remembering Tiffanee's email. Had he harmed any students? Being caught dealing drugs would explain his reason for leaving his teaching job.

Outrage replaced my fear and unleashed my voice. "What happened at your old school? Was everyone else able to leave it all behind them, too?"

"You can't believe everything you hear," he said. "I came here for a fresh start. You know how it is."

How dare he! His situation was completely different from mine.

Even in the dim light, I noticed the hard line of his jaw. "All your questions, Bobbie. If you don't stop, you're going to get hurt."

I flinched. What was that supposed to mean? I took a tentative step. "I need to get home."

CHAPTER TWENTY-EIGHT

William unclenched his fists and stepped aside. "By all means."

I stepped past him, my pace quickening at the unshakable feeling that he was watching. Without thinking, I sped to a jog, Darcy happily trotting beside me. This was a rare treat for him. He'd always enjoyed morning jogs with Dan. For me, our faster pace had little to do with pleasure and everything to do with an overwhelming urgency to return to the safety of my home. I needed to warn Rose.

As soon as I arrived home, I dug my phone from my pocket and pressed Rose's name on my speed dial. She wasn't going to like this. Still.

"Hey, girl," Rose answered on the second ring. "What's up?"

I was breathless from my rush to get home. "I need to tell you something, and I don't know how."

"Are you okay? You sound like you're huffing and puffing."

I gulped air, trying to slow down. "I ran into William."

"Isn't he great?" Rose's voice was almost as breathless as mine.

"You need to listen to me."

Rose's tone became wary. "I'm listening."

"You know the police are questioning him, right? Tiffanee was blackmailing him."

"I'm sure it's some stupid mistake."

Taking another gulp of air, I forged ahead. "I hope so. But we don't know that. He was dealing drugs at the high school."

An uncomfortable silence settled over our conversation. I resisted the urge to speak.

"No way. I don't believe it," Rose finally said.

"I'm not sure what to think. I mean, if he'd been dealing drugs, wouldn't he be in jail? But I think he threatened me." What had William said? That my questions would get me hurt. It certainly felt like a threat.

"No, I don't believe it." Rose's voice cracked. "William wouldn't do that."

I felt horrible. "You don't know him all that well, do you?"

"Yeah, so, I assume your warning is coming from a good place, and I'll try to remember that." Fire returned to her voice. "So, thank you, and stay out of it."

My cheeks burned like Rose had slapped them. "Rose…" What else was there to say?

"No, I mean it. I'm a big girl, and I was so happy today. Like, you know, I'd almost forgotten what it even feels like to be that excited over meeting someone new. It's been such a long time. I can take care of myself."

"We're talking about murder."

"William didn't murder anyone. He's too nice."

"Rose," I repeated. How could I convince her?

"I'm so sick of this investigation. It's turning you into someone who goes around suspecting everyone. I can't take it anymore. I can't. Count me out."

"But—" The phone clicked, and I sat in stunned silence.

Should I call her back? It's not like I'd expected her to feel grateful, but had she really hung up on me? An image of my friend's beaming face swam in my mind. I puffed my cheeks and let out a slow breath. How could I have been so stupid? But what else could I have done? I could only hope Rose wasn't falling headfirst for a murderer.

Chapter Twenty-Nine

The sun had barely crested the treetops when I dropped Darcy at the farm and waved goodbye to Nate. Traffic was light, and I drove my trusty Subaru as though on autopilot. I'd made this trip more times than I could count over the last twenty-five years. But this time felt different. It was like a magnet was pulling me home. With every mile I put between myself and Stonebridge, the force grew stronger, and I felt lighter as I surrendered to it.

I had spent the night tossing in my bed, a recurring dream playing through my mind—Detective Cram chasing me down Main Street, lights flashing, forbidding me to leave Stonebridge. No sooner had I fallen asleep than the sound of my pinging cell phone disturbed me. Getting an early start on the day, Alicia had been texting to confirm everything was a go for our night in the city. I felt giddy thinking about it.

I stroked the tail of my scarf, my thoughts returning to Rose. Making my getaway felt like a victory, but leaving our friendship in a shamble tied my stomach in knots. After two unanswered voicemails, not to mention several texted apologies, what more could I do? Rose was angry; that much was clear. I hoped a couple of days apart might soften her resentment. But what if I'd damaged our friendship permanently?

Traffic thickened the closer I got to the city. Cars wove between lanes, skirting and dodging—a typical day in Boston. I had learned to drive in the city and could jostle with the best of them. Cutting my wheel to the right, I wedged myself between two cars. "Slowpoke," I muttered. You can take the girl out of Boston, but there was no taking Boston out of this girl.

Approaching the Prudential Tunnel, my spirits lifted at the familiar city skyline. Everything was exactly as I left it, and my months in Stonebridge faded away. It was good to be back. Good to be home. I checked my rearview mirror, smiling, Vermont long out of sight.

The previous night, while sleeplessly lying in bed, a thought had popped into my head. *Stay in Boston. Don't come back.* I had rejected it at first. Impossible. Wasn't it? The idea wouldn't go away, replaying in my mind like a scratched record until a new thought joined it. *Why not?*

Moving away from the only home I'd ever known had been a mistake. What had I been thinking? I'd gotten caught up in the dream of my photography studio, of starting over. Now, I was so close, and my dream was almost a reality. Was I willing to throw it away?

I released a slow breath as I drove into the tunnel and glimpsed my reflection in the rearview mirror. Despite checking for cars darting between the lanes and navigating the fork ahead, I couldn't help noticing a lightness in my expression. I knew which way to go and was right where I needed to be.

This was home.

In the most un-Bostonian fashion, I signaled my exit from the tunnel and emerged back into daylight. My heart lifted. Moving home didn't have to mean surrender. It meant giving myself more time. Time to find a new studio and get settled again. I could do it, and I knew Emma would be thrilled. But for now, I'd keep my decision to myself, savoring it alone.

It was a beautiful late spring day—the kind of day I was convinced only happened in Boston. After parking in the garage, I nearly danced down Boylston Street, mingled with shoppers, tourists, and executives, and breathed the familiar scents of the city. This wasn't the clean pine-scented air of Vermont, but something more familiar. It was the sun on the pavement; people crowded together, their soaps and colognes and clothes intermingling; the odor of garbage in the alleys, which contrasted with the more pleasant aromas flavoring the air outside the restaurants' open doors. These were the scents of my childhood.

I strode toward Copley Square, my heart skipping a beat at the familiar juxtaposition of Trinity Church and the Boston Public Library against the looming backdrop of the glass skyscraper I would always think of as the Hancock Tower. I glanced at the benches near the library, remembering countless lunch hours. Then, I rounded the corner and headed toward Newbury Street.

A little way up the street, Emma was already seated on the sidewalk outside our favorite café. It hit me how much I'd missed her. I rushed to her side and squeezed her in a suffocating bear hug.

Emma laughed, escaping the too-tight embrace. "I'm excited to see you, too. I even got our favorite table."

The wrought-iron chair wobbled on the uneven brick sidewalk as I sat, drinking in the sight of my daughter. Her long blonde curls spilled over her shoulders, her blue eyes were clear of the all-too-familiar puffiness of our recent calls, and she wore that guileless smile of hers—the one she and Dan had always shared.

Emma touched my scarf. "That's so pretty. What happened to the other one?" Her voice drifted off as her hand fell to her side.

"The police still have it. I don't want it back, if that's what you're asking." I paused. "I'd like to stop by JoJo's boutique this afternoon. She received a shipment of scarves from a new artist. Abstract florals, and they look heavenly online."

"Sounds like fun. I'm so glad you came. Admit it, you loved leaving Stonebridge, even for a couple of days."

If she only knew. I laughed, not ready to reveal my decision. Not yet.

Emma tipped her chin. "Something's up. I know you, so spill the tea."

"It's nothing." I shook myself back to the present. "I'm just so happy to be here, away from all thoughts of murder."

Our server appeared from nowhere, his glance darting between us while taking our order.

"Who's your latest suspect?"

I filled Emma in on Tiffanee's sneaky camera habits, William's secret, Parker and Kendall's affair, and Harmony's suspicions that Hunter was too involved with Tiffanee.

"Blackmail and deep, dark, hidden secrets. If they never arrested the bookstore guy, is his secret worth killing for?"

"I doubt the good residents of Stonebridge would want a drug dealer running the local bookstore," I said.

"That other couple's story sure sounds juicy," Emma said.

"You're not wrong," I said. "A young guy whose wife is about to have a baby and an older socialite. They've both got motives." I left it at that, knowing Emma would worry if she heard about Kendall's visit or Parker's threats.

Our lunches appeared, and I poked at my salad, letting the subject drop. Thoughts of murder were ruining my appetite. "How are things with Ryan?"

Emma looked down, pushing onions to the edge of her plate. "Okay, I guess."

I held my tongue and watched the gears spinning in my daughter's mind.

"We're both trying. It's like you said, we're adjusting to being out of college." She stabbed a tomato and lifted it to her mouth. "Can we talk about something else?"

"Let's talk about this afternoon." I spied our hands resting on the table. "I have an idea. Let's see if the salon can squeeze us in for a manicure."

"That would be awesome. I miss that."

"It's settled. No cheating hearts or murders today."

Emma crinkled her nose. "The Cheating Heart Murders. It sounds like one of those silly mysteries you're always reading."

I jolted at Emma's words, wondering whether Tiffanee and Hunter's murders would look like a mystery novel if they hadn't been real. I pushed the thought to the back of my mind. No sleuthing either.

The afternoon flew by in a flurry of shopping and laughter. It was like I'd never left Boston. Sporting freshly polished nails—turquoise for Emma and bright coral for me—we'd strolled the sidewalks, our worries all but forgotten. With three new scarves in my shopping bag and a box of signature chocolate mice from L. A. Burdick's, my family's favorite chocolatier, both my heart and wallet were decidedly lighter.

Alicia was waiting on the sidewalk outside the North End restaurant when Emma and I stepped from our taxi. She had come straight from her meeting with a vendor, wearing navy trousers with a boucle jacket and looking like the savvy urbanite she used to be. Her erect posture and relaxed smile told of a successful meeting. After a round of hugs, she appraised me with a raised eyebrow.

"New scarf?"

"Mm-hmm." I was wearing the bright strip of floral silk like a headband. I'd changed at the hotel, where I'd checked in and dropped off my shopping bags. Dressed in a soft white halter top and linen skirt, I felt unquestionably Bostonian.

Alicia nodded her approval while signaling for the maître d'hôtel.

Emma peered down the sidewalk. "Don't forget Ryan is meeting us, too."

"Our table is right there." Alicia pointed toward the sidewalk patio. "Ryan will see us. These blasted shoes are killing my feet."

Emma and I gaped at Alicia's sensible low-heeled slingbacks and tried, unsuccessfully, to conceal our amusement.

"Ha, ha." Alicia drew out the two syllables. "What's with all these cobblestones, anyway?"

"Darn Boston for being so historic," I teased, remembering how we hadn't thought twice about cobblestones during our high school and college days. The Sullivan sisters hitting the town—in stilettos, no less—seemed like ancient history.

"Let's go sit."

Hesitant at first, Emma gave in, satisfied with the visibility of our table. She wore her worried expression like a sheath.

"Let's order a bottle of wine while we wait. What do you say, ladies? Chianti?" Alicia lifted a finger to flag down our server for a wine list.

Emma fidgeted while we chatted, and I placed a hand on her arm. "Let's enjoy the evening. Ryan probably got detained at work. You know how it is."

"Men," Alicia said.

The sommelier poured our wine, and I raised my glass. "Cheers. To a night in the city."

Emma's phone chimed. She read the text message, and her face fell. "Ryan's stuck at the office. He says to order without him."

"It happens." Alicia's gentle tone softened her curt words.

Beneath the table, I clenched my fists, fingers crossed. "I'm sure he'll do his best." I wasn't. I sipped my wine, preventing the words I really wanted to say from slipping out. The wine calmed me, but Emma looked crushed, and I was struggling to keep my temper in check.

"Let's do it up," I finally said. "Appetizer, soup, salad, entrée. Ryan will make it, eventually."

"I'm all for that," Alicia said.

Emma glanced from me to Alicia and back again, her face brightening. She lifted her menu and peeked over the top. "Let's start with calamari."

Alicia's eyes met mine in a knowing glance. Disaster averted for now. If not for the drama, the slow dinner of Italian cuisine on a brick sidewalk in my home city would be my idea of heaven. As our server cleared each course, Emma's mood plummeted. I wanted to wring Ryan's little white-collared, executive-in-the-making neck. He finally appeared when the server returned to recite the dessert menu. My watch glowed nine-thirty.

Emma jumped up and hugged him on tiptoe, smiling from ear to ear.

Ryan pulled on his tie. "I'm terribly sorry. New job. You understand."

I took in his dark gray suit and his red tie, loosened to match his disheveled hair. The smell of alcohol preceded our hasty hug. He reeked of it. No, I did not understand.

Ryan sat in the empty seat next to Emma. "How's it going, babe?" I had to hand it to him; he wasn't slurring his words. He held Emma's hand in her lap. When she leaned toward him, her smile faded.

"Can you excuse me for a minute? I think I need to use the powder room before dessert." Emma hurried away, nearly stumbling.

I waited until my daughter was out of sight to unleash my indignation. "What's the matter with you?"

With a sharp thrust of his chin, Ryan crossed his arms.

I spoke in a low, stern voice, "How dare you tell Emma you're working late and then show up here drunk? Completely drunk."

"Maybe you aren't familiar with today's office environment, but I was working. It got late, so we took it to the bar." He humored me with an impish grin that, without a doubt, charmed countless young women, my daughter included. I wasn't buying it.

The arch of Alicia's eyebrow said what she thought of my daughter's boyfriend, but she remained silent.

Heat crept up my neck, and I was sure my face was a splotchy red. How dare he treat me like I didn't understand office culture? I understood it all too well. It was the reason it had been so easy to quit my job. Getting drunk with coworkers, though—that had never been required.

"That is complete and utter malarky, and don't for one minute think you have me fooled. Emma deserves better."

Ryan opened and closed his mouth, leaving me to imagine the lame excuse he was smart enough to hold back. I'd always liked Ryan, and he knew it. My about-face, I hoped, put him on notice.

"Grow up," I said.

Ryan lifted his gaze, clearing his expression as he stood. Emma walked toward us and lowered to her seat. She glanced at each of us before raising her chin and giving Ryan a weak smile. "What did I miss?" Her face wore its telltale puffiness, but she'd glossed her lips with a fresh coat of soft pink lipstick.

When Ryan spoke, his voice rang with a false nonchalance. "We were catching up."

I twirled the stem of my wine glass, not trusting myself to speak.

"I'm sorry, babe, but I better get going. I have a meeting first thing tomorrow." Ryan dropped Emma's hand.

"You're leaving?" Emma's voice cracked. "I've been waiting all evening, and you just got here."

"Yeah, sorry. I'll call you tomorrow."

Emma's mouth made a small pink circle while she watched him walk away. Ryan's retreating back was barely out of sight when she turned to me. "This is your fault. What did you say to him?"

"Emma, you noticed how drunk he was."

"Yes, I noticed. It was none of your business."

I reached for her arm, but she jerked away.

"You said something to him, didn't you? That's why he left." Accusation filled her voice. "I'm going home. I don't even want to know what you said, but next time, stay out of it!" She stood, giving Alicia a quick hug, then in one swift movement, she whirled and stomped away, her curls bouncing with every angry step.

As the sound of Emma's heels faded, Alicia spoke in a monotone, dripping with sarcasm. "That went well." She tipped her head toward our server, who arrived with three desserts and three forks. "I hope you're still hungry."

I watched as the server placed the chocolate-laden plates on the table. There was nothing like wallowing in the comfort of sugar to mend an aching heart. "Between the two of us, we can definitely polish these off."

The gooey chocolate cake oozed with creamy pudding, but Emma's words rang in my ears. *Stay out of it.* It was the second time in as many nights I'd heard these words. From the people I loved most.

Chapter Thirty

Settled on the hotel's stiff sofa, my stomach was ready to burst. So much for the comfort of chocolate. I nursed a cup of herbal tea, my legs curled beneath me. The room was nothing special except for its fantastic view of the city skyline. I had swept the drapes wide open before settling in for our sleepover.

"Emma will come around," Alicia said after listening to me wail in a way I could only do with my sister.

Steam rose from the mug I held in my lap. Normally, I found the scent of chamomile and lavender soporific, but I was much too riled up. "What was Emma's plan? Go to the bathroom and cry, then come back with a fresh coat of lipstick, pretending everything was hunky-dory?"

"I think her plan was to not make a scene."

"You can't tell me you weren't feeling protective of her." My anger rose all over again.

"We have to let our grown children make their own mistakes, Bobbie." Alicia blew over the top of her mug. "All right, yes. I wanted to punch Ryan right in that smug smile of his."

I flashed an *I told you so* smile.

"Emma's all grown up," Alicia said in response. "She needs to fight her own battles."

Easy for Alicia to say. She had sons. Sons were different—not that I'd experienced it firsthand. I sipped my tea, its warmth soothing me. Okay, I'd messed up. While changing into my pajamas, I'd tried to call Emma, but my calls went straight to voicemail. I set my cup down and collapsed onto the cushions, thinking of Rose.

"There's something you're holding back," Alicia said.

I explained about my run-in with William and my call to warn Rose.

Alicia nodded. "You're on quite a roll."

"Don't I know it. I only wanted to keep Rose safe."

Alicia opened the box of chocolate mice, their little heads peeking over the top. The handmade mice were the signature confection of the chocolatier, and I knew the familiar treat would make her smile. "There's something else going on. Lay it on me." She pulled a tiny mouse from the box, holding it by its skinny ribbon tail.

I wasn't ready to talk about moving back to Boston. I shrugged, hugging the warm mug to my chest.

"Let's have it." Alicia's brown eyes chipped through the wall I was feverishly trying to erect.

"I want to move back home—to Boston." My hand flew to my mouth. I hadn't meant to say it, but my sister always knocked my guard down. Before Alicia responded, I surged ahead. "I love my new house, I do, and being close to you and Nate. But it's not working out. Everyone thinks I'm a killer. My best friend isn't speaking to me, and why did I ever think I could leave home?" I circled my index finger in the air. "This is the only home I've ever known." Hot tears threatened to spill.

Alicia set her mug on the coffee table and grasped my hand. "Would it surprise you if I told you I know how you feel?"

I nodded, unable to speak. What was she talking about? She was the strongest, most self-confident person I'd ever known. Well, except for our mother, who she clearly took after.

"What do you think my life was like when I first moved to Stonebridge? Nate and I were newly married, and we lived on the farm with his parents, for heaven's sake." Alicia chuckled as she reminisced. "Nate was busy establishing his law practice, and I was learning farm chores. Me, of all people. Everyone thought I was a snobby city girl—which, admittedly, I was—and there were more than a few of Nate's old classmates who were none too pleased he'd chosen me for his wife."

"I had no idea," I whispered.

"You wouldn't have known. You were finishing college and starting your own life with Dan." She paused. "The twins were born, and once we'd finally gotten them into school and bought the market, Nate's dad passed away. After a couple of years of trying to keep up with the farm and failing, we finally let the dairy go. It was hard, but I wouldn't trade any of it."

"I'm not you." I pinched my lids tight, a tear trickling down my cheek. "You've always been so strong, like our mother."

Alicia gave my fingers a gentle squeeze. "You're stronger than you know. You've been through a lot this past year. I don't know what I'd do if Nate took off for work in the morning and I got a phone call like you did."

I'd never forget that day. It had started like any other—getting out of bed in the morning, a hurried kiss as we left for work. Then, I'd been on my way to lunch when my phone rang. Dan's coworker had called to tell me he'd collapsed and been rushed to the hospital. By the time I got there, he was already gone. Dead from a brain aneurysm.

"I never got to say goodbye."

Alicia wiped my tears. "I know, sweetie. You expected this move to magically change things. But life doesn't work that way. You're following your own path right now. There are bound to be lots of twists and turns and bumps along the way. I think you need to see it through."

Tears streamed down my cheeks. I nodded, unconvinced I could stay in Stonebridge, but I promised myself to give it more thought.

Alicia let go of my hand. "I'm thinking the only way to get past this mess is to figure out who the killer is."

I swiped the tears from my cheeks. "Parker, it's got to be."

Alicia bit off the mouse's chocolate head. It amazed me she had even a smidgen of room left in her stomach. The lights of the city shimmered in the inky sky, and I switched off the lamp.

Alicia licked chocolate from her lips. "What about Tiffanee's email to William? Drug dealing is a pretty big motive, don't you think?"

"Sure, but William seems too level-headed. Besides, it would've all come out, eventually."

Alicia's expression turned thoughtful. "What if Tiffanee pushed too hard? Maybe he killed her in the heat of the moment. And, since your scarf was on the bench outside his store, he definitely had access."

"I really hope that's not true. William and Rose are adorable together. I want that for her."

"Okay, so we know that both Kendall and Parker lied," Alicia said. "They have a big secret, and I don't like the way he threatened us."

"They were fighting on the village green last night when I took Darcy for a walk. I wonder if finding out about Kendall's visit made Parker panic."

"It's kind of weird the way Kendall's come out of the woodwork suddenly. She's always been a customer in the market, but all these random sightings in the village are more than a little strange." Alicia dangled her headless mouse, peering at it as though it might squeak an answer.

"Kendall seems like someone used to getting what she wants. What if she demanded the photos from Tiffanee and Tiffanee refused?"

"She's like a spoiled child—an extremely cunning one."

An image of Kendall reading on the park bench popped into my head. "I can't picture her strangling Tiffanee by the river. She was wearing very pricey spiked heels."

"Not only that, but she'd have put herself in danger of a chipped nail." Alicia chuckled. "You're forgetting one person. The one person who we know had ties with both Tiffanee and Hunter."

"Penny." I sighed.

"You're being blinded by your soft spot for her."

My sister wasn't wrong about my soft spot, but I hadn't crossed Penny off my suspect list. Remembering my conversation with Harmony, I said, "She doesn't have a motive."

"No? Are you forgetting her secret baby?" The look of disbelief on Alicia's face made me want to push her eyebrows back down her forehead where they belonged.

"She was planning to tell Hunter about Hope. Harmony told me." *So there.* I sat back with a feeling of satisfaction I knew was childish.

"So she says." Clearly, Alicia was unconvinced. "All I'm saying is that you need to be careful."

I turned to face Alicia with my arms crossed. "The only suspects left on my list are the Righteous Sisters. What if they're behind the whole thing?"

"The church ladies?" Alicia laughed.

"Maybe they're behind the Stonebridge Scandal and leading the entire village on a wild goose chase. Maybe one of them is the killer. Maybe all of them."

"I wouldn't mind pinning it on Lorraine Adams."

"Right?" I laughed, knowing I was wrong, but couldn't help myself. "Lorraine might have been Tiffanee's aunt, but she's not very nice."

"Not a motive."

"Sure, but what if Tiffanee had something on her—something that would damage her pious image?"

"Hmm." Alicia seemed to consider the idea. "Nope, not buying it."

"All right then," I said. "Bernadine is Penny's mom. She seems kind of controlling."

Alicia sat upright. "That might not be as crazy as it sounds. But it's not much of a motive. And you never knew Tiffanee's mother. Believe me, Bernadine practically raised Tiffanee along with Penny."

"That leaves Vickie Sue, and honestly, she seems kind of nice."

"It's always the quiet ones." Alicia licked chocolate from her bottom lip.

"It's not her." An image of Vickie Sue's worried whispers in the bookstore played in my mind. She'd seemed genuinely scared.

"Too bad Jackson's alibi checked out," Alicia said. "But then, being a jerk isn't a motive, either."

I sipped my tea, thinking about Jackson. "What I don't get is why he keeps telling the detective things that incriminate me."

Standing, Alicia said, "I'd say we've narrowed it down to Parker, Kendall, and Penny. It's getting late, and I'd better hit the sack. I plan to get the heck out of Dodge before the infamous Boston rush hour."

I dove onto my bed. "Before I head home tomorrow, I'm meeting some friends. I may not be awake when you leave." I hadn't seen Cindi and Jenna since leaving Boston. They'd been my tribe, and I was beyond excited to catch up. I couldn't wait to see their reaction to the news that I might move back.

The next day, I left Boston enveloped in despondence. I felt lost. It wasn't that I couldn't find my way back to Vermont. I could do that in my sleep. But I couldn't shake the feeling of being adrift. My fingertips rested on the steering wheel, their cheerful coral lacquer mocking me. Had it been only one day since I'd been so buoyant, floating on my dreams of returning home? My heart sank to the pit of my stomach, along with my dreams. After living in Vermont for merely four months, Boston no longer felt like home.

Concentrating on the road ahead, I blinked away tears. I had scarcely been able to contain my excitement over getting together with my two former best friends. The trip from the hotel to my old neighborhood in Jamaica Plain was a few quick stops on the subway, and nostalgia overtook me as I sat in the jerky, screeching car. I couldn't help picturing my friends' expressions when I told them about my idea to move back to Boston, knowing they'd be as excited as I was.

Or so I'd imagined.

We'd met at our favorite coffee shop, a popular upscale bistro bustling with customers from sunup to sundown. It swam with the aromas of locally roasted coffee and homemade bagels I swore were every bit as good as ones from New York City. I was biased, but that didn't make me wrong.

It had been like old times at first. Cindi had barged inside, grabbing the one empty table in the small seating area. Customers sat at long, industrial-style tables, bent over their laptops—a fresh wave of coffee shop entrepreneurs. The only people who did that in Vermont were the weekenders. Well, and me.

"Get me a chai latte with almond milk." Cindi brushed crumbs from the table with a napkin as she staked our claim. Lively and full of chatter, Cindi and Jenna were exactly as I remembered them. Unlike me, they still had teenagers, and they bantered about the soccer team and the hot new English teacher their daughters had crushes on. I remembered sharing similar conversations over the years, but listening to my friends laughing over a flippant comment made by Cindi's youngest, I felt detached.

I stared out the window, lost in my thoughts, and Jenna tapped my arm. "You're so lucky Emma has already finished school. How is life in Vermont going?"

"Did I hear something about a murder? Did that happen near where you live?" Cindi leaned on the table, primed to hear a shocking tale.

"You heard about that?" I took in my friends' eager expressions and inhaled deeply, preparing to tell my tale of woe. But then, something held me back. Something made me want to keep that part of my life private. "Yeah, it was pretty close to me." A chasm opened between us, wide and deep. How had we gotten to a place where my two best friends knew nothing about my new life? It wasn't their fault, I knew, but still.

Driving back to Vermont, traffic was light. Miles rushed past, miles that morphed from city to suburb and eventually to dense forest. A heaviness settled in my chest. I couldn't move back to Boston. It was no longer my home. I feared before long, my friendships with Jenna and Cindi would be nothing more than exchanging Christmas cards and the occasional happy-face emoji on social media—if I ever reopened my profiles. I'd been naïve to think I could go back to my old life.

My phone rang, jarring me from my reverie. Refocusing on the highway ahead, I spied my console with barely contained excitement when Rose's name appeared.

Before I'd even had a chance to say hello, she rushed right in, her words clipped. "I thought you should know the police are snooping around your yard."

Chapter Thirty-One

My heart jumped to my throat. Why were the police in my yard? I was unable to speak before Rose continued. "That's all I know. It looks like they're searching for something." She was all business.

Still angry.

I counted to five, calming my nerves. "The rifle. They must be looking for it."

"Like I said, I don't know what they're doing, but I thought someone should tell you. I've got to go."

"Thanks," I said at the same time the call cut off. *Okay—definitely still angry.* My fleeting moment of hope was crushed.

What to do about the police? My mind swirled, but one coherent thought formed. *Call Nate.* Issuing a voice command, I was relieved when Nate's administrative assistant answered my call.

"I need to speak with Nate right away. It's urgent." Realizing how rude I'd been, I quickly corrected myself. "Sorry. Good afternoon. This is Bobbie Brooks. Is Nate available, please?"

Nate's assistant chuckled. "No worries. I'll see if he's free."

Drumming my fingers on the steering wheel, I tried to concentrate on the road.

Nate's voice came on the line. "What's going on? Have you left Boston?"

"I think I need help. The police are at my house."

"You're home already?" I pictured him checking his watch.

"Not yet. I'm on my way. Rose called me." My voice grew more feverish with each word. "She says the police are wandering around my yard. Why are they doing that? Don't they need a warrant or something?"

"You're driving? Stay calm. I'll head over to your house. And yes, they need a warrant. How long until you're home?"

I looked up, unsure of where I was. Mountains loomed before me, and I recognized the stretch of highway. "I just crossed the state border. It'll be about an hour."

"I'm heading to your house now. When I learn more, I'll give you a buzz."

I sighed with relief. Alicia wasn't the only one who wouldn't know what to do without Nate.

"Drive carefully. I mean it. We'll take care of whatever this is."

With each breath, I counted slowly to calm my heart. The police must be searching my yard for the missing rifle. What else could it be? I jolted. Another body? No way I could live there if they found a dead body behind my house.

Breathe.

I resumed my mental count. No, it had to be the rifle. But why my yard?

It wasn't long before Nate called with the news—they had found a rifle under a bush near my barn.

"I don't understand." I gulped a breath before continuing. "What made them think of searching there? It's not like I even know how to shoot."

"An anonymous phone call, apparently. You're what, about thirty minutes away?"

"Sounds about right."

"I'm going to run back home and get Darcy. I'll be at your house when you get here. I'll let Detective Cram know we'll be at the station in, say, forty-five minutes."

Nate's guestimate had been spot-on. Approximately thirty minutes later, I pulled into my driveway. A relieved sigh escaped upon seeing his familiar sedan parked in front of my house. Our conversation played through my mind in an endless loop. The police had found a rifle under a bush near my barn, the tip coming from an anonymous phone call. *How convenient.*

I jumped from my car and gave an automatic wave toward Mr. Miller's porch. Nate was already standing in my doorway, Darcy at his heels. Ruffling Darcy's fur, I bent to kiss his head. His wagging tail never failed to calm me. He didn't care I was such a mess.

"I know nothing more than what I told you on the phone." Nate's uncharacteristic dismissal of his usual cordial greeting made me more nervous than I already was.

I searched his eyes, hoping to find answers hidden in what he wasn't saying.

"Detective Cram is expecting us. Let's take my car; I need to head straight back to my office afterward. We can talk on the way."

I gave Darcy's head another scratch on my way out the door. I thought he was happy to see me, but he looked beat. Two days with his doggy cousins would do that. "Have a good nap," I said with envy while closing the door.

"Do you know anything about this rifle?" Nate asked as soon as I climbed into his car.

"No!" I immediately regretted my tone of voice. Nate was on my side. "Sorry."

"I had to ask. Let's confirm you don't own a rifle."

"You know me. I never even let Dan bring one into our house. He only went shooting when we visited you."

"I thought as much," Nate said. "Any idea how a rifle came to be in your yard?"

"Where was it, exactly?"

"Sticking out from under the bush close to your barn door."

"Basically, right near the threatening note."

"Seems an unlikely coincidence." Nate pulled into a parking space outside the state police barracks. "It should go without saying the police won't find your fingerprints on the rifle."

"I can't imagine how."

He sat for a moment before opening his car door, appearing to give it thought. "They won't be able to hold you. You've been away, and anyone could have planted the rifle." We walked along the sidewalk in front of the police station, and Nate stopped. "You remember the drill. Brief answers, and if I place my hand on your arm, stop talking."

"Got it."

An overwhelming sense of déjà vu came over me when we entered the building. Olivia greeted us, led us down the same nauseating corridor to the same white-gray cell of a room, and Detective Cram led me through a series of questions that left me dizzy. The most interesting piece of information I gleaned from the conversation was that Vermont had no firearms registration, which meant there was no way to trace the owner of the rifle. I was shocked to learn this, but Nate merely nodded, confirming the detective's words.

After answering what seemed like a multitude of meaningless questions and being told that running to Boston wouldn't save me from arrest, Nate and I walked back to the reception area. Annoyance and concern mixed in his soft hazel eyes. It was the concerned part I found worrisome.

We'd almost reached the door of the police station when Olivia's voice came from behind us. "It was nice to see you, Mr. Crowley. Have a pleasant evening."

Nate turned with a smile. "Same to you, Olivia. I suspect you'll be seeing more of us before this is over."

Olivia sported a fresh coat of lip gloss. She nodded, seemingly eager to please my attorney. "I hope—oops—I mean, thanks." Her face beamed as she picked up her ringing phone.

Nate and I stepped out to the sidewalk, his face an unreadable mask.

I wiped my slick palms on my jeans. "I was getting worried in there."

"I know you were," Nate said. "It seemed best not to engage too much. It's interesting he knew you were in Boston."

"I was thinking the same. But then, you know this village. We're all in each other's business."

Nate's forehead creased. "I don't blame you for thinking otherwise, but truthfully, he's a decent detective. His style could use a little work."

I huffed out a breath. "You're right about me thinking otherwise."

"At this point, he doesn't have enough evidence. Since your fingerprints won't be found on the rifle, you should be okay."

I swallowed, meeting Nate's steady gaze. "You know as well as I do there won't be *any* prints on the rifle. That's almost worse. He'll say I wiped it clean. He's building a case of circumstantial evidence. I could be arrested."

"I doubt it will come to that, but we'll cross that bridge if we need to." He paused. "I heard about you running into William the other night."

"Rose is barely speaking with me. I'm hoping she'll understand I was only trying to protect her."

Nate's expression was sympathetic, but when he spoke, his voice was somber. "William isn't the killer."

I couldn't believe Nate would deliver such a crucial piece of information as if it didn't matter. "What do you mean, William isn't the killer?"

Chapter Thirty-Two

I stared at Nate, waiting for an explanation. When he didn't say anything, I asked, "How can you possibly know?"

Nate drew in a deep breath. "Let's just say I'm his alibi," he said.

I let Nate's words sink in. Oh, attorney-client privilege. Was Nate helping William with the drug accusation? That must have been the reason William had been frazzled and closed the store early. I would be eating a heaping serving of humble pie the next time I talked to Rose. But first, I needed to tell Nate about Parker and Kendall.

Nate checked his watch. "You look like you have something you want to say."

I hemmed and hawed, knowing it was best to just spit it out. Nate would likely be angry when he heard about the photos I'd stolen from Tiffanee's house. Alicia was right. I was on a roll.

"I came into contact with one of Tiffanee's old memory cards," I said, ignoring Nate's skeptical expression. I told him about the photo of Kendall and Parker.

"Kendall Lee?" Nate scoffed. "You're way off base here."

"She has a lot to lose, though, doesn't she? She lied about not being in town the day Tiffanee was killed, and she stopped by my house on a fishing expedition. Darcy even growled at her. She's looking for Tiffanee's photos."

Nate didn't answer right away. Staring into the distance, he appeared to be mulling over my words. "Let me think on this," he said finally. "I've been friends with her husband for several years. It seems like a long shot, but I can't deny that Kendall is crafty. In the meantime, I won't ask how you came into contact with the memory card." He was quoting my words back to me, twisting his lips as he spoke. "Hang onto it, and please don't say or do anything to add ammunition to Detective Cram's case."

I saluted crisply, thankful he'd not only let my possession of the memory card go but hadn't specifically demanded I stay out of the investigation. I was already in too deep.

After Nate and I parted on the sidewalk, I walked straight home. As I trudged up my porch stairs, I raised my hand in an automatic wave to my next-door neighbor. At least, I assumed he was there, sitting in his usual chair, watching the village. I jiggled my key in the lock and froze, struck with a sudden thought. Letting go of the doorknob, I twisted to look at Mr. Miller, giving my idea a moment to percolate. My neighbor had his usual look of indifference, but from his daily perch, I was certain he observed everything happening in this little corner of the village. Had Detective Cram questioned him? One would hope so, but I wasn't feeling magnanimous. If I wanted the killer caught, it was going to be up to me.

With a new feeling of anger-fueled determination, I strode to my kitchen. Darcy lay on the floor, barely managing a tail thump when I entered. He had the zonked look of contentment. My plan needed a peace offering, a bribe for information. This was one of those countless times I wished I were more like Alicia. I flung my freezer open, sorting through my meager assortment of frozen items until I found it—one of my sister's coveted macaroni and cheese casseroles.

Perfect. Mr. Miller would need superhuman strength to resist this offering. Armed with my cheesy weapon, I slammed my freezer shut and marched back outdoors and across the lawn.

"Good afternoon, Mr. Miller." I announced my presence as if inviting myself to his porch was a normal occurrence. With my fingers crossed behind my back, I held up the foil-wrapped package. "I have more food than I can eat, and I thought you might help me out. It's Alicia's famous macaroni and cheese, which everyone thinks is delicious. I mean, of course they do, because it is." Good heavens, I was babbling. I closed my mouth and thrust the casserole toward my neighbor.

Mr. Miller remained seated, rocking slowly. I shifted from one foot to the other. Maybe this hadn't been a good idea. I stepped backward, losing my nerve, when he reached out and lifted the frozen package from my hand. "Well, now, I'd be a fool to turn down anything Alicia Crowley made."

"For sure," I said. "I hope you enjoy it." I leaned against his porch railing, observing the village green across the street. "You know, it's funny how different our view is even though we live right next door." I wasn't making small talk. The difference truly surprised me.

The massive maple tree sitting across from my house did little to obstruct my neighbor's panorama. From Mr. Miller's porch railing, the village green spread out before me with its white gazebo and crisscrossing sidewalks. My gaze followed a path leading to the shops lining Green Street on the opposite side, including Long Trail Booksellers and Harmony's Heart and Harmony Yoga Studio. Following the line of his porch railing to the side opposite my house, the church's front lawn ended at the corner where Main Street and Bridge Street intersected. Mr. Miller's porch was an ideal place to keep watch on the daily happenings in the village.

"Is that so?" Mr. Miller drew out the words.

I spun around and thought I detected the barest hint of a smile. "Someone planted the rifle in my yard while I was away. *The* rifle."

"Yup." He continued rocking. "An awful lot of ruckus back there today."

"I don't own a rifle," I said. "I can't help wondering who owned one and wanted both Tiffanee and Hunter dead."

A low rumbling, which I thought resembled a chuckle, sounded from behind his grizzly beard.

"What's so funny?"

"You wonder who might own a rifle?" He chuckled again. "Around here, rifles are like woodstoves. Most houses have at least one."

"Do you?" I asked.

With a slight dip of his chin, he continued rocking.

Whether my neighbor owned a rifle was beside the point. I needed to stay on track. "I don't suppose you saw anything. Suspicious, that is."

Mr. Miller rocked for another moment. I thought he might ignore my question completely. Then he gave a slight nod and said, "The morning that fella was shot, I might've seen someone out back."

My breath caught. "Did you see who it was?"

His head moved slowly from side to side. "They were like a shadow moving through the trees. Dark clothes."

I tried to hide my disappointment. "Do you think that's when they hid the rifle?"

"Could be," he said.

I waited for him to say more. But after a moment, he stood and uttered a begrudging thanks, and headed to his front door.

"Heating instructions are on the sticky note," I called to his back as the door banged behind him.

That had gone as well as could be expected. Encouraged by his chuckle and almost smile, I lumbered back to the sidewalk, lost in thought. The morning Hunter was shot, Mr. Miller had seen someone in the woods. Assuming they'd planted the rifle by my barn, where had they gone afterward? The woods ended behind Rose's café. Walking between our back yards would have been risky, unless they'd known we were at yoga class.

It would have been easier to backtrack through the woods, cross Main Street at the corner of Bridge Street, and join the crowd on the village green. I gasped at the idea. The scene had been mayhem, the perfect place for a killer to hide.

Chapter Thirty-Three

The next day, I worked my way through a pile of laundry and household chores I'd neglected over the past several days. If it hadn't been for our photography club meeting that evening, I would have been content to stay in my sweats, camp in front of my television, and gorge myself on a humongous bowl of buttery popcorn.

Indulging my mostly non-existent introverted side was not to be. I dressed for the meeting and tied one of my new scarves around my ponytail, hoping the colorful silk might miraculously lift my spirits. An ominous gray sky mirrored my mood when I ran to the village market for refreshments. Upon my return with a package of cheerfully frosted cupcakes tucked under my arm, the clouds opened, and a torrential rain buffeted my house.

As I pulled a white stoneware platter from my cupboard, Darcy slinked past me, his belly brushing the ground. He was one of the most laid-back dogs I knew, but storms turned him into a cowering bundle of nerves. He'd probably spend the rest of the evening trembling on the floor next to my bed.

"Poor baby." I patted his head and washed my hands before returning to my task of arranging the cupcakes. Then, remembering how Jackson had devoured all the cookies at our last meeting, I set a pretty pink one aside for later. Alicia had specifically recommended them, and I wasn't about to miss out on the sugary confection. I couldn't wait to snuggle beneath my blankets with a book, a cupcake, and a hot cup of tea. My club members would soon arrive, and that particular treat would have to wait.

Still proud of myself for mastering my complicated coffee machine, I scooped beans into the grinder, thinking about Rose. I hoped to get a private moment with her, one where I could apologize. I owed her that much. Hopefully, she'd forgive me.

The coffee machine gurgled, filling the kitchen with its warm scent. I'd spent too much time with Tiffanee's photos, going back to them after crossing Williams's name off my chart of suspects. As a result, I'd neglected to prepare my own for the meeting. With everything that had happened at our photo shoot, I was sure the few pictures I'd snapped needed some serious work before presenting them. An idea took form. I'd use my raw images to walk the group through my editing process, inviting them to help. The club was about learning, after all.

Footsteps sounded on my porch as I carried the coffee carafe to my living room. "Come in," I called, setting it next to the cupcakes before racing to the door. When the door swung open, Rose, Alicia, and Penny blew in like a storm. They stomped their feet and shook their umbrellas while I hung their jackets on the coat rack. Only Alicia seemed unfazed as she pulled her blonde ponytail from under her sweater.

"Whoa." Jackson came running up my porch steps. "I didn't think we had monsoons in Vermont."

"No Darcy?" Alicia asked, a dog biscuit in hand.

"Thunder." I gestured toward the stairs, and Alicia responded with a knowing smile before joining the other members in the living room. Rubbing their hands and chattering about their trek in the deluge, they gathered to pour themselves coffee and settle on my couches while I prepared my computer to project to a wide screen. I was relieved to note they had all brought the requested flash drives.

Jackson devoured a cupcake, a second one balanced on his thigh. Penny sat next to him, nibbling an edge of frosting, while Alicia poured a steaming cup of coffee. Rose was silent, her hands folded in her lap.

"Before we begin, does anyone have questions or something they'd like to share with the group?" Undeterred by their silence, I forged on, determined this meeting wouldn't turn into a repeat of our last one. "Before we review our photos, let's have a discussion about constructive criticism."

Jackson scoffed. "We're all adults here."

"That's true." I managed a tight smile. "As adults, we know how destructive it can be to tear each other down." I thought back to Tiffanee's harsh comments about Penny's lack of a camera before adding, "This club is a safe place for learning and sharing ideas."

Penny sat with her arms crossed. "What if we don't want to share?"

My eyes sought the young woman's, whose baggy T-shirt and slumped posture made her look dejected. Clearly, not the vibe I was going for. When I first started with photography, sharing my work had been the hardest part. Learning about lighting and composition had been nothing compared to opening myself to criticism. I understood Penny's hesitation. I also understood her need to get past it.

"You don't have to share," I said with a firm voice. "But if you decide not to, I'll need you to think about what you hope to learn and why you're here."

Alicia placed a hand on Penny's arm. "Bobbie's right. We can help you look at your photos differently. It's the best way to improve."

"Since photography is art, feedback is not about whether we like a particular image or a photographer's style, but what part of the image speaks to us—what works and how the message could be clearer. As we get to know each other better, we'll also become familiar with each other's artistic styles."

With a click of the mouse, I opened one of my unedited photos to an image of a flower. "Admittedly, this is not a great photo. Let's use it as an example for a quick critique. What might make it better?"

"The exposure is terrible. You should give it some oomph." Jackson garbled his words through a mouth full of cupcake.

The harshness of his comment wasn't the example I was hoping for, but I sucked it up and smiled. "Excellent suggestion." As a group, we decided on the correct exposure. Then, Rose and Alicia both made suggestions on different ideas for cropping the image.

"As you can see," I said, "everyone has their own vision. Ultimately, the photographer chooses, because only they know the story they want to tell." I observed the group's thoughtful expressions. "Photos are visual stories. Your suggestions have helped me take a new look at my image. From here, I can decide what further editing I'd like to do."

The members nodded, including Penny, whose knee bounced to the rhythm of her clicking tongue ring.

"Any volunteers to go first?" I understood their reluctance. A tense moment passed before Jackson volunteered, handing me his flash drive.

We worked our way through Jackson's and Alicia's images. The members expressed surprise at the different styles of photography. Alicia had shot larger landscape views, while Jackson made a study of light and shadows hitting the nuts and bolts of the bridge's structure. The discussion was lively as the photography enthusiasts explained their photos and accepted ideas. I stood back, allowing the conversation to flow, interjecting only when I wanted them to dig deeper.

"Okay, Penny, you're up," I said.

"You haven't gone yet." She gripped her flash drive.

"I'll be using mine to show the steps of my editing process."

Both Alicia and Rose offered words of encouragement, while Jackson said, "Come on, they can't be *that* bad."

To my surprise, Penny looked up with a pinched smile and handed me her flash drive.

Alicia playfully nudged Penny as I projected the first image. "Wow, Penny, you took that with your phone?"

"The contrast of the sparkles on the water with the darker interior of the bridge is fantastic," Rose said. "What if we deepened the shadows just a bit more?"

"I was wondering the same." I took in Penny's slouched shoulders, her hesitation. "It's lovely the way it is, but Rose's suggestion might put more emphasis on the river. What do you say?"

Penny nodded. The club suggested several variations before Penny chose the one she liked best. It was a minor change, one that accentuated the setting sun glimmering on the river.

"It's time to vote on our feature image," I said.

"What about yours?" Jackson asked. "We haven't seen them yet."

"Mine won't be included in the vote. After seeing all of yours, they're hardly contenders. The layout for our calendar allows for one large feature image with smaller images from each photographer. Since Rose didn't attend the shoot, she can go out on her own if she likes and submit one later."

"I nominate Penny's," Alicia said. "They were all fantastic, but I think Penny captured the best part of a pretty terrible evening."

Jackson's expression darkened, but he didn't argue. For the first time that evening, Penny allowed a wide smile.

"Time to see yours, Bobbie," Alicia said.

"Bear with me. I'm afraid I'm not as organized as I should be." I opened my photo catalog. "This is the perfect example of do as I say, not as I do. What I have planned is to walk you through the steps of my editing process. With experience, you'll develop your own. We'll even discuss creating presets to streamline it."

I found my file from the previous Thursday and opened it, scrolling through the images of the village green before stopping at my photos of the covered bridge. The room was silent. Penny appeared to be staring at the screen. The click of her tongue was louder than usual through her parted lips. I couldn't help wondering which image had captured her attention.

Projecting my first photo of the bridge, I said, "The first things I'll check when opening an image are lens distortion, white balance, and distortions coming from perspective. If you look closely, you'll see the shadows in this photo have a bluish cast to them. The way a camera interprets light is often surprisingly different from the way our eyes perceive it, and this change alone can have a tremendous impact on how the image looks and feels." I stopped speaking to scan the room. Sometimes, the more technical aspects of photography were confusing. Satisfied they were all with me, I continued. "My style is to make my photos as realistic as possible, but some photographers might go for a more artistic effect and choose to make the shadows even bluer. There's no incorrect choice, as long as it's informed and deliberate." I walked the group through various methods and tools for setting the white balance.

After making the initial corrections, I still had a photo in dire need of critique. "Have at it. Time for the teacher to learn from the students."

The group critiqued my photos with the same animated zeal as the others. My fear they'd be intimidated was unfounded. When we finished, I closed my computer and returned the flash drives while the members chatted amongst themselves, making suggestions for our next photo shoot, as well as the group Rose planned to set up online for sharing photos. I let out a long breath, my tension leaving with it. The Stonebridge Keep It Snappy Shutter Club was feeling like the club I'd dared to dream of—the club I had plastered flyers all over the village for.

As everyone rose to say goodnight, I thanked them for their candor. "Next meeting is two weeks from tonight. We'll talk about upcoming photography challenges and choose the location for our next shoot. Please come with ideas for both."

While the members grabbed their jackets, I tried to stop Rose, hoping for the chance to apologize. But when Alicia opened the door, William was standing on my porch. He looked uncomfortable, his posture rigid and his fists clenched at his sides. The rain had stopped, and the cool evening air had that fresh, earthy scent that came after a storm.

"Hey, William." Rose's cheeks flushed. "I wasn't expecting you."

His expression softened as he looked at Rose. "Would you mind waiting a minute? I'd like to speak with Bobbie first. Then maybe we could go for a walk?"

"For sure." Rose blushed. "I'd really like that."

"I'll wait with you," Alicia said as they stepped out to the porch with Penny and Jackson.

Stepping inside, William closed the door behind him. "I owe you an apology." He lowered the hood of his rain jacket. "I made you uncomfortable the other night, and Rose let me know, in no uncertain terms, she was most unhappy you felt threatened. That wasn't my intention."

I swallowed and reached for the tail of my scarf, rubbing it between my fingers. Despite Rose's anger, she'd been defending me. My heart swelled, and when I lifted my eyes to meet his, I saw the sincerity of his words.

"I should apologize as well. It was unfair of me to jump to conclusions."

A smile played at the corner of his lips. "It's hard not to. I had hoped for a chance to get settled before everyone found out about the student's accusation. My bookstore seemed like a good way to become part of the community. I miss being part of something." His face relaxed, softening, and in that instant, I understood why Rose had never believed he was a killer.

"That makes two of us," I said.

"Thank you for understanding. I won't keep you. Have a good night."

I wished him the same as he joined Rose on the porch. I shut the door, locking it behind him before performing a pirouette in my entry hall. Had that been a successful meeting or what?

The wind continued to howl outside while I called up the stairs to Darcy. Reluctantly, he crept down and followed me to the kitchen, where I let him out back. Noting the empty platter, I was glad I'd had the foresight to set a cupcake aside. I put the kettle on the stove and listened to the wind whistling through the leaves. It provided the perfect backdrop to tuck myself in for a cozy night of reading.

Chapter Thirty-Four

My bedroom was dark, but for the dim light from the yellowed shade of an antique lamp on my nightstand. I snuggled beneath my blankets, pillows propped behind me, a mug of herbal tea clenched in one hand, and a new thriller in the other. My eyes were glued to the page, flying over the words, unable to devour them quickly enough. I lifted the mug to my lips with a shaking hand. I'd forgotten it was empty and had been for the last several pages.

As I set the cup on my nightstand, I looked up from my book. The wind had picked up again, rattling my windows. I jerked at a shadowy movement outside—tree limbs swaying in the wind, silhouetted by the streetlight.

Darcy lay at the foot of the bed—all ninety pounds of him. Dan wouldn't have allowed it, but when I'd crawled into bed, Darcy's pleading eyes had worn me down. To be honest, it hadn't taken much. His warm presence was reassuring. I leaned forward and ruffled his fur before nestling beneath my comforter and returning to my book.

The heroine had entered a dark, creepy warehouse alone. *No, get out of there.* I shivered. No way I could ever be that brave. But this story was fiction. Real people didn't do that. I ran my finger down the page, finding where I'd left off, and continued reading. The heroine prowled into the deepening darkness. My heart was already pounding, but when something thumped outside, I jolted upright, my quilt clenched to my chest.

"Darcy, someone is on the porch," I whispered. He snored soundly, curled at my feet. Now that I was with him, it seemed his earlier fearfulness had disappeared. I chided myself. *Get a grip.* It must have been a broken tree limb falling against the house. I settled back, catching my breath. Reading a thriller was a bad idea. I closed the book and reluctantly set it on my nightstand before switching the lamp off. The heroine's escape would have to wait.

After a fair amount of tossing about, I settled in, smoothing my tangled sheets. Then, from below my bedroom window, another thump came, softer than the last one. I gripped the blanket to my throat, listening. Another light thump and then another. Footsteps. There was no mistaking the sound. Something, or someone, was on my front porch. Darcy lifted his head, his ears perked. Then, silence.

Paralyzed with indecision, my mind raced. The front door rattled, and I flung the covers off me, reaching for my phone. Had I locked the deadbolt? I couldn't remember. Darcy let out a low growl, his body tense and his fur forming a stiff ridge along his neck.

With shaking hands, I grabbed my phone. My finger hovered over the keypad, hesitant. Was I being hysterical? I was convinced the wind wouldn't rattle the doorknob. No sooner had I punched in the numbers 9-1-1, than a crack came from outside. Something slammed against my roof. The hall light went out. Blackness surrounded me.

Sitting on the edge of my bed, I spoke with the emergency dispatcher, my voice a faint whisper. "I think someone is t-trying to break into my house," I said, my hands shaking. The calm voice on the other end of the line was meant to reassure me. It might have worked if Darcy hadn't risen to high alert. With his attention trained on the open bedroom door and stairway beyond, I knew I should be worried.

The rumble in Darcy's throat grew steadily louder while I listened to the dispatcher, whispering answers to questions I barely heard. Downstairs, glass shattered. Darcy jumped from the bed and dashed to the hall, barking.

"Darcy, wait!" I commanded. I grabbed Dan's bathrobe and pushed my arms into the sleeves while rushing out to the hallway. The sound of footsteps came from downstairs—light, but unmistakable. I caught up to Darcy, grasping his collar while fumbling with my phone to enable its flashlight.

When we reached the landing, Darcy barked and pulled from my grasp, bounding down the stairs. I followed, reaching the front hallway in time to see a dark figure, more like a shadow, running toward the kitchen. Racing forward, I shined my flashlight, catching the slightest sparkle as the figure ran out the kitchen door and into the night.

Under my slippered feet, something crunched. Shards of glass glittered in the moonlight. The back door was wide open, its window shattered, and the screen banged in the wind.

It felt like hours passed as I waited, sitting on my bottom step. What I wouldn't have given for Rose to be sitting there with me. She couldn't change what had happened, but having her by my side would have made it all seem okay.

Through the sidelights, a tall figure in a broad hat appeared on my porch. I unlatched the deadbolt and opened the door to Detective Cram.

"Is the intruder still here?" He stepped into the foyer and made wide sweeps with his flashlight.

"They ran out the back door."

"You stay here," he ordered, then strode toward the kitchen. "Power lines are down all over the village."

I held Darcy's collar while I stroked his fur and waited. I didn't think he'd run after the detective, but my dog made no secret of his hostility toward him, and I couldn't be sure.

The wind continued to toss the tree limbs. Clouds raced across the sky, providing momentary glimpses of the moon. A branch tapped against my roof, its incessant scraping adding to the chaos in my mind. That branch was coming down, if I had to climb a ladder with a saw myself. I slumped forward, resting my elbows on my knees.

When Detective Cram returned, he had a young police officer in tow. "They ran away before we got here. We inspected the area outside, but nothing looks disturbed. We'll come back for another look in the morning. It's too dark right now."

I rested my forehead on my knees.

"We can try to secure your door, if you like, but you'll need to call someone to repair the glass. The sooner, the better."

"That's fine," I said. "There should be some plywood in the barn." I stood to retrieve the key from my hall table and handed it to him.

After giving the key to his officer, Detective Cram drew a notepad from his pocket. "Can you tell me everything that happened and what you witnessed?"

With my arm around Darcy's chest, I told him about the noises and the crash of the breaking window. "I didn't see much. When I came downstairs, someone was running to the kitchen. I tried to follow, but they ran out the back door." When I looked up, meeting his gaze, my mouth fell open in surprise. There was no sign of the detective's usual sneer. His expression was almost…caring? Was it possible he had a heart?

He cleared his throat. "Can you describe the person?"

"I don't think so. It was dark, and they were wearing a dark hoodie, I think."

"Large? Small?"

I straightened. "Smallish. I'm sorry, that's really all I could see." I replayed the scene in my mind, unable to remember anything else.

"That's good. Even the smallest detail could be helpful." Detective Cram waited patiently while I thought, his belt buckle glinting. "I saw the tiniest flash of something sparkly."

"Like what? A buckle, a watch, a gem?"

"I really don't know. It could have been any of those things, or even a reflection. It all happened so fast."

"Is there someone you can call tonight?"

Was there? Alicia would insist I go to her house. The thought filled me with a deep sense of weariness. I was too tired for a long, drawn-out discussion and thought it unlikely the intruder would return. It was time I ended my damsel-in-distress routine. Time to rely on myself.

"I'll be fine," I said with more confidence than I felt.

After a sleepless night, I sat on my porch, wrapped in a quilt against the morning chill. Nursing a cup of lukewarm coffee, I watched Stonebridge come to life. Detective Cram had arrived with the early rays of the sun like a strutting rooster. Any goodwill I'd imagined in his expression the night before was gone.

Once again, I'd recounted the events as if they'd happened to someone else. And when Cram had all but accused me of breaking my window in an effort to subvert the ongoing investigation, I couldn't even muster the energy for anger. Eventually, he'd driven away, leaving me feeling listless.

I stared across the village green and lifted my feet, hugging my knees. Shopkeepers arrived for work, the glow in their windows signaling the beginning of another day—another day with no answers. Inside my kitchen, a hammer pounded, and a drill whirred. Connor had planned to get an early start in my studio, but was fixing my kitchen door instead. The ruckus made my head throb. Even so, I was grateful. Despite everything, I knew I was blessed. I needed my heart to feel it more.

My phone rang, jolting me from my thoughts.

"Hi, Alicia. Everything is fine."

"Are you trying to convince me or yourself?"

I cringed at the head-splitting whine of Connor's drill.

"Fantastic. It sounds like Connor is there," Alicia said.

"He's been a godsend," I said.

"Why didn't you call me last night?"

"Because there was nothing to be done, and I can't have you running over here to save me every time something happens, and—I don't know—I'm so tired. I am so very, very tired. I know what you're going to say, so don't. Detective Cram thinks I did this myself. I remain his number one suspect."

"He's got a case of tunnel vision."

"It's not like you to call rather than text, so I'm guessing there's something more."

Alicia was silent for a moment, uncharacteristically hesitant. "You won't like this, and I probably shouldn't tell you right now."

"But..."

"But Emma called me last night to let me know she broke up with Ryan."

A lump lodged in my throat. "She must be devastated. Why didn't she call me?"

"Why do you think? She's still mad at you. I suspect she called me because she knew I'd tell you. I'm sorry to be heaping more on you, but I knew you'd want to know."

I burrowed more deeply into my quilt. "I'll call her."

"Not a good idea," Alicia said. "You can't fix this for her. She needs to work it out herself."

"I have no intention of fixing it." A spark of anger flared, nudging my melancholy aside, if only for a moment. I hated that my sister could always be so practical. The last thing I needed was for her to tell me how to deal with my daughter.

"I'm glad to hear it. Emma needs a little space. She'll come around."

I let my frustration out on a long sigh. Alicia was right, but knowing that didn't make me feel better. No matter how old Emma was, I would never let go of being her mother. Being shut out of her life hurt.

"Look, I'm sorry everything is piling up on you. Emma and I had a long talk. She's good. I assure you she is."

Of course she was. Long ago, Alicia had taken care of my romance dramas. She was good at it. "Thank you for being there for her. Breaking up with Ryan is a big deal."

"Between you and me, she's well rid of him, and I think she understands that. She's going to be a-okay."

"I wish she would speak to me."

"Just give her time, okay?" Alicia's voice had softened.

The drill's shrill whine started again, the sound blowing through the open window.

"So, last night? Someone broke into your house? Is anything missing?"

"As far as I can tell, only my laptop," I said.

"You didn't recognize him or her?"

"It was dark, but they looked small."

"Petite? Like Penny?" Alicia asked.

"Or Kendall. Even Parker, I guess. He's not very tall." I was so tired of this case, of rehashing everything over and over. An incredible feeling of ennui settled over me, and I continued in a low monotone. "Maybe it's not related to the murder."

"What else would it be?"

"I don't know. Kids robbing my house of a valuable piece of equipment? It was an extremely nice MacBook. I take it to the coffee shop all the time."

"I don't buy it. It's too big of a coincidence. Besides, we don't have many robberies like that around here."

"That's what Detective Cram said."

There was noise in the background, customers talking. Alicia's voice filled with impatience. "I've got customers waiting. Keep me posted." My phone clicked. Once again, I was alone.

I continued to rock on my porch, setting my now-cold coffee aside. Next to me, Darcy's throat let out a soft rumble, and I looked up to find Kendall on the sidewalk in front of my house. Her lips curled into a soft smile that didn't look fake.

"I overheard Alicia on the phone just now," she said. "Someone broke into your house?"

I stroked Darcy's fur while regarding my visitor. Hanging at her side, she held a reusable shopping bag with a baguette poking out the top. Just like the morning of Hunter's death, she appeared dressed for a jog in her black leggings and running shoes. Dark clothes, my neighbor had said.

I stood up and walked to my porch railing. "That's right," I said. "My laptop was stolen."

"Just your computer? What was on it?"

I watched her expression closely, confused by what appeared to be genuine concern. "Photos, mostly," I said. "Among the other usual things."

"Someone took your photos?" Her hand flew to her chest. "What do you think they'll do with them?" If she was acting, she was putting on an award-winning performance. She looked worried, and I couldn't help wondering whether she was worried about someone else having her incriminating photo, or worried about being caught.

"Your guess is as good as mine," I paused, considering my next question. "When did you find out about the photo of you and Parker?"

"I don't know, a couple of weeks ago? Parker told me about it. Then, a day or two later, Tiffanee showed it to me."

Parker had lied. I wanted to feel a sense of triumph, but didn't. Besides, I'd already suspected as much. I turned my attention back to Kendall. "She was blackmailing you." It wasn't a question.

Kendall's eyes narrowed. This version of her was one I was more familiar with. "It's not like I'd fall for that. I demanded she give me the photo."

"But she didn't." Again, it wasn't a question. "If you had my laptop, what would you do with it?"

"You can't possibly think I took it," she snapped. Then, letting out a long breath, she added, "If that photo was on your computer, I'd destroy it. It's nothing but trouble."

I nodded slowly. "It's not that simple. The photos are still on the memory card. Besides, my photography software stores the images in the cloud."

"You mean the photos on your computer can't just be destroyed?" Her fingers shook as she grasped and smoothed her ponytail.

"Afraid not." I almost felt sorry for her. "If it makes you feel better, my laptop requires a password or my fingerprint to open it."

"I've got to run." With a jerk, she turned and looked in all directions before running across the street.

I watched as she got into her car and wondered if she'd broken into my house, thinking that destroying my laptop would take care of the incriminating photos. Across the green, Harmony set her sandwich board on the sidewalk, and yogis trickled out her open door. Rose's unmistakable red topknot appeared with the rest of the class. Shops had opened and the quiet village filled with the energy of a new day. As confused as ever, I gathered my cold coffee and warm quilt and trudged back into my house while shooting off a text to Alicia.

We were right - Parker lied

Chapter Thirty-Five

Music played at The Crow, and I bobbed my head as I hummed along. The atmosphere was lively, and I was happy with my spontaneous decision to sit at the bar while waiting for my takeout dinner order. It had been ages since I'd been brave enough to sit at a bar alone. Probably pre-Dan. But there I was, giddy with an inexplicable feeling of something unfamiliar. I wasn't sure what it was. Something light and free and—not me.

I lifted my glass, pushing back a wayward strand of hair before sipping my wine. Hurting from my conversation with Alicia that morning, I'd shaken my lethargy by kneeling in the mud next to the barn and yanking weeds to the whirring of saws. I stretched my legs and smiled. They were sore, the good kind of sore that felt like accomplishment. Let the killer try to hide a rifle now.

William slipped onto the stool next to mine. "Enjoying the music?"

With a nod, I smiled, relieved to feel relaxed in his presence. "Just killing time while I wait to take my dinner home. How about you?"

"I'm meeting Rose for dinner." He glanced at his watch, his cheeks flushing. "I'm early."

"Sounds like fun." I hoped I sounded more convincing than I felt. "Rose is great," I added, meaning it. I still hadn't had a chance to speak to her. Her café had been unusually busy all day, and Ethan had a school commitment that kept him from helping.

"I heard you had some trouble last night."

I touched the silky tail of my scarf. "You could say that."

"I'm usually too busy to pay attention to village gossip, but customers were talking about it." He lowered his voice. "Funny that it happened right after your meeting."

"You think so?" I straightened, setting my glass on the bar.

"The timing makes me wonder."

I waited, but he didn't elaborate. "How so?"

"I heard your laptop was stolen. Was that all?"

"As far as I can tell."

William shifted on his stool. "Does it strike you as strange they didn't steal your camera as well?"

"Thank goodness for that. I'd be lost without my camera equipment." I shuddered at the thought.

William's deep brown eyes appeared lost in thought. "Rose said you showed photos last night. You still have the memory card, the one with the photos you showed the club?"

I nodded as I watched William's brow furrow. "I put it back in my camera after our meeting."

"Perhaps my assumption is wrong. The intruder would need your memory card."

"Do you think someone wanted the photos I shared last night? That the thief is a member of my club?" It was unthinkable. Then I remembered Penny's interest in the photos on my screen, and Alicia's voice echoed in my mind, warning me of my soft spot. The intruder was small. Penny fit the description.

"It's worth a thought." William turned his attention toward the door, and his expression brightened. I looked up as Rose appeared, her bright floral blouse easy to track as she jostled her way through the crowd.

She paused at the hostess station where Harmony stood with a man I'd never seen before, an impossibly handsome one at that. I greeted Harmony with a waggle of my fingers, surveying the man—tall and fair with a short, scruffy beard and tousled hair that was almost black. Harmony raised her hand in response, and the man looked up, meeting my gaze with eyes that were a startling shade of green. I froze, mesmerized, as our eyes locked. I couldn't seem to look away. But then, he didn't either. As William stood up beside me, his arm grazed mine. It was just enough to snap me out of it. I clamped my drooping jaw shut, and mortification took over. I spun around so quickly that I needed to grasp the edge of the bar to keep myself from spinning right off the stool. Had I *seriously* gawked at a strange man? I raised a hand to my burning cheek. What universe was he from, anyway?

Rose approached, a curl playing at the corner of her lips as her glance flitted between the mystery man and me. My heart leaped at this glimmer of the old Rose, the Rose who would rush over and dish with me about Harmony's stranger. Her gleeful expression disappeared as quickly as it had come, the sparkle in her eyes dimming as they settled into something neutral and much less personal.

The sound of a deep voice came from the crowd as Harmony's friend greeted the hostess. "Howya," he said. Okay—definitely not from Stonebridge. Did I detect a brogue in that one seemingly simple word?

"What's going on?" Rose flashed William with a beaming smile.

"We were talking about the break-in at Bobbie's."

"Oh, yeah. I was sorry to hear about that. You could have called." Never had Rose sounded less sincere.

"Thanks," I said. "It was fine." It wasn't, though. I wanted my friend back.

"I was telling Bobbie I think she should check her photos from your meeting last night. The timing makes me uncomfortable."

"Penny," Rose whispered. "It has to be." She twirled a curl around her finger. "Or Harmony. Or maybe that Kendall chick."

"We ruled out Harmony," I said. "You really think it could be Penny?"

Rose settled on the stool next to William. "She's been keeping secrets. Remember how she said she couldn't help with the investigation?" Tapping a finger to her chin, she added, "Or, like I said, it could have been Kendall. She's cunning as a fox."

Penny *had* been keeping secrets, even if I couldn't blame her for not wanting Hunter in her life. And then there was Kendall. *Cunning as a fox.* Rose didn't even know the half of it.

"Where did you say your camera was?" William asked.

"In my backpack near the front door. The intruder had come in from my kitchen at the back of the house." My squeaky floorboards had creaked with the sound of tiptoeing in my living room below. Then, Darcy—"Darcy barked and ran down the stairs," I added.

"That's it," William said. "Whoever it was must have turned and run away before getting there. You should examine the photos you showed at your meeting."

The hostess approached, gesturing she was ready to seat William and Rose. For an awkward moment, I marveled at the silent conversation my friends appeared to be having. While I vacillated between awe and envy over their advanced couples-style communication, their wordless discussion ended.

Out loud, William asked me, "Would you care to join us?"

Every fiber of my being wanted to jump at the opportunity, but only for a split second. No way would I crash Rose's date. She deserved this.

I declined their reluctant invitation, pretending not to notice their lack of protest. "I already ordered dinner to take home. And I think some time alone will do me good."

Never in my life had I thought I'd utter those words and mean them. Alone time wasn't something I normally craved. I was still a little jumpy from the previous night's break-in, but my words rang true all the same. I had so many things to sort out, and I needed to embrace this new feeling—whatever it was.

As night fell, I expected uneasiness to settle in, but the break-in already seemed like a fuzzy dream. I snuggled into the corner of my couch, surrounded by my books and photos and everything that made my house feel like home. Being alone had its benefits, too. The fact it had taken me a lifetime to learn this made me an incredibly slow study. But I couldn't help enjoying the strangeness of it all while I ate straight from the takeout container and watched the sappiest chick-flick I could find.

Darcy tried to climb on the couch with me, probably remembering the other day when I'd snuggled with him.

"Oh no, you don't. I'm eating dinner."

That didn't stop him from sitting on the floor next to me and begging with those puppy dog eyes of his. I couldn't help it. I was a hopeless sucker. No sooner did I dangle a morsel of chicken in front of his nose than he gobbled it down and begged for more.

"Ingrate. A simple thanks might be nice." When he tilted his head in response, I couldn't resist. I handed him another piece. As companions went, he wasn't half bad.

I missed Rose and Emma like crazy and vowed to do whatever it took to mend my bridges. The wild, light sensation that had started at The Crow continued throughout the evening. I wasn't ready to let it go.

It wasn't until later, when I was getting ready for bed, I puzzled over my conversation with William. I wanted him to be wrong. Surely, nothing in my photos would spark a break-in. Like he'd pointed out, the timing was suspicious. Remembering the bright red block letters, I watched in the mirror as my mouth dropped open. The intruder in my barn. The warning note. That, too, had happened after a club meeting. The back of my neck tingled at the coincidence. Kendall and Parker weren't part of the club. Did that rule them out? Soft spot or not, Penny still didn't feel right.

What am I missing?

The sun waned as I kneeled on the ground the next afternoon for another round of yanking weeds. I'd spent the morning sipping coffee on my patio, nursing a pounding head. Since then, the physical labor, as well as my man-against-obnoxious-vegetation tenacity, was proving to be an effective method for avoiding the source of my headache—William's suspicions. It wasn't until I stood, feeling woozy, that I realized I'd skipped lunch. The day was nearly gone.

I massaged my lower back. All my years of living in the city had taught me little more than how to buy potted flowers from the garden center. I was proud of my hard work. The beds around the barn were nearly weed-free and ready for something pretty. Flowers? Alicia would help with that.

"We're taking off." Connor and a friend stepped out of my barn. "The wiring is almost done. Tomorrow, we can hang light fixtures. I think you're going to like it." Connor's face beamed, clearly pleased with his work.

"Great." I stood, wiping dirt from my knees, and forced a smile. He was making fast progress with the renovation. Soon, I'd be running my own photography business. I should have felt more excited and couldn't help noticing Connor's look of disappointment at my lackluster response. Instead, I was preoccupied with the task I was avoiding, the task I knew I needed to complete. My photos awaited my attention.

Arching my back, I looked up, wishing I could float away on the puffy clouds. I'd procrastinated long enough. Pulling weed after stubborn weed, William's words had rung in my head. I was convinced he was right. The answer to my intruder, and possibly the murders, was hidden on my camera. It was time I faced them. As I longed for the solution, I couldn't help feeling scared of what I might find.

I set my tools inside the barn, locking the door behind me. The windows in the coffee shop were dark. It had been three long days since I'd visited Rose. Nothing would have made me happier than to grab my camera and take it next door. Rose would make reviewing my photos less frightening. I let out a long sigh and trudged across my patio. This was something I needed to do alone.

After retrieving my camera from my office, I grabbed a container of yogurt and sat at the kitchen table. Nerves made my fingers shake. The LCD monitor lit up when I pressed the playback button. I smiled at the images of the bear cubs' antics. As cute as they were, it was mama bear who caught my attention—the intensity of her gaze. My neck prickled with the memory.

With only three images of the covered bridge, I easily scrutinized each. There was nothing I hadn't noticed before. I ate a spoonful of yogurt before hunching back over my camera, scrolling through the images again, moving back and forth several times.

Nothing.

Maybe I'd imagined Penny's interest. Or maybe that's all it had been. I set my camera on the table. The light was too dim; the screen was too small.

I shuffled to my refrigerator, poured a glass of iced tea, and took a long gulp. Without my computer, I felt lost. Then I remembered, my photos were in the cloud. I could view them on my tablet's larger screen. After topping off my glass, I strode to the living room and settled on the couch.

I was missing something. But what? I opened my editing app and scrolled backward, inspecting each image before swiping back to the photos I'd taken on the village green. I could almost feel the warm sun on my face, my excitement over spring's late arrival, and the upcoming photo outing. Letting my breath out slowly, I remembered snapping photos of my new home and my bright yellow door—photos of hope.

Settling back, I curled my feet beneath me. William must be wrong. There was nothing sinister lurking in my photos. Idly, I slid my finger across the screen one more time. Most of the images were nothing special—the photos of a woman wandering, feeling hopeful and content.

I stopped at my favorite, the image of my cottage framed by the towering maple tree. Even from a distance, the contrast of the door with the last hurrah of lavender lilacs was cheerful against the white porch railings. What if I brought them closer? Whenever possible, I eliminated any element of a photo that wasn't part of the story.

In the bottom corner, a small, blurry patch of purple and pink drew my eye. The colors were pretty, but also distracting. Preparing to crop the image, I paused. Something wasn't right. I remembered snapping photos of spring flowers the afternoon of Tiffanee's murder: yellow daisies, pale lavender lilacs, and lots of tiny white flowers I didn't know the name of. Pink and purple, though? I used the magnifier tool to enlarge the corner of the image. Leaning closer, my hands shook. I couldn't believe it. She'd lied. My fingers lost their grasp, and the tablet slid to the floor with a thump.

It wasn't possible. And yet, it was. The blurry patch of purple and pink, they weren't flowers. Not real ones, anyway. In the corner of my photo, a tote bag sat on the ground near a park bench, the tail of my missing scarf hanging over the top. My neck prickled.

Mama Bear.

I ran to the kitchen and grabbed my phone from the table. My fingers trembled as I typed. It took several tries to get it right. I hit the send button.

I know who the killer is

Chapter Thirty-Six

My heart pounded, my breath heaving in my chest. I darted to the front hallway and stepped into a pair of sandals. Darcy rushed to my side, always up for adventure.

"Sorry, boy. You're staying here."

My fingers fumbled with the straps. Seconds dragged as the buckles refused to fasten. I glanced at my clock, surprised to find the afternoon gone. Part of me knew there was no reason to rush. My sense of urgency was only in my imagination. But when I saw my scarf in the photo's corner, an image of the next victim popped into my mind. I needed to find Harmony. I needed to warn her before the killer struck again.

Frustrated with my stubborn sandal straps, I paused. I should call the police. For what? To invoke another sneer from Detective Cram? He wouldn't believe me. All I had was a photo of my scarf. Besides, it wasn't like I was planning to confront the killer. The thought calmed me, and I fastened the buckle. The detective could wait.

Sprinting out my door, I gave Mr. Miller a cursory wave, imagining his responding harumph as I ran across Main Street. On the other side of the village green, windows were already dark, the shops closed. Visitors continued to mill about, enjoying the cool evening. I dashed around them as quickly as my legs would carry me, my lungs burning.

Please let Harmony be there.

As I prepared to cross Green Street to the row of shops facing the village green, from out of nowhere, a hand grabbed my arm. "Whoa there, Nancy Drew. What's the rush?"

I shook my arm from Travis's grasp, ignoring his impish grin. "Not now, Travis." With my teeth clenched, I felt my face contort into a grimace I was sure made me look feral.

"Sorry." He drew out the word with his hands raised in mock surrender. Free of his grip, I scurried past.

The windows of Harmony's studio were dark, the shades drawn. I wiggled the doorknob. It held tight.

"Harmony!" I pounded on the door. Like most business owners, she likely remained in her shop long after closing. "Open up. I need to talk to you."

My knuckles throbbed, but still no answer from inside. *Think, Bobbie, think.*

I pressed my ear to the door, unable to hear above my beating heart. I took a large gulp of air, held my breath, then let it out slowly. There was no reason to think Harmony was in peril, but I couldn't shake my sense of dread. A young couple strolling along the sidewalk looked askance at me, as if hugging a locked door wasn't normal. I waved and smiled, hoping I didn't appear completely maniacal. My legs took over, and I sped away, running around the building.

The surrounding forest shaded the parking area behind Harmony's shop. Next door, a faint light filtered through the window of Long Trail Booksellers, providing an eerie gloom to the alley. Stepping onto Harmony's back stoop, I reached for the door, pulling my hand back with a jerk. The door was ajar. In every mystery novel I'd ever read, finding a door ajar meant *turn around and run, now!* I let out a shaky laugh. This wasn't fiction. Didn't authors just make stuff up?

Patting my pocket, I reached for my phone. No signal. None. No way to call for help. How had I forgotten this? Right across the green, the signal was fine. But on this side, it was dead. *Seriously, Vermont?* I held my breath. Now was not the time to curse spotty cell service. Or panic. It wasn't like I needed help, anyway.

I peeked into the dark hallway and whispered Harmony's name. I waited a beat, but no answer came.

"Harmony," I said again, louder this time. "I need to talk to you."

Thinking she must be in her shop, I pushed the door open, jumping when it screeched. Inside, a narrow wooden staircase was lit from above. At the end of a short hall, another doorway led to Harmony's studio. I inched forward on tiptoes, my palm against the bumpy plaster.

The studio looked different, dark, and empty. One yoga mat lay abandoned on the floor. Standing outside the cavernous room, I eyed the lone mat and called for Harmony once more. A shiver ran up my spine. Something was wrong. Very wrong.

Racked with indecision, I froze. Inner voices warred with each other. One told me to go home. The other worried about Harmony. She might be hurt. Or worse. My worried voice won. I couldn't leave. Releasing my grip on the doorframe, I took a tentative step forward. Then another.

Inside the studio, the scent of lavender, rosewood, and patchouli hung in the air. Soft music floated from Harmony's shop, drawing me forward. It was supposed to be calming. Still, my gaze fell on the empty mat, and my heart pounded.

I crept through the studio, stopping where a curtain separated it from the shop. I called for Harmony once more. The music was louder from where I stood. The tinkling sound of chimes provided a backdrop to the singer's mournful tune. Harmony wouldn't have left the music on.

Trembling, my fingers grasped the silky fabric, and I steeled myself. I pulled the curtain back, and my eyes met Harmony's. The shake of her head was barely noticeable—a warning that came a moment too late.

"You may as well join us." I recognized the dispassionate voice of the killer.

Squaring my shoulders, I drew in a long, steadying breath and stepped forward.

Chapter Thirty-Seven

"Hello, Bernadine." My unwavering voice surprised me.

"We've been waiting for you. What took so long?" Her tone held no threat. It was as if she was inviting me for a cup of tea.

When I'd seen Bernadine's tote in my photo, I'd wanted to kick myself. How many times had she said she couldn't stay late at the bookstore because she needed to babysit Hope? And yet, that afternoon, she'd been on the village green with her friends. I took another step forward.

"Stay there." Bernadine swung a rifle, pointing it at me.

I jumped back, raising my hands in the air. "You have a rifle?" My mind spun. Had the police released it? Surely, they wouldn't give it back to the killer.

The cackle of Bernadine's laugh made me cringe. "Obviously, you're not from Vermont. It's called a shotgun." Her mouth twisted. "And no, this isn't what I used to kill Hunter."

With my eyes trained on Bernadine, I edged toward Harmony.

"I said, don't move." Bernadine's voice was rough like gravel, betraying no sign of the gossipy-yet-mild-mannered church lady.

I froze, knowing better than to argue with a weapon-wielding woman who was clearly unhinged.

"Good girl," she said. "Now stand over there." She pointed her shotgun at a spot a few feet from Harmony.

Nothing raised my hackles more than being called a *good girl*. Heat rose up my neck.

"Now!" She gave me a quick jab, and I jumped to obey. With a twisted smile, Bernadine lowered her shotgun. "There, that's better. You only need to do as I say."

She'd placed Harmony and me just far enough apart to inhibit strategic whispering—not that Harmony seemed inclined to do either. Gone was the calm yoga instructor I needed if we hoped to devise a plan to get out alive, assuming there was the slimmest possibility of that.

With my hands raised, I pivoted to face the killer. Harmony's fear seemed to feed our captor. I lowered my hands and took a steadying breath. I had no intention of providing mama bear more food. Our only chance was to stall.

"What's your plan, Bernadine?"

"What's my plan?" Bernadine mimicked me. "Why don't you tell me, smarty pants? You seem to think you know everything."

With all the confidence I could muster, I brushed off her mocking tone. "I don't see that you have one."

Bernadine's lips curled. She raised her rifle, aiming it straight at my head. "I tried to warn you, but you wouldn't stay out of it. Now you'll have to die like the rest of them."

Her bland, no-nonsense tone chilled me. She'd already killed twice. She had nothing to lose.

I scanned the shop. There was no way out. Bernadine stood between me and the back exit. The path to the front door was a maze of tables topped with new-age paraphernalia. A shotgun blast would beat me to it. I stared into the long barrel and gulped down panic. I was trapped.

Keep her talking.

I was certain she had a story to tell. Listening to its sordid details was better than dying. What other options were there? I looked at Harmony, who now had her palms raised, her long, dark lashes shadowing her cheekbones. Was she meditating? Pinning her with the hottest glare I could muster, I attempted telepathy to make her snap out of it. It didn't work.

I gave up and faced Bernadine. "What inspired you to strangle Tiffanee with my scarf?"

Bernadine licked her lips and aimed a deranged look my way. Hannibal

Lecter had nothing on her. I shuddered.

"That *was* inspiring, wasn't it?"

I nodded, forcing myself to agree. "Very inspired," I said.

Seemingly pleased by my answer, she continued. "Of course, I had no way of knowing you'd be so careless, but your scarf added a nice touch."

Biting back what I really thought about my scarf being used as a murder weapon, I smiled encouragingly. If this was a game, I wasn't enjoying it. Not at all.

Bernadine, however, clearly relished her role. "Watching you squirm under suspicion was rather enjoyable. You really shouldn't have been so nosy."

Thinking of everything she'd put me through made my anger flare. With a shaky breath, I reined it in. I knew what I needed to do, and it involved stroking Bernadine's ego.

"The way you cast suspicion on me was certainly…inspired." Satisfied she didn't detect my lie, I laid it on thicker. "It's amazing no one ever suspected you. That must have taken planning."

I sensed a shift in Harmony. A slight flicker of her lashes. It offered me a glimmer of hope. I needed to believe she was paying attention.

Thankfully, Bernadine didn't seem to notice. "Oh, but I didn't plan to kill her. I only meant to talk sense into her." There was a ghoulish pleasure in her voice that sent shivers down my spine.

Beneath half-closed lids, Harmony shifted her gaze from Bernadine to me. I thought I detected a slight nod, to which I gave a slight nod back while prodding Bernadine to continue.

"Oh?" I prompted.

"Yes. Tiffanee told Penny she was planning to go to the bridge early, you see." Bernadine's eyes lit as she warmed to her story. "She wanted to scope things out before your little meetup. Just like Tiffanee, always competitive, always needing to outshine everyone else."

I nodded, offering Bernadine my rapt attention.

"As I said, I only wanted to talk to her. I thought she might listen to reason. I should have known better. That girl was always so headstrong. Such a bad influence on my Penny." Bernadine swung her rifle at Harmony. "You weren't much better."

Harmony jerked, a soft cry escaping. With a steady stare, I implored her to help. We needed a plan. I'd hoped that while I kept Bernadine busy, Harmony could think of something. She didn't so much as glance my way. Apparently, my extrasensory communication hadn't improved over the past few minutes.

I turned back to Bernadine, fitting the last pieces together. "You tried to talk to Tiffanee to make her stop threatening Penny? That's what she was doing, right? Threatening to tell Hunter about Hope?"

Bernadine took a quick breath and pointed her rifle at me. "Very good, genius. If Penny had wanted Hunter to know about Hope, she'd have told him herself. That drunk had no place in our lives, and there was no way I'd let him take the baby."

"Drunk? Hunter had a drinking problem?" I thought back and pictured his glassy eyes the night I met him at The Crow. He had a temper, too.

Bernadine's tongue ran slowly along her upper lip. Bile rose in my throat. The taste of fear. This was no casual conversation, but it was my only hope.

"I didn't know Hunter was Hope's father," she said, ignoring my question. "But then you came into the bookstore with your photo. The resemblance was impossible to miss—Hope's white-blonde hair and those adorable little dimples."

"Did Penny tell you Tiffanee was threatening her?"

"Ha!" Bernadine's sharp laugh was full of disdain. "I eavesdropped. It's the only way a mother learns anything. I heard Tiffanee tell Penny the father had a right to know." Her eyes narrowed. "As if she knew anything about it."

"But you were too late, weren't you?" I asked. "Tiffanee had already told Hunter."

Bernadine ignored me, lost in her tale. "Tiffanee was always playing games. I begged her to leave Penny alone. You know what she did?" She blinked, her wide eyes filled with disbelief. "She turned her back on me and laughed." Bernadine's face twisted, her cheeks reddening. "That's when your scarf came in handy. I had no trouble looping it around Tiffanee's skinny throat and squeezing."

"That's not how she died." The story was exhausting me.

"She struggled, of course." Bernadine started where she'd left off. "That's when she lost her footing, doing me the favor of tumbling down the hill and hitting her head on a jagged rock. She was unconscious. I figured her bleeding would do the rest. They say she died from the blow to her head." A look of delight transformed Bernadine's face—and not in a good way. "You see, I didn't actually kill her."

I reared back. "You left her to die?"

"Bobbie, Bobbie." Bernadine clucked her tongue. "What else could I do? I worried she wouldn't die fast enough. It was a chance I had to take."

There was a finality in her voice, and I still had no escape plan. My pulse racing, I picked up the thread. "You removed Tiffanee's memory card."

For a moment, Bernadine didn't say a word. Her gaze was unfocused. I groaned to myself. What would she do when she finished her story?

She blinked, her eyes darting back to me. "Yes. I took the memory card from Tiffanee's camera. I picked up her bag, too. There was no telling what else was on that card. Then I went home to take care of Hope." She shrugged like it was just another day.

"You returned the bag to Tiffanee's house?" I asked.

"I figured the police would think she left it at home."

She'd been right, but I'd known better. With the lens cap tucked into an outer pocket, I knew Tiffanee had been carrying her bag.

"Where's the memory card now?"

"I destroyed it and threw it in the trash. No one will ever find it." End of story, or so it seemed. Time for panic.

With her rifle pointed at my face, Bernadine turned to scan the room. It appeared she, too, was lacking a plan. I took a tiny step toward Harmony. She did the same. With a quick tilt of her head, she gestured to a shelf behind me. I furrowed my brow in confusion. Although thankful she'd come back to life, I couldn't decipher her message. She gave another quick jerk of her head. Heavy stoneware lamps lined the shelf.

My mind spun. *Think, Bobbie.* It wasn't until Bernadine turned her back that I understood. The stoneware was heavy, making it the only weapon within reach. With good aim and perfect timing, I could take advantage of Bernadine's distraction and throw one at her. If I did it just right, it would knock her out cold. It wasn't much of a plan, but it was the only one we had. As I reached toward the shelf, Bernadine turned, swinging her rifle.

I jumped. A lump lodged in my throat. I couldn't breathe. We needed more time. "You thought Hunter saw you near the bridge?" My voice was hoarse. I persisted. "Or did you only want to keep him away from Hope?"

The room was growing dark. Window shades blocked any remaining sunlight from entering the room. We'd soon be trapped in the dark with a rifle-swinging lunatic. Should we live that long. I gulped air.

Focus.

With an unnerving calmness, Bernadine resumed her tale. "Penny's father was a drunk. Anyone could understand how I'd never let my granddaughter suffer the way Penny did before the bum finally took off. William admitted he might have seen Hunter that night. I couldn't take the chance he'd seen me. Let's say I covered all bases when I took care of him."

Harmony's quiet squeak was just loud enough to divert Bernadine's attention.

Frantically, I surveyed the room, memorizing the various displays. The table of mantra bracelets was at my side. I peered at one which read *FEARLESS.* I remembered Harmony's words. *You'd be amazed at their positive energy. Truly powerful.* It felt like a sign.

I continued my inventory. The lamps were the heaviest items in the shop. A well-thrown lamp seemed unlikely to win a battle with a bullet. It was all I had.

"I was so disappointed to realize Hunter is Hope's father." Bernadine spat her words with disgust. "How could Penny have been so stupid?"

I hadn't forgotten the clammy feel of my hand in Hunter's, along with his leer. I could almost empathize with Bernadine. But I wasn't interested in victim blaming. Nothing justified murder.

"Enough with the chit-chat." Bernadine's voice made a deadly shift from unhinged to commanding. "Walk over there, behind the cash register."

Time was up. Keeping my hands low behind me, I fumbled to grasp a lamp. When my finger pressed against one, I felt it teeter. *No, no, no...* I suppressed a gasp.

Finally, it stilled, and my knees nearly buckled with relief. I clutched it with both hands. Heavy and solid, its slightly bumpy texture made it easy to hold. I shuffled slowly toward the cash register. Taking stock of my captor, I figured she was about my age. Somewhat overweight, she huffed and puffed with every step. I only hoped that buoyed my chances.

I had almost reached the front of the shop when Bernadine turned her back to me.

Now!

I hurled the lamp, grazing Bernadine's arm. She whirled with a suddenness that surprised me and bared her teeth like a bear prepared for attack. With three long strides, she thrust her shotgun's butt into my head. Time slowed as I hit the floor, first my knee, then my elbow, then my head.

Major miscalculation. The room went black.

Chapter Thirty-Eight

When I came to, darkness surrounded me. I blinked, my cheek resting on a hard, smooth surface. I felt groggy. *Where am I?*

I tried to lift my fingers to soothe the throbbing pain in my head, but discovered my hands were bound behind my back. I couldn't tell how long I'd been out—presumably long enough for Bernadine to tie my ankles and wrists.

Slowly, the room came into focus. Broken pottery shards lay scattered on the floor. Just beyond, Bernadine's black sneakers came into view. From somewhere behind me, Harmony's soft, musky scent mingled with the earthier aromas of the yoga studio. I raised my head. A stabbing pain shot up my neck.

I wriggled onto my side, trying to lift myself. Giving up, I tried to pull my wrists apart. Whatever Bernadine had used felt surprisingly smooth. I stopped. Every movement brought pain. My breath heaved. Bernadine appeared preoccupied, humming to the unearthly music playing through the shop's speakers.

Although I couldn't see her, I sensed Harmony was near and whispered her name. She answered by wedging her feet beneath my shoulders and nudging me until I could sit up. I scooted back to lean against the wall, shoulder-to-shoulder with her.

"Nice try, by the way. Sorry it didn't work." Despite everything, the hushed sound of Harmony's voice calmed me.

I nodded painfully, still groggy.

Harmony shifted. "We should meditate."

That woke me. "Are you kidding me?" I struggled to keep my voice low. "We need a plan."

"It will come to us." She lifted her face and chanted softly.

Great. Just great.

Bernadine ambled across the room. The crunching sounds of the broken shards beneath her shoes grated on my nerves. She stopped, peering at us, and chortled at Harmony's serene posture. An oil lamp illuminated her face with a ghastly glow. It reminded me of childhood camping trips and spooky stories around the campfire. I'd always thought Alicia made the scariest faces. That was before Bernadine.

"You're awake." Bernadine stooped to hold the lamp close to my face, the oily scent of its flame filling my nostrils. "Too bad you weren't more like Tiffanee, dying quietly."

I met my captor's eyes and tipped my chin in defiance. One last show of bravery. The scene had played itself out, reaching its inevitable conclusion. A yoga studio in Stonebridge, Vermont, was where I'd die. Soon, I'd join Dan, much earlier than planned. The thought was oddly comforting. If I wanted to, I could just give up.

I waited for my life to flash before my eyes. Except it didn't. Despite my odds, I wasn't ready to die.

"Your variety of murder methods is impressive," I muttered, reasoning the lit oil lamp meant fire was next on her murderous agenda.

"I got the lamp idea from you. Thanks for that." Bernadine bent forward, panting. Her foul breath nearly suffocated me as she spoke. "It's not like I'm a serial killer."

I reared my head, cringing at her words. Her definition of a serial killer seemed to differ from mine. As she straightened, I stretched my legs in front of me, reaching for her ankles. If I could send her crashing to the floor, she'd hit her head on the way down.

It nearly worked. Bernadine stumbled. Just as quickly, she regained her balance. Her eyes flashed as she grabbed her shotgun and poked its barrel to my forehead. She spoke through clenched teeth. "I should shoot you right here." Then she shrugged, set her shotgun on a table and smiled a smile I thought could only belong to a devil.

"But I won't." Bernadine's voice sounded playful. "This is going to look like a terrible accident." Humming to herself, she lifted a bottle of oil. "Too bad Harmony was so careless. Such a tragic mistake." Splashing oil on the floor, Bernadine snaked her way through the shop to the studio door.

"You won't get away with this," I said. "When they find us tied up, they'll know it wasn't an accident." My defiant words offered me no comfort. It wouldn't matter. I'd be dead.

"I used Harmony's pretty silk curtains. They'll burn before you're found. Besides, no one knows I'm here." She stalled in the doorway. "I do feel bad for you. But I'm sure your meddling will be forgiven." With that, she slammed the lamp to the floor with a crash and watched, seemingly transfixed by the leaping flames. Her voice sounded far away as she left the way I'd come in minutes before. "This will be over soon enough."

I nudged Harmony. "We need to get up." The time for meditating had passed. "Maybe you have a yoga move that can help?"

Her expression was exasperatingly serene. I watched the flames grow as they snaked toward us. Harmony rocked forward and back.

"What are you doing? We need to get out of here now!"

The room was growing hot. Smoke rose.

Her rocking gained momentum until she rose to her feet. *Good plan.* I attempted to follow her lead. With my ankles bound and my wrists behind me, I couldn't get the leverage I needed. I lacked the strength of my agile friend.

"Rock a little harder." Harmony's voice was amazingly calm despite the growing flames. A hazy glow filled the room. Soon, we wouldn't be able to breathe.

"You better leave without me." I wasn't giving up, but I didn't want to hold Harmony back. Unsure of how, I thought she might possibly get help.

"Wait, do you hear that?" Harmony whispered.

Outside, I heard voices. And barking? Darcy? But that couldn't be.

Someone pounded on the door. "Harmony? Bobbie? Are you in there?" It was Rose.

Harmony and I exchanged a quick glance before shouting. "Go around back."

"Ten-four," a male voice called.

The flames appeared to stall momentarily. I thought Bernadine might've missed a spot with the oil. It would only be seconds before they leaped forward, catching again. My heart raced, and I rocked as if my life depended upon it. Likely, it did. I could do this.

What was taking Rose so long? Had Bernadine caught her, too? The smoke was thickening. Its acrid taste filled my mouth. I coughed. I closed my mouth and rocked back once more, pouring as much momentum as I could into my forward movement. It brought me to my feet and then some. My triumph was short-lived as my momentum toppled me forward. With no hands to brace my fall, this was going to hurt. I barked a maniacal laugh.

"I've got you," Harmony said, hopping in front of me to prevent my fall.

The smoke had thickened. Holding my breath, I hopped alongside Harmony. Progress toward the door was excruciatingly slow.

"Bobbie! Harmony! Are you in here?" Rose's voice swam through the smoke.

"In here!" Harmony and I shouted together.

Rose appeared in the studio doorway, accompanied by William. "Jeepers! What happened?" Not waiting for an answer, she shook her curls and skirted the flames to reach us.

William made a quick study of the room and jerked his head toward the front door. Gathering yoga mats in his arms, his voice held a calm authority. "Take them out the front. I'll keep the flames from coming closer."

Rose wedged herself between Harmony and me. She wrapped her arms around our backs, holding us steady while guiding us through the smoke to the front door. Behind us, mats made a thwacking sound as they hit the floor.

"Where's Darcy?" I asked, suddenly panicked. "I thought I heard him outside."

"He was with me a minute ago," Rose said. "He must still be outside."

Time stood still while William rushed forward and flipped the lock. The smoke was so heavy, I didn't think I could take another breath. When he pushed the door open and helped Rose guide us down the stoop to the sidewalk, I couldn't help gulping the cool evening air.

Sirens wailed, rounding the corner at the village green. The sidewalk filled with curious onlookers. My knees buckled, and I dropped to the curb, Rose and Harmony beside me.

Rose picked at the silk that bound my wrists. With a frustrated groan, she looked at William. "It's too tight. I need scissors."

From across the village green, Detective Cram's spiked plumage bobbed toward us. He bumped into William as he halted on the stoop and scanned inside the yoga shop. Stepping to my side, he lifted his nose with a sniff. "I should have known you would be involved."

"You're welcome." I didn't bother looking up. My days of trying to win over the loathsome detective had passed.

"Holy moly!" Rose said. "Were you in there with the killer?"

"Bernadine." I suppressed a nervous laugh. "If you can believe that."

"Bernadine? I'm so confused." Rose stared at Harmony.

"You thought it was me?" Harmony slumped against my shoulder and laughed—a laugh filled with as much relief as humor. "Far out."

"Bobbie had ruled you out, but I still don't understand why you weren't at yoga," Rose said. "If you don't mind me saying so, you were a mess."

"Sad but true." Harmony blinked. "I was looking for Hunter. He was staying at my house. In the morning, when I went to his room, he wasn't there. I figured he went to Penny's house to meet Hope like he'd threatened to do." She stared across the village green as she spoke. "But he wasn't there either. When I crossed the bridge, I heard someone running in the woods. Thinking it was Hunter, I chased after him. Whoever it was had disappeared." She stopped to look at me. "I told this to Detective Cram. But he thought it was you."

"Of course he did," I said. "Why didn't you tell me?"

"I didn't know what to think. You were too involved. It seemed best to let the police figure it out."

The scene Harmony described was easy to picture. "That's probably when Bernadine put the rifle by my barn, hiding it before walking behind the church and crossing the street to join the garden club. It would have looked like she'd come straight from her house. Remember?" I prompted Rose. "They were planting flowers on the green when we walked to yoga."

Rose nodded. "I remember. But Harmony, where were you all that time?"

Harmony rested her forehead on her knees. "Meditating by the river. I sensed something bad had happened. I wasn't ready to face it."

There was a commotion behind us, and a gruff voice called out, "Got her." We turned in time to see my crotchety next-door neighbor and Travis walk from behind the building, holding Bernadine between them. Darcy trotted alongside them, snout in the air.

Mr. Miller held one arm while Travis twisted the other behind Bernadine's back. "She was trying to sneak off." Lester's voice was both strong and clear. He lifted the shotgun with a satisfied smile.

My mouth opened at the sight of my friend's ex-husband and my elderly next-door neighbor. Mr. Miller? Travis? I'd have thought them an implausible duo, but I was grateful for both of them.

"Your dog's a hero," Travis said. "He blocked her from getting into her truck. I didn't know Labradors could look so menacing."

"He's a killer." I laughed. As soon as I spoke, Darcy ran to my side, his tail wagging. His long tongue reached out and licked my face. With my hands still tied behind me, there wasn't much I could do. I didn't care.

Together, Travis and Lester led Bernadine to the sidewalk and thrust her toward Detective Cram. With a curl of his lip, Travis didn't bother to disguise his contempt. "How about making yourself useful for a change?"

William cut the silk from our wrists and ankles with scissors he'd retrieved from his bookstore. I twirled my sore wrists and lifted my hands to my face. I was going to have a terrible bruise on my head. It was preferable to being shot. Wrapping my arm around Darcy's back, I hugged him close. Dan's dog was a hero.

From the far side of the village green, Penny ran toward us. She stopped in front of Bernadine as Detective Cram clicked the handcuffs closed.

"Mama?" Penny's voice was little more than a squeak, but the gathering crowd silenced at her appearance. She took a step forward and repeated her plea.

Bernadine stood rigid, her tight-faced expression full of disdain. "Weak," she said. "You've always been weak. I did it for you."

Penny appeared to crumple, and I resisted the urge to run to her. No daughter should have to listen to those words. Not ever. Swiping her cheeks with the back of her hand, Penny looked at me with a small, sad curl of her lips that felt like an apology. I met her gaze, remembering the table of mantra bracelets, and lifted my chin in a gesture meant to convey strength, courage, and defiance—fearlessness.

Facing her mother again, Penny squared her shoulders and pushed back her veil of hair. "You did it for yourself." Her voice wavered. She stood taller, as if gathering strength before continuing. "You weren't protecting me. You were protecting your control over my life—and Hope's. This time, you went too far." With her head held high, she pivoted on her heel and tossed one last glance over her shoulder. "Goodbye, Mama."

"Right on," Harmony said, her dark eyes sparkling as Penny scuffled across the green, ignoring Bernadine's sputters. "That's been a long time coming."

"Okay, wow. Major wowzers." Rose's voice echoed my awe.

As Penny strode away, I was relieved to see Mackenzie's bright pink hair rushing toward her, arms wide. What would her life be like without her mother? Better, I hoped. I made a mental note to call Emma. We needed to reconcile, stat. I wasn't taking no for an answer.

Lightheaded, I rested my face in my hands, and Rose drew me to her side. I turned and hugged her. "I've missed you." A ridiculous understatement. Reluctantly, I let go. "Now, I think I better have a paramedic examine my head." Noting Rose's crinkled nose, I laughed. "Don't you dare say it."

Chapter Thirty-Nine

"I'm staying with you tonight." Rose guided me across the village green. "You're on concussion protocol, so don't even bother protesting."

The paramedic had wrapped a bandage around my head, which seemed overly dramatic, considering there was no blood. But my forehead sported a nasty lump, courtesy of Bernadine's rifle, and I was happy to hide the reminder.

"I'd like that." It had only been a few days—days that had felt like weeks—since Rose and I had last talked. Now, the mystery was solved, and we could put it behind us. For that, I was immensely grateful.

"It's settled, then. Ethan is spending the night with Travis, and I have no better place to be than with my best friend." Her blue eyes twinkled as she spoke, and I wrapped my arm around her waist, drawing her close.

Crossing Main Street, I noticed a familiar truck parked in front of my house. "Looks like Alicia stopped by. She didn't need to do that."

"Girl, you've got to be kidding me," Rose said. "You sent that text to Alicia. You know, the one about knowing who the killer was. She was shopping in Rutland, which sent her into a frenzy. Then, she texted me, which sent me into a frenzy too. Pretty soon, the whole village was hunting for you."

"The whole village?" My cheeks flushed.

"You know what I mean."

Laughter and chatter drifted through my living room window as we climbed the porch stairs. "Is Alicia throwing a party at my house?"

The words had barely come out of my mouth when Nate threw the door open and called over his shoulder, "Hey all, our unlikely heroine is home!"

I stopped, blinking back tears as Emma rushed forward, throwing her arms around me.

Alicia set a wine glass on the coffee table and sped toward me with her arms flung open. "Group hug." Nate and Rose joined in, and for the first time in weeks, I felt secure.

When we pulled apart, Emma giggled, wiping a tear from the corner of her eye.

"How did you know?" I whispered.

"As luck would have it," Alicia said, "Emma was already on her way to see you when I got your text."

Smoothing her curls from her face, Emma said, "I felt terrible with the way we'd left things. And even though you were totally in the wrong, I wanted to make up."

I gathered Emma into another hug, thinking I might never let go. Reluctantly, I released her and stepped back, trying to maintain my composure while I took it all in.

With a gesture to my bandage, Alicia's eyebrow rose in a slow arch. "Not one of your better scarves."

My fingers sought the white gauze, and I laughed. "I'll be sure to remedy that."

"Come in and sit down. We've been so worried."

A chorus of well-wishes and the comforting aroma of Alicia's cooking met me when I entered my living room. Tears blurred my vision as I looked around, stopping on my favorite photo of Dan among the jumble lining my fireplace mantle. I missed him terribly; I always would. This evening, taking in his familiar smile, something felt different. It felt like encouragement and hope and acceptance all rolled together. I regarded my guests with a weak smile.

Connor leaned on the curled arm of the couch where Jackson and William sat, the latter rising to join Rose. I couldn't help noticing the flush on Rose's cheeks when their eyes met. Relieved I hadn't completely ruined their budding romance, my face broke into a jubilant smile, which seemed to make her cheeks brighten even more.

"*Mon Dieu*," Jackson said. "You scared us all to death."

The room whirled around me as everyone spoke at once. Emma led me to the other couch, and Nate brought me a glass of iced water while Alicia, ever efficient, plumped a pillow behind my head. Not to be forgotten in the chaos, Darcy ambled across the room and placed his head in my lap, his tail wagging. When I'd dreamed of my first party in my new home, this certainly hadn't been it. And yet, it was perfect.

Connor had left his spot on the couch's arm and reappeared in the kitchen doorway carrying a tray steaming with hot cocktail meatballs and bacon-wrapped dates. Leave it to Alicia to have appetizers at the ready. After setting the platter on the coffee table, he leaned to give me a hug. I rested my head against the pillow while the sound of voices swam around me. Rose and Alicia were telling the story of my text message and the ensuing maelstrom. They spoke in a volley of words, everyone's heads moving back and forth between them. Then a third voice chimed in, one I'd never heard in my house before. There in the doorway stood my harumphing next-door neighbor with a smile so unexpected, it took a moment to register.

He pointed a gnarled finger at Rose. "Then, our red-headed coffee maven came pounding on my door."

"Because I figured you saw Bobbie leave." Rose crinkled her nose at him. "You pretend you're not paying attention, but if anyone in the village knows what's going on, it's you—or Alicia." Rose turned to Alicia with a wide grin.

"Humph," Mr. Miller said, and the room filled with laughter.

"What I still don't understand is how you figured it out," Jackson said. The room grew silent.

I raised my head and explained how Rose and I had discovered Penny's connection with Hunter. "And then—"

"No, wait. Back up," Emma chimed in. "You and Rose went to a biker bar?"

"Rose even had a burly biker dude drooling over her. But that's a different story." One we'd all have a good laugh over later.

With their fingers entwined, William squeezed Rose's hand. "Without a doubt, the man has good taste."

Rose blushed. "Anyway, it made sense to us that Hunter was Hope's father."

"And then, there was the coincidence of Bobbie's computer being stolen right after her club's meeting." William joined in the narrative.

I nodded. "If I had been more organized, no one would have seen the photo showing my missing scarf hanging from Bernadine's tote bag. I projected it on my large screen, but I was so busy on my computer I didn't notice. Penny must have spotted it."

"You're saying Penny didn't want Hunter to know about Hope, but Tiffanee figured it out and was threatening to tell him?" Jackson rubbed his chin. "Why would Bernadine care?"

"She probably thought she was helping Penny," Rose said.

"That, and she's always been controlling," Alicia added. "I doubt she wanted to share Hope with someone like Hunter, especially after the trouble she had with her own husband."

I returned to my story. "Tiffanee had already told him. That was why he was here. Then, Bernadine heard William say he might've seen Hunter on his way home that night. If that was true, he'd have been near the scene when Bernadine killed Tiffanee."

William scratched his chin. "Now I understand how you figured out Bernadine was the killer. Why was it so urgent to find Harmony?"

"So you don't think I'm a complete lunatic," I began. The room filled with another round of laughter.

"You?" The sarcasm in Rose's voice echoed the sentiment in the room.

Everyone had stilled, holding their collective breath, and I beheld the caring faces surrounding me. How could I have underestimated what they meant to me—all of them? Related or not, they were family.

"Anyway," I started, smiling as I shot Rose with my sternest side-eye. "Harmony has always been protective of Penny, and when I talked to her, I don't know. I got the feeling she was figuring things out. I thought it was only a matter of time before Bernadine went after her." My throat felt scratchy, and I sipped my water. "I can't explain it, but it was like a voice inside telling me to warn her. And I assure you, I hadn't planned to confront Bernadine. Definitely not in a dark studio with a gun pointed at me." I shuddered, my fingers reaching for my bandage. If it wasn't for the welt on my head, I might have thought it had all been a bad dream.

"Your premonition saved my life." Harmony's voice startled me. She stood in the entry hall with Penny, whose veil of hair couldn't disguise the puffiness of her downcast eyes.

I ignored my dizziness and rushed over to gather both into a tight hug. Tears threatened yet again.

"I'm so sorry," Penny whispered. "I never thought my secret would come to this."

Reaching out, I grasped Penny's hands, and tears spilled down my cheeks.

Harmony gave Penny a gentle nudge. "We brought you something."

Penny reached into her bag and pulled out my stolen laptop. "I wasn't thinking about how much I would frighten you. When I saw the photo of your scarf in my mom's bag, I got scared." Her voice dropped to a whisper. "I panicked."

Taking my laptop, I placed it on the hall table. I was speechless. The stormy night, the shattering glass—it had nearly frightened me to death. But Penny was a victim, too.

"I guess my mom and I will get matching orange jumpsuits."

"That won't do. Nate, isn't there another option? Probation? Community service?"

Nate's expression turned thoughtful. "I'll take you to the police barracks tomorrow. I don't think there's any way around being charged, but under the circumstances, jail time seems unlikely."

Harmony gave Penny a reassuring smile. Penny's chin tipped in a tentative nod.

"Come in, girls. Eat." Alicia waved them into the living room. "We have plenty of food for everyone."

I sank back onto the couch. My body ached, and I was tired, but with Alicia acting as hostess, I allowed myself to sink into my couch's warmth and close my eyes to the voices filling my home.

There was one last piece. Sitting up, I pointed at Lester Miller. He appeared startled, and my guests went silent. "You," I said. "Does this mean you're going to wave back now?"

"Humph," Lester answered, but not without a twitch of his lips beneath his thick white beard. As everyone laughed, I sat back, satisfied, resting my aching head on the soft cushion.

Gradually, the guests left. Laughter turned to subdued whispers while I rested, watching the activity through half-closed lids. Rose gathered plates and glasses from the coffee table and placed them on an empty tray.

Alicia walked into the living room, wiping her hands on a dish towel. "Thank goodness this night is almost over." She scanned the room and smiled. Rose lifted the filled tray and started back to the kitchen, only to be intercepted by Nate.

"Allow me." He lifted the tray from her arms.

Connor looked at Emma, who was curled next to me. "I'm meeting some friends at The Crow for a beer before it closes. Do you want to come?"

Emma perked up, then sat back again. "I'd better stay here."

"Go have fun while I rest," I said. "We can talk in the morning."

Emma placed her hand on my arm. "Are you sure? You shouldn't be alone."

"I'll stay with your mom until you get back," Rose said. "We have some catching up to do, and I promise to keep close watch. The paramedic gave me instructions."

"Great," Connor said. "I think you'll like my friends. They're super chill."

Emma smiled shyly. "Maybe one beer."

"Thanks for your help," Alicia called to Connor as he strode past with Emma, patting my arm before leaving.

Nate dropped onto the couch with what appeared to be a mixture of relief and fatigue. "When I told you everything would work itself out, this wasn't quite what I meant." He fixed me with a wry smile.

"What can I say?" I laughed. If only I'd had his faith.

"All's well, I guess." He shook his head. "This might seem like a strange time to mention it, but I've been meaning to tell you about a web designer who is setting up his business in the village. He won't be here full-time until the fall, but you mentioned needing to create a website."

"Definitely." Now that this episode was over, I could finally focus on my future.

"From what I've seen, this guy is good. Ciarán Donovan. He's already working with Harmony, and he'll be updating my website, too."

With an elfish grin, Rose tapped my arm, her eyes sparkling. "Ciarán Donovan? He wouldn't happen to be tall and handsome with dark hair and a wee bit of a brogue?" Her imitation of an Irish brogue wasn't half bad.

My cheeks burned, remembering my near fall from the bar stool. Our shared glance hadn't lasted for more than a moment, but I'd never forget those mesmerizing emerald eyes.

Nate laughed. "I suppose some would describe him that way. He's a heck of a nice guy—a widower, I think. No, that's wrong. He's divorced, coming to Vermont to escape the city. Anyway, I thought you'd be interested in knowing about his new business."

I nodded, ignoring the playful sparkle in Rose's eyes, the same playful sparkle I'd longed for the night before. "Thanks. I'll get his contact information when I'm ready. Finishing the studio renovation comes first."

"Sounds like a plan." Nate stood. "I'll call you tomorrow. The police will want to interview you in depth."

"I'll be home soon." Alicia walked Nate to the door before turning to Rose and me. "I hope you don't mind if I stay for a glass of wine."

"Please do. I don't think Bobbie will be much company, but I'll have a glass with you." Rose patted the cushion next to her. "It's the three of us together again, kind of like our dinner at the start of this mess, except without the unsolved murder. Thank goodness."

Alicia strode to the kitchen. When she returned, she topped off my water glass and set two wine glasses on the coffee table before filling them with a pale, luminescent pink. "Cheers." She raised her glass and clinked Rose's.

A soft breeze wafted through the window, carrying the gentle scent of roses. We were silent for a moment, allowing the events of the day to sink in.

"I'm so glad this is over." Alicia's voice was laced with fatigue as she sank into the couch. "Don't ever do that again."

I'd never seen my energetic sister so tired. The ordeal had been hard on everyone.

CHAPTER THIRTY-NINE

"You got it," I murmured.

"When I got Bobbie's text today..." Alicia said.

"And I got yours, only to rush over here to find she'd run off. Then Darcy escaped, taking off like a bat out of—well, you know the saying. Jeezum Crow! I thought I might have a heart attack." Rose giggled. "You should have seen Lester Miller when I banged his door down. "

Alicia's tone became serious. "Thank you for everything you did today. You put yourself in jeopardy, and I think that tidbit got lost in all the commotion. Don't think I didn't notice."

Rose flushed, her cheeks turning a bright crimson.

"You're a good friend to Bobbie."

"It goes both ways." Rose's voice was soft.

"Hey, you two," I said. "I'm still here, you know."

"How about a super fun change of subject?" Rose bounced in her seat. "Did I see sparks flying between Emma and Connor?"

I shifted. "Did I miss something? I mean, we all know Emma's always had a girlhood crush on him."

Alicia and Rose exchanged knowing glances.

"Looks to me like Connor just noticed Emma's no longer a little girl," Rose said.

But Emma was still getting over her breakup. Surely, she wouldn't jump into something new this soon. Not even with Connor.

"Your gears are grinding." Alicia leaned into my side. "Stop right there. Emma has a good head on her shoulders. You should know. You put it there."

I slumped back into the cushion with an audible sigh. I was tired of my sister always being right. If Bernadine had shown me anything, it was the invisible lines mothers should never cross.

"I can think of other sparks worth mentioning." Alicia grinned mischievously. "The air around Rose and William sure crackled with electricity."

The freckles on Rose's cheeks stood out, but a wide smile stretched across her face. She twirled one of her curls before tucking it behind her ear.

"All I can say is touché." Alicia drained her glass and stood. "I'd better head out. Are you sure you don't mind staying until Emma comes home?"

"I don't need a babysitter," I mumbled as I sank further into the cushions.

"No arguments," Alicia said. "Just for tonight."

Rose pulled a colorful paperback from her purse. "I'm good to stay. Maybe I'll even read for a while." I smiled, knowing Rose rarely read for pleasure. Maybe William would change that.

Alicia leaned to hug Rose. "Thanks again. I mean it." She wrapped her in a tight embrace before speaking to me. "I'll be by in the morning."

When I spoke, my voice sounded far away. "I'm so lucky you're my sister."

Chapter Forty

Two weeks later…

I strolled the village green with Darcy and my camera, enjoying the aimlessness of it. My eyes were drawn across the street to the little white farmhouse cottage with the bright yellow door and the adorable barn-turned-photography studio. My studio renovation was nearly complete, and appointments for senior class portraits were trickling in. A new sign hung from a post by the driveway, its carved letters painted sky-blue to match my shutters—**In the Moment Photography**. I wanted my clients to feel comfortable in front of the camera, ready to capture the special moments in their lives, no matter what they were. But more than that, my business name was a reminder to myself to focus on the now.

A shiver ran up my spine every time I stopped to reflect on all the drastic changes in my life that went into making my dream a possibility. Moving to Stonebridge had never felt so right.

"Hey, girl." Rose's short legs strode across the village green, a to-go cup in each hand, her florescent pink blouse making her look effervescent, as always. "Another bea-u-ti-ful day." She lifted her face to the sun. We sat on the park bench, Darcy wriggling in the grass near my feet. "Kind of like—"

Kind of like the day Tiffanee was killed.

Rose didn't need to finish her sentence. I knew exactly what she meant. It wasn't like that, not really. I stroked the tail of my scarf. And though its presence reassured me, it wasn't my scarf that made the day different, either.

It was me. I felt different—stronger, more self-assured, more at home. As Rose had said on that first warm afternoon, feeling at home was something that had to come from within. I turned to my wise friend, grateful to have her by my side.

"Are you looking forward to our camera outing tonight?"

"I'm especially glad you'll be able to come too." I sipped my coffee, thinking about how far our club had come in the last couple of weeks. Spring was turning to summer in southern Vermont. The air was warmer, drier, less buggy, and a profusion of wildflowers blanketed the fields. Harmony planned to join us as our newest member, a welcome addition to our club.

"Looks like the terrible trio is now a dreadful duo." Rose nodded to a park bench where Lorraine and Vickie Sue sat.

"It's kind of sad." I'd come to accept the Righteous Sisters as one of the many quirks in my newly adopted home. Without Bernadine, a piece seemed to be missing. She was being held without bail, and I couldn't help wondering how she was making out. Had the end justified the means? "Penny is doing astonishingly well."

"Nate worked something out?"

"It looks that way. She's been helping me set up my studio. The Jacobsens gave her all of Tiffanee's camera equipment, and I'm considering hiring her as an assistant, assuming she's interested."

"That's great. The whole thing is still so hard to believe."

"Penny's been through a lot, and she feels guilty. She hadn't intended to hide Hope from Hunter forever. When she found out she was pregnant, she wasn't in a good place. She wanted to get settled, to show she could support Hope before telling him." I let out a long sigh. "It's all so tragic."

"I'm glad she has Mackenzie to help her through this." Rose sat forward and waved her hand. "Hello, Mr. Miller." My neighbor stomped past, the unhooked buckle of his overalls clinking with each step.

"Humph," he grumbled.

"Such a woodchuck." Rose crinkled her nose and giggled.

I was pretty sure I detected a slight curl to his lips. And yet, it didn't matter. Mr. Miller's harumph was the way he greeted people. Why had it ever bothered me?

There was only one question remaining in my mind, and I wasn't sure if Rose had the answer. "Did William ever tell you how Tiffanee found out about the drug dealing accusation?"

"Turns out that was William's fault. He'd accidentally mixed his separation papers from the high school with a bunch of invoices. He gave the whole pile to Tiffanee."

"Ouch. That was a tough mistake." I sipped my coffee.

"William is glad to have it all in the open. You do know the student recanted, right?" A hard, protective edge crept into Rose's voice. "He could have kept his job, but being only one of two Black teachers at the school, he was tired of feeling like he was being held to a different standard. Anyway, he'd always toyed with the idea of owning a bookstore. Lucky for me, the timing was right."

"I'm not surprised. William is no drug dealer. The school's loss is Stonebridge's gain."

Rose stood. "I'd better take off. Ethan has another baseball game. I'm driving him over before coming back for our photo shoot. Travis is taking him home."

No sooner had Rose walked away than my phone buzzed with Emma's jazzy ringtone. I petted Darcy's head, and we walked over to the gazebo, where I settled on its steps.

"Hi, Mom," Emma said as soon as I answered the video chat. Her clear blue eyes twinkled. "I called to wish you a super fun, murder-free night."

"Thanks, I'm excited about it." This outing would be a fresh start for the club.

"What's the destination?"

"The old stone mill building. Harmony claims the sun glints off the rusty metal roof in the late afternoon. She's extremely artistic."

"Sounds interesting." Emma's sarcasm wasn't lost on me.

"To a photographer, yes. There's nothing more compelling than the way light and shadows play with texture. Anyway, how are you doing?"

"I'm good. Really. I talked to Gran this morning. She's relieved this whole episode is over, and she says she wants to come visit this summer."

Involuntarily, my gaze moved to my house. The studio should be ready by then. Surely, if Fiona could see my new business, she'd be excited for me. Maybe she'd even be a little proud. "This summer should be good." With a laugh, I added, "I bet she needs to escape the Florida heat."

"Why do you act like Gran has an ulterior motive? She just wants to come see us. She's super excited about your new studio."

I sighed, thankful Emma and her grandmother were close. Grudgingly, I admitted to myself that I'd like to see her too.

"Other than wishing you luck, I wanted to let you know I'm planning to drive up this weekend. Will that work?"

My heart skipped a beat. "Definitely. Let's plan a day trip. I hear there's a book festival in Woodstock."

"A day trip sounds good," Emma agreed. "But I have plans for Saturday night. One of Connor's friends is throwing a party at her uncle's house on Stratton." Her cheeks flushed.

"Sounds like fun." I couldn't help the wary tone in my voice, thinking about Rose's and Alicia's comments about Connor and Emma. "So, you and Connor?" I paused, biting my tongue.

"Slow your roll, Mom." Emma's voice was a warning. "Connor and I are friends. That's all."

I mimicked zipping my lips. "I'll butt out. Promise."

Emma smiled.

I let out a slow breath. Emma looked happy, happier than she had in months, long before she and Ryan started having trouble. As much as I wanted to, I couldn't protect my daughter from every hurt, and I knew I shouldn't try.

I lifted a hand in surrender. "I promise to say no more. You know you can talk to me, don't you?"

"Of course," Emma said. "There's nothing to tell. Connor knows all about Ryan, and he knows I'm not ready for a boyfriend. Not yet, anyway." A pink flush rose to her cheeks.

"I can't wait for your visit."

"Me too. Here's the deal. I'm driving up tomorrow afternoon. Maybe we could go to The Crow for dinner—just the two of us?"

"It's a date. Be prepared to dance. They have live music on Fridays."

"Perfect. Oh, and Mom." Emma's expression became serious. "I'm really sorry I kept pressuring you to come back to Boston. Vermont is your home now. Your photography studio is going to be super cool. Dad would have been proud of you."

Tears welled, and Emma grew blurry as I swiped my cheek. I had dreamed of hearing these words, but hadn't dared hope they'd come this soon. "Thank you," I whispered. "That means so much more than you could ever know."

We hung up, and I leaned back on the park bench, snapping a photo of my little white farmhouse.

I rubbed Darcy's belly. "What do you say, boy? Is it time to go home?"

He rolled over, his tail thumping in the grass.

We were still figuring it all out, but we were settling into our new home in Vermont. And I got the feeling Darcy was happy, too.

Acknowledgements

When I started writing this book, I expected it to be a solitary activity. Little did I know I'd meet so many incredibly wonderful people along the way. It truly took a village.

A special thanks to my editor and publisher, Shawn Reilly Simmons, and the entire team at Level Best Books. I'm truly grateful and proud to be an LBB author.

To Dawn Dowdle of Blue Ridge Literary Agency, thank you for not only taking a chance on me, but for welcoming me into your BRLA family. You will be forever missed.

A huge thank you to my earliest critique partners, Clarisse, Lucy, and Maureen. I know how terrible those early pages were! Your wisdom, patience, and kindness will be appreciated forever.

The biggest of hugs to my Inky Fingers writing group. Every month I look forward to our get-togethers. I can't even begin to tell you what it means to me to be part of this group! Leah, Paula, Jessica, Andrew, Chris, and Beth—you are all amazing writers and friends! Your friendship, encouragement, and kindness will be forever in my heart.

To my photography friends, who graciously came along on my adventure. You were my earliest newsletter subscribers, cheerleaders, and guinea pigs while I figured it all out. I can't thank you enough for your encouragement, patience, and support. Sarah, León, and Barb—cheers!

To my ARC readers. Thank you so much for your willingness to read a book by an unknown author. I understand the commitment you made and appreciate it more than you know.

To Vermont and the lovely residents of Jamaica. You were my happy place and a soft place to land during some hectic, stressful years. Quaint, quirky, and exceedingly charming, your beauty inspires me daily.

To my mom, for whom this book is dedicated. Thank you for allowing me to use your name. I hope you love Bobbie as much as I do and that your library in heaven has a huge mystery section! Maggie and Laura, there are bits of you within my characters. Thank you for your love and support. And Greg—I saved you for last. You're my rock. You believed in me more than I believed in myself. There are no hugs big enough to thank you for all your support. I love you.

About the Author

Kara Lacey is the author of the Camera Club Mysteries. Along with her husband, she lives in a tiny village nestled in the beautiful Green Mountains of Vermont—the inspiration for her novels. Kara is a photography enthusiast who also enjoys hiking, skiing, and getting cozy with a good book. When she's not at her laptop creating havoc for her characters, you can find her rambling through the forest with her husband and spirited Labrador retriever, camera in hand.

Kara is a member of Sisters in Crime, Sisters in Crime-New England, and Mystery Writers of America. She is also a co-Member at Large for Vermont SinC NE writers.

SOCIAL MEDIA HANDLES:

https://www.instagram.com/karalaceyauthor/
https://www.facebook.com/karalaceyauthor/

AUTHOR WEBSITE:

https://karalaceyauthor.com

www.ingramcontent.com/pod-product-compliance
Lightning Source LLC
Chambersburg PA
CBHW020611110726
47899CB00002B/473